RIVERS
OF
SHADOW

RIVERS OF SHADOW

LEO HUNT

CANDLEWICK PRESS

First U.S. edition 2016

Library of Congress Catalog Card Number pending
ISBN 978-0-7636-8994-0

16 17 18 19 20 21 BVG 10 9 8 7 6 5 4 3 2 1

Printed in Berryville, VA, U.S.A.

This book was typeset in Palatino.

Candlewick Press
99 Dover Street
Somerville, Massachusetts 02144

visit us at www.candlewick.com

For Mum and Dad

(visitors)

One of the things I learned last year was that life doesn't give you a friendly warning when everything changes. There's no five-minute call before the ice breaks under your feet. The first time you realize everything's about to change will be when it's already happening.

My secret life starts again one Monday morning in second-period math. I'm not even pretending to pay attention, looking up at the ceiling, imagining that the brown water stains above me are the map of some uncharted islands. It's spring; exams are breathing down the back of our necks, and the teachers won't let us forget it. The sun, making a rare guest appearance in North East England, is shining through a gap in the clouds. The room is too warm. On the desk in front of me: textbook, worksheet, a pencil capped with a bacon-pink eraser. My shadow is hard-edged and vividly present. The girl on my left-hand side has her head propped on one hand. She hasn't moved for a good five minutes. It's not a room where anyone's expecting something exciting to happen.

Mr. Hallow, our math teacher, has one of those pale, awkwardly proportioned faces that look like you're viewing them through the bottom of a dirty bottle. He's drawn a triangle in green pen on the whiteboard, and he wants someone to find its angles. Since I made the mistake of meeting his gaze while I was thinking about how weird his head looks, he chooses me.

"Luke Manchett. Could you find the way out of this dilemma?"

"Sure," I say.

I stand, my chair's rubber-tipped legs making a high squeal on the floor tiles. The only one of my classmates looking at me is Kirk, and when he catches my eye, he quickly looks down at the floor. I'm treated as an embarrassment, an inconvenience that everyone's determined to pretend isn't here. It wasn't always like this, hard as it may be for anyone to believe. I started school last year in a great position, ready to play a winning hand. I was on the rugby team, best mates with Mark Ellsmith and Kirk Danknott, went drinking in the park with the Dunbarrow High A-list. I even had a shot with Holiday Simmon, though I doubt she'd be willing to admit that now.

All that changed last October. I'm a freak now, and

everyone knows it. I'm a freak with a freak girlfriend, and I have a freak mum and a dead freak dad and a freak dog and I live in the Freak House at number one Freak Street. Kirk and me used to be close as anything, friends for years, and now he won't even look me in the eye.

It does hurt, but after what happened last Halloween, I can't totally blame him. I am a freak. I'm not like Kirk, not like Holiday or anyone else, and I never will be again.

Mr. Hallow holds out the green felt-tip as I approach, appraising me gravely, like I'm a young squire hoping to be knighted. I take the pen, clammy and warm from his touch, and stand in front of the whiteboard. I haven't listened to a word he's said all lesson, but fortunately this doesn't look like an especially tricky problem. The classroom is bright, sunlight pouring in through the back windows, and the whiteboard is slightly reflective. I can see a dull mirror image of myself, the class behind me visible as slumped silhouettes. Half of them are asleep, or close to it.

I touch the pen to the board.

"Mr. Hallow?" comes a voice.

"Where have you been?" he asks, irritated.

I turn and see Holiday Simmon, Queen of Dunbarrow High School, standing in the doorway. Holiday being late for class is rare enough, let alone missing a lesson and a half. She advances into the room and stops just in front of Hallow's desk, followed by a strange girl.

"This is a visiting student," Holiday tells Mr. Hallow. "I'm supposed to guide her around this month."

Nobody's paying attention to me now, so I decide I'll hold off on uncovering the mysteries of Hallow's triangle. The boys are all definitely awake now, and they're looking at the new arrivals like caged dogs anticipating their meat ration. Holiday is, by anyone's standards, a beautiful girl. She's tall and blond, always expertly groomed, with the easy confidence that comes from knowing you'll never be second best. She even somehow manages to make our shapeless gray school sweaters look stylish. Taking all of this into consideration, Holiday still seems commonplace compared to the girl who came into class with her.

The visitor is more striking than beautiful, but she's able to hold everyone's attention as she stands beside Hallow. She's petite, barely up to Holiday's shoulder, with a delicate-looking face and slim, tanned arms. She's not in uniform; instead she wears a white sundress and white Converse All Stars, needing only a visor and a racket to look completely at home on a tennis court. An optimistic outfit for an English spring. Her hair is daringly short and more white than blond, the kind of white you'd normally associate with ninety-year-old women. A silver ring glints in her nose. Her grin targets everyone in the room simultaneously, and her teeth are even and bright.

"Hello, everyone!" the new girl says, like she can't

imagine being anywhere more exciting than Room 3G on a Monday morning. "My name's Ashley Smith, but you can call me Ash. I'm sixteen years old, I'm from California, and I am so excited to meet you all!"

"What is this about?" Mr. Hallow asks.

"Sir, this is Ashley," Holiday explains again. "She's an exchange student. She's living here in Dunbarrow with my family, and I'm her guide at school, too."

"Exchange program?" Hallow splutters. "Miss Simmon, there is no exchange program. What are you talking about?"

"I'm here as part of the William Goodman Foundation's American-European Cultural and Educational Enrichment Program," the visitor, Ash, tells him cheerfully. She has that thing where your voice makes every statement sound like a question. "It's for teenagers with challenging backgrounds, to help us get perspective and aid us on our personal journeys? And it's really super-great on college applications. I come from Marin County in California, and I was really lucky to be able to come and visit here for a month, to live in your beautiful and historical town!"

The idea that someone would be willing to give up life in California, even for a month, in order to travel here, Dunbarrow, North East England—and not only that, but that they'd be excited about it—seems to baffle Mr. Hallow so much, he can't form an objection.

"We've got a note from the Head," Holiday adds. "She said to bring Ash here because she'll be taking all my classes with me."

It makes sense that Holiday would have exclusive early access to this glamorous stranger. Ashley Smith just doesn't fit in this room, this math class. It's like seeing a zebra galloping in a supermarket parking lot.

"This is extremely irregular." Hallow sniffs. "An exchange student, arriving near the middle of spring term, with exams just around the corner . . . I suppose if the Head agreed with this, I can't . . . Who is the lucky student we sent to Marin?"

"Mark Ellsmith," Ash says. "I never actually met him—he left a few days ago. But we talked online. I told him some good spots."

Despite the fact that Mark used to be one of my really good friends, I don't think we've spoken since Halloween. He's Holiday's boyfriend now, still captain of the rugby team, with the body of a Greek statue that got a spray tan. He'll get on just fine in California, I'm sure.

"Well, I see. Good for Mr. Ellsmith," Mr. Hallow says. "Girls, I really think you've taken up enough of our lesson already. And Holiday, I do wish you'd told me about this earlier if you knew you were going to miss some of my class. Speak to me at the end."

"Of course, sir," Holiday says.

"Anyway, I'm sure Mr. Manchett is dying to get on with the problem I gave him. Aren't you, Mr. Manchett?"

I'm not sure if Hallow thinks calling us Miss and Mr. is funny or what. Nobody ever laughs. I'd say he's got at least a decade to go before he retires, so whatever keeps you sane, I suppose.

"Can't wait," I say.

Holiday brushes past me without saying a word, without looking at me — I've come to expect it, her acting like we never laughed together or flirted, like she never invited me up to her room — but Ash looks me in the eye, smiling. Her eyes are a strange gray, I see as she passes.

"Nice to meet you, Luke," Ash says cheerily, and follows Holiday to some empty seats right in the middle of the room. They settle themselves down, a beam of sunlight striking them, making Holiday's hair glow like amber and Ash's white head shine in a way that seems lunar, unearthly.

"Mr. Manchett, if we could move this along?" Hallow says again.

"Sorry," I say, turning back to the board. I try to focus on math, collect my thoughts, but something strikes me as odd: How does Ash know my name? She called me Luke. Mr. Hallow only used my last name. She didn't hear anyone call me Luke.

Maybe Holiday already told her about me. She gave

Ash a first-day briefing on who not to sit next to at lunch. That's probably it.

I look at the green triangle scrawled on a white background, and that's when it hits me. There's a sudden roaring in my ears, blood rushing to my head, bursts of color and light in my eyes like the spots you see after you've looked at the sun. Behind it all, I can hear a high ringing sound, like someone struck a glass bell.

I've seen this triangle before. I've seen every triangle before; I've seen them all. Last Halloween, I saw every combination of three lines. In the Book of Eight I saw every shape we have words for and some that we don't. They're all inside me, coiled up inside my mind, waiting for a chance to come spilling out like vomit. They were in the Book, and they're in me now as well. The shapes and sigils flow over everything. I've seen the Book and I saw other things, too. A gray silent shore. My mother standing over me holding a knife. I've seen eyes as black as tar, and I've seen eyes that burned like the heart of the sun. I've met a man with unlined palms, and I saw my dead father walking in mist. I've met a baby without face or name. I met the dead and I spoke with them, too, and I saw where we all go in the end, the darkness behind a pale-green door.

The ringing noise fades, and I find I'm lying down. Someone's put a soft object, a school sweater, I think, under my neck and head. I'm looking at the ceiling of the classroom and about a dozen frightened faces. Mr. Hallow is leaning right over me, snapping his fingers.

"His eyes just moved," someone says.

"Luke—"

"I never seen nothing like that!"

". . . messed up . . ."

"Luke," Mr. Hallow says loudly. "Luke Manchett. Can you hear me?"

"Yes," I say.

Everyone's looking at me like I grew an extra head or something. I can't see Holiday or the new girl anywhere.

"What happened?" I ask.

"Can you tell me where we are?" Hallow asks.

"Math," I say. "School. What happened?"

"You had some kind of . . . attack," he says.

"What exactly did I do?" I ask.

Mr. Hallow swallows. His eyes flick to one side, seemingly without him realizing he's done it. I turn my head slowly. When I see what happened to the whiteboard, my heart skips a beat.

The original math problem is still there, somewhere. It's almost impossible to see underneath everything else that's been drawn on the board: magic circles, sigils, spiky incantations in a language I don't recognize. There's a design like an eight-pointed star, and a symbol I last saw tattooed on the palm of a ghost's white hand. There are layers upon layers of letters and symbols, all drawn with scary precision. I close my eyes, but when I open them, the writing is still there.

This will be all over school. This might even make the news.

"You were talking, as well," Mr. Hallow says. "But we couldn't understand what you were saying."

"How long—"

"Ten minutes," he replies.

I don't reply. I sit up, and bright spots flash in front of my eyes again. I feel like I might faint but don't.

I thought this was over. I've had dreams, sure. I've had dreams nearly every night since Halloween, since I shook hands with the Devil and sent my dad on to wherever he went to. Sometimes my dreams are just pages of the Book of Eight, and sometimes I wake and find I'm at my desk writing words I can't understand. But it's never been like this before. Never in daylight.

"What . . . what's going to happen?" I ask.

"I don't know," Mr. Hallow says. "I don't know."

It seems clear to everyone that I shouldn't go to my next class, so they sit me down in the nurse's office while someone calls Mum. The office is small, with pink walls, and smells of antiseptic. There's nobody else here. The nurse checked my eyes with a handheld light, asked if I felt sick, then gave me a glass of water and went somewhere else. I'm not a medical expert, but it seems like a pretty low standard of care.

My name is Luke Manchett, and I'm still sixteen years old. Until last year, I thought I was pretty normal. That was before my dad died, and I discovered he was actually a necromancer, a dark magician with eight ghosts that he kept as his servants. With Dad gone, the ghosts—his Host—belonged to me instead.

They were a weird bunch, with titles instead of proper names, like the Judge, the Vassal, the Heretic. One of them, a ghost called the Shepherd, wanted revenge on Dad for enslaving him, and since Dad was already gone, he came after me instead. With the help of my now-girlfriend, Elza, and my dog, Ham, I managed to fight the Host off. See, Dad also left me his copy of the Book of Eight, a book of magic that I'm not even sure is really a book at all. It seems to work more like a doorway into a place your mind was never meant to go.

I read the Book of Eight and it gave me a ritual to summon the Devil, who broke my Host and sent them back into the world of the dead. I met my Dad's ghost that night as well, on the border between life and death, and the Devil said I could either send Dad to Hell or set him free. I let Dad go, but in return, the Devil told me that I was in his debt. What that means, I'm still not sure. I think it's fair to say it was one of the more eventful nights of my life.

Someone is opening the door to the nurse's office. I sit up straighter, doing my best to look alert and healthy. Unless there's someone at the hospital with a working knowledge of necromancy and the Book of Eight, sending me off for testing isn't going to help. I really just want to go home.

The face that peers around the door is pale and freckled, with perfectly arched eyebrows, dark-green eyes, a thundercloud of black hair looming over it. Elza Moss slips into the room, letting the door slam shut behind her, and rushes over to me.

"Luke, what happened?"

I reach out to her, and she hugs me so tight, I can barely breathe.

"Elza—"

"Luke! Don't just hug me! Tell me what happened!"

"I don't know."

"Are you all right?" she asks.

"I feel normal now, yeah. Does everyone know?"

Elza doesn't reply. She sits down beside me, slips her hand into mine.

"They actually . . ." Elza swallows. "It's best you hear

this from me. Someone was actually filming it. You're already online."

"What?"

"I don't know who did it. But *Boy Gets Possessed at School* is already on several thousand views. I think you're going to reach a mass audience."

"That's . . . just great. Perfect."

We have only a few more months left at Dunbarrow High before our exams, but I have a feeling they're going to be long ones.

"You just have to ignore it," Elza says. She rests her head against me. "They don't understand what we've gone through. They're just . . . they couldn't have done what we did. Ignore them."

"Yeah," I say. I don't want to say it out loud, but Elza never really had any friends to start with. For me, being an outcast has been a painful transition. It hurts that we have to eat lunch on our own, walk home from school every day alone. It hurts to have to take an alternate route to avoid walking through the park on the weekends so I don't run into Kirk and his mates, who've told me in no uncertain terms that I'm not welcome there. Elza seems to have this nearly invulnerable armor and has become immune to sneers and laughter, but no matter what, I can't seem to help myself from noticing how people here look at us. Things are great with Elza, and I'm not sorry for a second that I met her—it was probably the only good thing to come out of that mess last Halloween—but your only friends shouldn't be your girlfriend and a deerhound.

I think morning break must be over now. I can hear people moving in the halls, kids shouting, rushing past. Everyone thinking about normal things, living their normal lives. Me and Elza are shut in this quiet room, alone.

The fluorescent lights flicker.

"Seriously," Elza says again, "what happened? People said you were writing something. What was it? Something from the Book of Eight?"

"I was supposed to solve this geometry problem. Hallow gave me the pen, and then I got this rush. . . . I was back inside the Book again, felt the way I did in your room that time after I came up out of it. I didn't know I was writing, but I could see the symbols, feel them. I felt like I could say those words if I wanted to. . . . It's hard to explain."

"But the Book is gone. You threw it away. Right?"

This isn't exactly true.

"I've had flashbacks sometimes," I tell her instead. "Whatever I read in the Book, it's still inside me. It's not going anywhere. But what happened today is new."

"You never told me anything about flashbacks," Elza says sharply.

"It's just been dreams. Nothing to worry about."

"You know you can tell me this stuff, right? You can tell me. I'm your . . . You ought to tell me. This is important."

"I'm telling you now, Elza. This is me telling you."

"OK," she says. "Whatever. Sure. So why now? Why today?"

"I don't know."

"No ghosts that you saw? You didn't hear from . . . you know?"

"Who? My dad?"

"Berkley."

My dad's lawyer. The Devil. When I first met him, he—it—had taken the form of a man, Mr. Berkley.

"No," I say. "Thankfully. Nothing since . . ."

I'm about to say *since he came to my house, spoke to Mum,* but I never actually told Elza about that. She doesn't know I've still got the Book of Eight, that it's buried in the corner of the field next to my house. After what happened on Halloween, after we'd won, we were so happy to be alive that I never found the right time to mention it. As the months went by, I just felt like I wanted to put it behind me.

"Well, good," she says. "The less we hear from him, the better. So nothing at all? Normal Monday morning."

"There was this girl."

"What girl?"

"She came in with Holiday. Exchange student."

"Oh," Elza says. "Where from?"

"California. She's called Ash. Five foot nothing, bleached white hair. You haven't heard about this?"

"Nobody tells me anything around here," Elza says. "So what did she say?"

"Just said hi and sat down."

"Well, that hardly sounds very sinister."

"I suppose not."

"But you're OK?" Elza asks again, squeezing my hand. I kiss her.

"I'm fine," I say. "It was probably nothing."

"Yeah," Elza says. "I just wish . . . I wish you'd never read that Book, Luke. I wish I'd never —"

"If I hadn't, we'd probably both be dead. We did what we had to."

We sit together until the noise from the corridor outside fades, and there's not even the sound of stragglers hurrying in from the far yard.

In the end, I get sent home. Mum comes straight from work to pick me up. I'm actually feeling fine and could probably manage the walk back to Wormwood Drive without help, but I want a day off from school, so I don't stress this point too much. Mum has a really disconcerting habit of looking you in the eye if you're having a conversation with her while she's driving.

"I think it's because of the meat you eat," she says as she pulls out of the school parking lot, barely glancing at the road.

"What makes you say that?" I ask.

"Hormones," Mum says darkly.

Mum's name is Persephone Cusp (back to her maiden name now that Dad's gone, although I'm stuck with Manchett), and she's been making some changes in her life. Back in October, Mum was in a bad way and had been for a long time. She was ill and would spend weeks in bed with headaches, ice pressed to her forehead, curtains drawn. After Halloween, that changed. The doctors, who never seemed to really know what was causing her cluster headaches anyway, call it "an unprecedented recovery." Personally, I suspect Mum's wellness is connected to one of Dad's ghosts—my own brother—who I sent over into Deadside along with the rest of his Host, but it's not really the sort of thing you can bring up at the hospital.

"They take these poor animals," she's saying to me, "and they pump them—are you listening?—they pump them with hormones. It makes them grow faster, get fatter. And the hormones, when you eat meat, they go into you."

"I need protein for lifting."

One thing I've missed since Halloween: nobody to

spot me, and nobody to celebrate my gains. Elza has made it clear she'd rather pierce her eardrums with a pin than listen to me talk about "moving bits of metal around," and while Mum is less hostile to exercise as a concept, she just fundamentally doesn't get it.

"You can get protein from beans and lentils," Mum says.

"I don't want to eat beans. They're no substitute for bacon."

"Well, I don't know. You can be vegetarian and still eat protein, Luke. And you won't be supporting the ghastly industrial farming complex."

"Yeah, I'll look into it."

Mum's weirdness is long-standing and deep-rooted. She's thin, with straw-colored hair, and a desire to wear ponchos that borders on the disturbing. When she first met Dad, she was permanently barefoot and living in a van.

We drive past the town square. I can see the usual pensioners, ambling around, all dressed in some variant of beige. A mobile-phone salesman having a cigarette outside his shop. A woman with a toddler on an elastic leash. A dead man with bloodstains on his uniform.

I still have second sight; it didn't vanish along with my Host. Elza says that she thinks once your brain gets used to seeing the world that way—the true way—it's nearly impossible to go back to how you were before. So I can see dead people. It's honestly stopped bothering me. They usually just walk around, sit down, stare at nothing. Some of them are a bit gruesome-looking (there's this one ghost in Brackford who me and Elza call Half Head, for reasons that become obvious as soon as you see her), but they're really not frightening. It's better not to let on that you can see them, because they're usually crazy, or boring, or both. One of the weirder side effects of second sight is that a lot of shows on TV and movies actually have ghosts wandering around during some of the scenes. There's a discussion thread on the Second Sight Support website Elza posts on devoted to sightings. I watched a football game the other week, and there was a man in what I think was a Civil War uniform standing beside one goalkeeper the whole game, trying to talk to him. It was really distracting.

"Look," I say to Mum, "I don't think it had anything to do with being a carnivore."

"Yes, of course, love," she says. "Are you feeling OK now?"

"I'm all right. Sort of light-headed. There's a car coming."

"I'll see if you can go to the doctor this afternoon," Mum says, glancing back at the road just long enough to swerve out of the way.

"What exactly did they say happened?" I ask.

"They said you had a seizure," Mum says. "Has that ever happened before?"

"No," I say. "And I don't think I need to go see anyone. I'm just stressed. Exams."

Normally, invoking exam stress is a good way to get Mum to forgive me for things, like leaving cereal bowls in my room until the remains dry harder than cement, or forgetting to close the kitchen door before I let Ham back in from the field—which once led to an unfortunate incident where he came in fresh from rolling in cow pies and jumped on her lap while she was wearing cream-colored pants—but it doesn't seem to be cutting it this time. Mum gives me a sustained and serious look, apparently with full faith that nobody else will want to use either of the lanes on this road in the near future.

"This is really serious, love. You didn't see any flashing lights? Dark spots?"

"I'm not getting your headaches, Mum."

"I hope not," she says. "I've just . . . I was always worried that I would give them to you, somehow."

"Cluster headaches aren't hereditary," I say.

"You're seeing a doctor," Mum says. "Today, if we can manage it."

"We're coming to the intersection," I say.

"I know," she says, and brakes with just inches to spare.

I wonder if there is something really wrong with me, but our doctor isn't going to find anything unusual. I'll end up getting diagnosed with epilepsy or something else and given pills that will do nothing to solve the problem. I know why I had that blackout: I read the Book of Eight, and I saw stuff in there that normal people were never meant to see. And it's still inside my head, festering away in my subconscious, ready to erupt at the slightest provocation. How to deal with that, cure it, I have no idea.

"I suppose," Mum says, almost to herself, as we make our way along Wormwood Drive, "it might be nothing to do with the meat anyway. It could be because your school's using those fluorescent lights."

I decide some questions are better left unasked.

Our place is nothing too fancy: front and back garden, short gravel drive. A few trees, some grass, flowers, the usual garden stuff. Inside we've got more fairly normal stuff: carpets, walls, furniture of varying sizes, a large dog. As soon as Mum opens the door, he leaps past her and tries to knock me down. In a friendly way, of course.

"Get down!" I shout. "Ham! No! I'm a sick man!"

Ham yelps with delight and practically somersaults in the driveway. In Ham's world, me coming home from school a few hours early is like Christmas and his birthday rolled into one. Ham likes eating, sleeping, running in small bursts, being petted, and having his ears rubbed. He doesn't like the dark, shots, loud noises, vacuums, cats, foxes, fireworks, and people blowing air into his ears while he's asleep (which, of course, I would never do). He's lean and gray, with long, smoky hair and big eyes with pupils the color of marmalade. We've been partners in crime since I was small, just after Dad left.

"Why don't you lie down, love?" Mum asks. I don't need telling twice. I sit down on the sofa and put rugby on. Ham comes and hunkers down in front of me and I rest my feet, still in gray school socks, on the gray fur of his back. He's warm, and I can feel his heartbeat pulsing up through my toes and into my legs.

Mum gets an emergency appointment with our doctor, and I get a more in-depth version of what happened in the nurse's office this morning: light shone in my eyes, lots of questions. He asks if this has ever happened before; I say no. In the end, we get an appointment with some specialists at the hospital next Monday to get a brain scan, and Mum takes me home.

I lie down and watch more TV and try not to think about everything that happened today: Ash and Holiday, Mr. Hallow, Elza, the shapes that I saw in my mind's eye when I looked at the triangle on the board. I just want to relax and ignore that small abrasive voice in my head that tells me something's wrong, that things are about to change again, that whatever happened this morning is just the start. Ham shifts in his sleep. Despite her earlier objections, Mum makes me a decent pizza, with salami on it.

I lie in bed but I can't sleep. The sky outside my window is dark and clear, glittering with stars. When I think back to those weeks before Halloween, when my whole life changed, what I remember is gray: overcast skies, the gray clouds heavy with rain, the gray mists that swirled around me and Dad and the Devil on whatever shore we walked upon.

I keep thinking about the Californian girl, Ash. There was something weird about her. The last time I felt this so strongly was when I met my dad's solicitor, Mr. Berkley, and he turned out to be someone who was very dangerous indeed. I didn't listen to my intuition then, and it went badly for me. I don't want to make that mistake twice. There's something about that girl. She doesn't fit in at Dunbarrow at all. Why would you go on an exchange to this place? Why would the school agree to it this close to our exams?

I get out of bed and search for "Ashley Smith" online. There's about a hundred thousand results, none of which gets me anywhere. She certainly isn't one of the better-known Ashley Smiths. I scroll through the related pictures for a while, looking for a glimpse of her distinctive face and short white hair, but I don't find anything.

I sit for a moment, my laptop's fan purring in the dark, my room lit only by the faint creepy light of the screen, and then I search "William Goodman Foundation."

This time the results lead me somewhere. The foundation has a web page, a bland PR-sanitized white void plastered with stock images and clean blue logos. The foundation is "a nonprofit organization devoted to improving the lives of young people worldwide." This claim is accompanied with stock photographs of young people laughing in some kind of coffee bar somewhere. Ash is nowhere to be seen. It doesn't say, anywhere, what the foundation specifically does, or who runs it, or how I might contact the foundation about their activity in Dunbarrow. The website is, essentially, a friendly locked door.

I turn off my laptop and head down to the kitchen. It's about one in the morning. Ham's lying in his crate next to the washing machine. He doesn't get up, but he thumps his tail eagerly as I approach. I kneel down and rub his warm belly.

"All right, boy?" I whisper.

Ham grumbles and rolls onto his back. I sit there, petting him, and think some more. Maybe Elza is right; maybe Ash is just an exchange student, a cheerful Californian transplant. My attack could've come at any moment, and might have been brought on by the whiteboard's geometry alone. Maybe seeing the green pen caused it? The Book of Eight was green, after all. It's totally possible. Magic, from what little I've learned, seems to depend on the movement of the planets and stars. Perhaps they were in a bad configuration, and Ash just happened to walk in with Holiday? Correlation isn't causation.

No.

There's something wrong. She knew my name, but I don't know how. I couldn't find her online, and the foundation that arranged her trip could be run by anyone. For all I know, this is Berkley again; he (or it) seems to like cloaking his activities in the semblance of human process. He enjoys dressing up as a man, wearing a man's face, pretending to do a man's business. From what I've seen of him, it would be exactly like the Devil to set up a charity called the Goodman Foundation. I imagine he'd get a big laugh out of that.

I decide to take Ham out and stand under the stars, get some night air. If this really is Berkley again, there's no way I can avoid what's coming. He's not someone you can hide from. If he wants something from me, it can't be anything good. I'll just have to be ready and do my best.

Ham hears the jingle as I unwind his leash, and he gets up, grunting, and thrusts his head into my legs. I put on my raincoat and a woolly hat and softly open the door, leading Ham out into the back garden. There's a fair amount of moonlight, illuminating the stone wall, the garden shed, our apple trees. There's a crisp, fresh smell in the air. Almost April.

We walk out through the back gate and into the grass field behind our yard, which is occasionally used for grazing sheep. There are tall trees at the far end of the field, coming into leaf after the winter, their long branches dark against the orange city glow on the horizon. Beyond this field are more fields, then trees and wild moorland that stretches on for miles. Somewhere off in the distance, I hear the cry of an owl. Ham, a coward of infamous proportions, whimpers a little, but I pull him onward and he calms down.

After a few minutes' stroll we reach the far side of the field, the spot where I buried the Book of Eight. The flat stone is still there where I left it, almost five months later. The site is undisturbed. Although I could hardly claim the Book was the greatest source of my problems, it was the first magical thing I ever saw, and it seems to have had the longest-lasting effect on me. I buried it about a foot deep, in a toolbox, along with my dad's sigil—a strange black ring that was the focus of his magical power—and his other eight rings. That's where they still are, sleeping down there under the stones and mud and grass.

I don't quite know why I came out here. I think I wanted to check on the Book, to make sure it had stayed buried. Maybe I thought the plants here would've turned black, or the hedge would be growing leaves shaped like pentagrams. There's nothing out of the ordinary. It's just a field, just a flat stone from our wall.

The owl cries again, louder this time, a haunting, hollow noise. It sends a prickle of fear down my neck. I suddenly feel exposed, out here in the darkness. I'm glad I wasn't born a field mouse.

Ham, far from mouse-size, is pressed up close to me. He's whimpering and whining, quaking against my thigh like a vibrating phone you're ignoring.

"It's an owl, boy," I say. "It's a bird as big as your head. You're fine."

He whines louder. As I look down at him, I realize I can see my breath in the air. There's a chill around us, a cold that's reaching down into my guts, my marrow. I've felt cold like this before.

I turn slowly, feeling like I'm in a dream, and see a girl standing between us and the house. My heart is thumping, a hard-core rave rhythm, big whooshing bass reverberating up into my chest and skull. Ham snarls, baring his teeth. I can't make the girl out properly; she's about halfway down the field, but she's definitely looking at us. She's wearing what looks like a short dress, way too skimpy for a clear night like this. She is definitely a ghost.

Like I said, the dead are usually harmless. The town ghosts keep to themselves, don't usually pay you any attention. Some of them are confused, try and talk to you, asking about buses that stopped running back in 1956 or jabbering about the inheritance that wasn't divided the way they wanted it to be. That's annoying, but I can deal with it.

This girl is probably one of them. The ghosts who stick around on earth, in Liveside, aren't the sharpest knives in the drawer. Mostly they don't realize they've died, or are too afraid to go onward into Deadside. I feel a bit bad for them, but they're not scary.

There's something about this girl that I don't like, though.

"Toughen up," I hiss at Ham. "You're a necromancer's familiar, remember? You eat ghosts for breakfast. Literally. Let's get back to the house." Elza put hazel charms in the bushes to keep my house spirit-free, but their effect doesn't reach this far out into the field. Even if this ghost does want trouble, we just have to get past her, into the yard.

We make our way toward her. I don't see any point in trying to be stealthy; she's clearly seen us. My feet rustle in the grass. The owl calls out again and again in the trees behind us, a mournful siren. The closer we get to the girl, the colder the air becomes. My breath balloons in white clouds.

She's closer now, still a dim shape, but I can make her out more clearly. She's small, almost child-size. What I thought was a dress is actually a hospital gown, pale green, stopping just above her knees. Her hair is long and unruly, spilling down over her shoulders. It looks like it hasn't been washed in a long time. She's gazing up at the stars now, her body turned away from me. We stop about a room's length from her, enough distance to give me time to react if she's not so friendly. To be honest, I'm not sure what I'll do. Elza used to have a wyrdstone, a stone with a hole through it that warded off spirits, but it broke when she used it against my dad's demon, and we haven't found another one yet.

"Hello?" I say, projecting my voice through the cold air toward her. "Can I help you?"

The girl turns to look at me with curious eyes, and my heart nearly stops.

The ghost has Ash's face. She has the same nose, same eyes, same pursed lips. She has Ash's figure, too, I realize: they're exactly the same height. Only her hair is different, darker and longer and tangled around her face like a lion's mane. As she turns to face us fully, I see that her left arm is missing. The hospital gown hangs limp from her left shoulder, sleeve empty.

"Ash?" I whisper. "Ashley Smith?"

The ghost smiles and says something I can't understand. She's speaking another language, singsong, jaunty. It's not French or Spanish or any of the languages they teach at school. She holds her hand out to me. Ham growls.

"I can't understand you. . . . Do you speak English?"

More nonsense. The one-armed girl smiles again, points up at the stars.

"Are you . . . Ash? Do you know Ash?"

She says something else, more animated. I look up to where she's pointing. There's nothing in particular there. Just blackness, and some small points of light.

"Yes . . ." I say uncertainly. "The stars are nice tonight." I don't understand what's happening. Is this Ash, somehow? Why is she talking like this? What language is that?

She walks toward me, single hand outstretched. I'm not so sure I want to touch her. She doesn't seem exactly threatening, and most ghosts are perfectly harmless, as I said. But last year I met a few that weren't.

I take another step backward, Ham scrambling to keep my body between him and the one-armed girl. She steps forward, almost skipping, holding her hand out like she wants to dance with us. I'm smiling, keeping my body language friendly and open, trying to move back and side-ways so we can get ourselves past her and into the protective influence of the hazel charms. I don't exactly know what I'm afraid of, what I think she'll do. I was safe from my own Host, for the most part—their binding prevented them from harming me directly—but there's no protection here.

She's asking me a question, coming at us a little faster. We're weaving around in the moonlit grass, neither of us quite running, and I feel for a moment like I'm playing tag back in lower school, that thrill of dodging and diving—

Ham suddenly yowls and bucks and tears his leash free of my grasp. I'm turning to see what happened, and then it feels like a supersonic train made of ice hits me in the back, and I'm flung to the ground. It's a hard blow, and I want to stay lying down in case something's broken, but years of rugby have gotten me used to getting up after a hit. Whatever got me came up behind us while I was keeping my eye on the one-armed ghost.

Ham's already running; I can hear him yelping, heading for the house. Surprise, surprise. I heave myself up, whirling around, my ribs squealing with pain inside my chest. I'm gasping, trying to get a breath, raising my fists up as if that'll help me.

A second ghost is standing between me and the one-armed girl, her body held erect, radiating authority.

This spirit is a woman, dark-skinned, with a sheer flow of black hair and a long white robe. Her feet are bare, and her big toes are decorated with golden rings. She's tall and proud, with a face like an obsidian statue, and her eyes are black as tar pits, like bottomless holes bored in her face. I've only seen one other spirit with eyes like that, and he was my father's Shepherd, a ghost who was very old and very powerful. To complete this intimidating picture, the ghost has a spear stuck through her chest, with dark blood clotted around the wound. The point juts several feet out of her back. No prizes for guessing how she died.

I'm unsteady on my feet. My breath is coming shallow, and it burns like I'm taking little gasps of magma rather than air. I've got nothing: no spells, no Host, no sigil. My dad's things, my only source of magic power, the only way I could defend myself, are buried in a box half a field away. The one-armed girl stands behind the tall ghost, looking upset. She's saying something in her nonsense language to the dark-skinned woman, who doesn't take her black eyes from me. The woman shakes her head in dismissal.

I hear the owl crying again in the far trees.

"I don't want to hurt you," I say to them. "I have . . . I have a great Host. I am a powerful necromancer. I don't want to hurt you."

"You cannot harm us," the woman says. Her voice is

smooth and low, implacable, with the strong tinge of an accent I can't place.

"I am Luke Manchett," I say, edging away from her. "I am the son of Horatio Manchett. I am a powerful necromancer. I demand to know your business in my town."

"Remove yourself, sorcerer," the woman says. "Return to your abode."

She stands completely still, but I can tell we're moments away from her doing something unpleasant to me. Knocking me to the ground was just a way to get my attention. My attempt to intimidate her has utterly failed. The spear jutting from her chest seems almost accusatory, mocking me, as if to say, *You think anything you could do to me would be as bad as this?*

The one-armed ghost is saying something again, plaintive, gesturing up at the sky. With an unmistakable look of irritation, the black-eyed woman turns her head and responds in the same singsong language.

I take the opportunity to run, adrenaline taking over, crossing half the field in what seems like no time at all. I vault over the garden wall and collapse onto the grass, gasping, holding my chest as my muscles burn and burn. Ham is lurking in the shadows by the kitchen window, his leash dangling from his collar. He doesn't even come over to see if I'm all right.

Forget about the William Goodman Foundation. If

I needed any more proof that Ashley Smith from Marin County is up to something, I just got it. As for the woman with the spear in her chest . . . if she wasn't a bound spirit, part of someone's Host, I don't know what she was. Being bound to a living person makes spirits more powerful. Normal ghosts don't punch you hard enough to lift you off your feet. Normal ghosts can barely rattle a window frame. I feel like I got hit by a car.

I get to my feet and look over the garden wall. Far away, at the opposite side of the field, I can see the woman, her white robe easily picked out in the moonlight. The smaller figure, the girl, follows her closely. I think they're holding hands. I lean there on the wall, watching for any sign they might know about the Book or be looking for it, but they walk right through the hedge without a glance at the spot where I buried it. I stand out in the garden for a long time, a bruise flowering on my chest. When I'm sure the spirits aren't coming back, I get a spade from the garden shed and head back out into the field again.

(the blank house)

Elza exhales a lungful of smoke, frowns up at the trees around us. It's early morning, before homeroom. I asked her to meet me here, our spot, in the graveyard of Saint Jude's. We're sitting at the side of an old mausoleum, surrounded by trees. We've been coming down here over lunch for months, and no one's ever mowed the grass or plucked any weeds in all that time. I doubt anyone else ever comes to this part of the graveyard. Elza finishes off her cigarette and drops it into the dirt, grinding it out with her boot. I look at the angel statue that looms over the graves, its face hidden by foamy yellow lichen. I remember looking at it the first time Elza ever brought me here.

"So what did you do after that?" she asks me.

I pause. "Put Ham inside. Tried to sleep," I say.

"So do you think they knew it was your house? Were they coming after you?"

"I don't think so. If they'd wanted me dead, I'd be dead. They caught me away from the hazel charms. I had nothing. This ghost, the woman with the spear through her . . . she was ferocious. Someone's bound spirit, I'm certain. Part of a Host. I couldn't understand what the girl was saying. She wanted something, but they didn't want to kill me."

"This girl, with one arm? You're sure it was this American girl? Ash?"

"It wasn't exactly Ash. The hair was different, but the same face, same build, same everything. Do ghosts ever look different from their bodies?"

"I don't know. When your Host forced you out of your body, you looked exactly the same . . . but maybe if they'd controlled your body for years, it would've started to look different? Hair grown out, something like that? I presume ghost hair doesn't grow?"

"Yeah," I say, "maybe. Maybe this girl, Ash, she had the same problem as me. Maybe she inherited a Host, and they forced her out of her own body?"

"So whatever's driving her body around, it isn't Ashley Smith. It's something else," Elza says.

"OK," I say. "But the Ash ghost, she seemed . . . I don't know . . . happy? Like she was trying to say something about the sky? It's hard to explain. I mean, I was scared of her at the time, but looking back . . . I think she was just excited."

"And this other ghost, the woman, she only appeared later?"

"She knocked me down and stood between me and the one-armed girl."

"Like a bodyguard," Elza says.

"That kind of vibe, yeah. I felt like I got between a mother bear and her cub."

"Maybe this has nothing to do with you," Elza says slowly. "Maybe Ashley Smith is just part of something else that we don't understand? The world doesn't revolve around us. I don't expect the supernatural world does either."

"She came into my class and called me by name. She—it—wants something from me."

"Yes." Elza sighs. "I expect she does. It seems a bit too much to hope that she's flown halfway around the world to visit Dunbarrow by some weird coincidence."

She looks down at the ground.

"Hey, are you all right?" I ask.

"I'm fine," she says. "I just . . . I really thought this was *over*, you know? You nearly died. I nearly died as well. I thought that was it. Haven't we been through enough? The last five months have been so great, I just thought . . ."

I kiss her on the forehead. "They have been great. Whatever's happening, we'll get through that as well. I promise. Ash can't be worse than my dad's Host."

"Yeah, we hope," she says, muffled by my shoulder. We sit there for a while, with my arm around her.

"So what do you think we should do? Should we, like, talk to Ash?"

"What?" Elza laughs. "No, I don't think so. What are you going to do, just walk up to her and start talking about ghosts? She, it, whatever, will pretend she doesn't know what we mean. Our one advantage is she thinks we don't know."

"The ghosts could've told her I saw them. She knows I know. Like, *we* know that she knows that we know."

"A perilous wedding cake of deceit," Elza says. "You're probably right. But we have to be careful. We don't know what she wants or what she's capable of. This girl might not even be remotely human. She might even be something to do with Mr. Berkley. We don't have a wyrd-stone. I'm almost wishing you hadn't gotten rid of your dad's stuff. . . ."

I don't say anything. I dug up the toolbox last night. The Book is in the bottom drawer of my wardrobe right now. Still in the toolbox I buried it in. I didn't want to risk Ash, or whoever's behind these ghosts, getting their hands on it. I'm wondering if this might be a good moment to reveal this to Elza, and then I decide against it. This isn't the time to start an argument about that.

I've actually got my dad's sigil—the black ring that was the focus of his power—in the inside pocket of my jacket. Problem is, without a Host to back me up I'm not sure how powerful it is. I feel like it might be the magical equivalent of an unloaded gun.

"Oh, I forgot to mention," Elza's saying, "it doesn't seem as exciting now, but I did some research of my own. Your old mate Mark Ellsmith? Who according to Ash is in California on exchange? His social media's been dead quiet since a couple days ago. No updates."

"You think . . . ?"

"I don't know. Somehow I don't think he'd go to California for a month and not post a single photograph. Imagine all the opportunities for shirtless pictures. Shirtless at passport control, shirtless by the pool, shirtless crossing the Golden Gate Bridge. Plus we're only a few months from exams. Plus what kind of exchange program takes one student? The timing she chose for all of this just makes no sense at all."

"So where's Mark?"

I didn't always get along with Mark, even when we were mates—I played rugby with him, had to keep on his good side—but the idea that something bad happened to him because of me and Elza, without him even understanding what he was caught up in, makes me feel like I've stepped on a splinter of glass.

"My thoughts exactly."

Elza takes out another cigarette. She examines it, turning it over in her hand, then puts it back in the pack. "Has Ash ever seen us together?" she asks.

"I don't think so. But I mean, she seems to be staying with Holiday. She'll tell Ash who you are if Ash asks about you."

"It's not a great plan, but how about I try to stick close to them in school today? Just observe and report. I'll see if I overhear anything useful."

"All right," I say. "Let's just try and play this cool."

Ash isn't difficult to find. She's become an overnight sensation at Dunbarrow High. At morning break you can see her, dressed in white, sitting at one of the outdoor picnic tables with Holiday and the other popular girls. I'm at the other end of the lot, over near the cars, keeping an eye on her, just wondering. She knows I can see her, but never even glances at me. All I want is for her to slip up, show me something abnormal, prove to me that she's more than a cheerful Californian schoolgirl. In the light of day, watching her across the yard, all our evidence seems less substantial. For all I know, Ash can't see ghosts, has no idea there's a spirit with her face roaming the fields of Dunbarrow at night. Those ghosts might be hunting her, not me. Maybe there's a necromancer after *her*, and we're the only ones who can help her. All we've got are little pieces of the puzzle, and Ash just looks so blissfully confident and happy, sitting with Holiday Simmon and Alice Waltham, throwing her head back to laugh at something they're telling her. I know appearances can deceive, but her surface is still throwing me off.

Elza is struggling in her surveillance mission. She has many admirable qualities, my girlfriend, but blending into crowds isn't one of them. Her thunderhead of black hair foils any attempt to stay anonymous. She's lurking under a tree near the picnic benches, leaning against the trunk, pretending to read a paperback, but she's been on the same page for five minutes already.

After a while the bell rings for the second morning period, and Ash strolls into the main building with a flock of girls around her, Elza hurrying after them like a sheepdog in combat boots.

Lunchtime is the same story. Ash is at the center of a crowd, no doubt regaling them with stories about California. Her popularity actually functions as a defense: it's difficult for Elza to get near her without being instantly noticeable. I can see Alice Waltham and a couple of the other girls getting snippy when Elza tries to sit at the table nearest them in the dining hall, and eventually she gets into a full-blown argument with them and leaves. Ash watches her go.

I'm barely able to focus on my classes. My ribs hurt, and my sleepless night has left me feeling like my head's full of wool. I'm too tired and weirded out to pay attention to anything that's happening, even when Kirk does an impression of my fit during history and gets sent out. I basically stare at the floor, going over and over the previous night in my mind: the one-armed girl, the black-eyed woman, the way she sent me flying through the air with a single blow. I don't remember my Host being able to hurl people around like that. Just how powerful is that spirit? Should I tell Elza I've still got my dad's things? She's going to want to know why I kept that quiet since November. Would it even help us? I know the sigil can control my own Host, but I've got no idea what it'd do to someone else's. The Book of Eight would tell me, but the idea of ever looking inside that thing again makes me shudder. Last time I read the Book, it sucked my mind into its pages for three days. We still don't know why, or how I came out of it when I did.

At the end of the day, Elza's waiting for me on the road by the school gates, cigarette held loosely in her left hand. I pull her in for a kiss.

"I thought you said you didn't want to kiss me when I was smoking," she says when we break apart.

"Rules are made to be broken," I say.

"I know I should stop," she says, giving the cigarette a guilty glance.

"I'm not going to make you. You know that."

"Well, I'm sorry. Today was stressful."

"Did you overhear anything?"

"Mostly no. Let's just wait here a moment."

"Sounds good to me," I say, pulling her in for another kiss.

"Seriously," she says, laughing, "give it a break. We have to watch."

I lean against the tree trunk beside her, casting my gaze over the kids leaving through the front gate, heading downhill, packs of girls with bags flapping by their hips, boys shouting and kicking balls around in the road. I actually resent them, I realize, these people who don't seem to have a care in the world. I know really they're all worried about acne or girls or boys or exams or their families, but it's hard to feel any sympathy when you're trapped inside a whole different set of problems.

"Holiday always leaves through this gate, right?" Elza asks.

"I mean . . . probably?"

"It was hard to get close to them," Elza says, "and to be honest, they weren't talking about anything interesting. Ash is hardly going to tell Holiday and her friends that she's a necromancer or a demon host or whatever she might turn out to be. She was mainly telling them about the bands she's seen in San Francisco. If she's acting, she does an exceptionally good impression of a nice, brainless California girl."

"So what are we doing here?"

"We're about to head back up to school. I heard Holiday talking about this charity fashion show they're rehearsing for. It seemed pretty clear that Ash was expected to stay and help out. They were discussing skinny jeans versus straight-legged jeans for like *twenty minutes*, I swear. . . . Anyway, they should all be in the main hall."

"So . . . ?"

"If they're there, it means we've got a few hours while Ash and Holiday aren't at home. Then I think we should go to Holiday's house and see what's going on there."

"How is that going to help?"

"I'd like to get a look at the current state of the Simmon household—preferably while Ashley Smith isn't around. I mean, aren't you worried about them? It's a whole family. We could at least ask when they decided to have Ash stay, how long she's with them, et cetera. I think it's worth trying."

I still sometimes have trouble believing I have a girl-friend who says stuff like *et cetera* in everyday conversations.

"She'll know we went up there," I say.

"She already knows that we know. We think."

"All right. What if we don't find anything, though?"

Elza shrugs. "Then we try something else. We talk to her?"

"Yeah, maybe." Even though I suggested confronting Ash this morning, it now sounds like a pretty unlikely strategy. But we don't have anything better. After another few minutes, we head back up the hill to Dunbarrow High. Most of the students are gone now, and there's no sports practice on Tuesday. It used to be the night we all met in the park. I remember those days, when my biggest worry was getting there before Kirk hogged all the alcohol. We make our way around the side of the school and sneak through the shrubbery toward the row of windows that look into the main hall. I can hear some pop song playing from behind the glass. We press ourselves against the brickwork, peeking into the hall. The lunch tables have been packed away, and there's a low wooden walkway protruding out into the room. Nobody's doing any fashion stuff at the moment; they're all laughing at some video on Holiday's phone. Ash's bright-white hair is clearly visible to Holiday's left. There's a big rack of clothes pushed up against one wall.

Watching them through the window, I still can't get myself to see Ash as an evil being.

"Well," Elza says quietly, "they're there, all right. Now let's make a call at Holiday's place."

I've only been to the Simmons' house once before, for what turned out to be among the most memorable parties of my life. I still remember the way, up to a big mock-Tudor mansion at the top of Wight Hill, the kind of neighborhood where you can imagine the residents meeting to discuss fining someone for having a hedge above the height specified in the residents' agreement. We walk up the gravel driveway to Holiday's sunburn-pink front door, still in school uniform. Elza pushes the doorbell before either of us can think better of it.

Holiday and her mum both have this thing where they can make anyone feel easy and welcome, no matter how surprised or unhappy they actually are to see them. I feel like I could be wearing a ski mask and waving a gun in Mrs. Simmon's face and she'd still give us the exact same smile.

"Luke? And Elza? How lovely to see you."

"Hello, Mrs. Simmon," Elza says, smiling back. "Are Holiday and Ashley here?"

"Oh, I'm afraid they're out at the moment," Mrs. Simmon says cheerily, although there's a subtle change in her expression when Elza mentions Ash. "They're still at school, rehearsing for Holiday's show."

"Oh, of course," Elza says. "How silly of me."

"I haven't seen either of you in a long time," says Mrs. Simmon. "Not since . . . Halloween, I think?"

There's an awkward pause. My Host came to the Simmons' house during the Halloween party, used everyone there as part of some kind of black-magic ritual that I still don't understand, and brutally killed the family cat for good measure. Mrs. Simmon doesn't know this is my fault, but I feel like she connects me with it in some hazy way.

"We've been busy studying, haven't we, Luke?" Elza says.

"Yeah," I say. "Big year."

"It's such a stressful time for you all," Mrs. Simmon says. "I bet you can't wait until it's all over. I know you'll both do fine."

"Thank you," I say.

"So, Mrs. Simmon, we're very sorry to be a bother," Elza says, winding some hair around her right hand, "but Holiday borrowed a DVD from me about a month ago. She said she'd give it back to me if I came by this evening, but maybe she forgot she wouldn't be here? So I was thinking, since we already walked over, maybe we could just go up to her room and get it?"

This story makes no sense at all, because Holiday never speaks to us and surely never speaks about us, and why would it be so important that we get the DVD right here and now? Holiday could bring it to school tomorrow. I fully expect Mrs. Simmon to raise some or all of these objections, but instead she just smiles even wider and says, "Of course!" and lets us into the house. Despite her leather jacket and combat boots and smoky bomb-blast of hair, which make her look like she's starring in a public service announcement about the Dangers Of Sniffing Glue, Elza has an incredibly winning way with adults. They just seem to trust her.

"Thanks so much," Elza says as we walk through the kitchen. "We need it for class, you see?"

Last time I was here, there were people standing motionless in every room and a circle of murderous ghosts waiting for me outside. I still shudder when I catch a glimpse of the garden through the kitchen windows. I remember the demon's hand reaching out, clutching that dark red rope of light that joined my body with the corpse of the cat . . .

"Luke?"

Mrs. Simmon is staring at me with alarm. I force a smile.

"Sorry," I say. "Just my mind wandering."

"So how long is Ash staying with you?" Elza asks.

Mrs. Simmon frowns.

"You know, I'm not exactly certain. But she is a lovely girl."

Elza frowns as well.

"I thought she said it was a month?" I say.

"Oh, of course," Mrs. Simmon says, almost gratefully. "A month! She's here for a month."

"What made you sign up with the Goodman Foundation to be her hosts?" Elza asks.

"Oh, you know. It's empowering for young women to get out into the world. She's a lovely girl. So polite. I think it was Holiday's idea originally. They started talking online somewhere. She's very fond of Ashley."

"Ash is just so . . ." Elza searches for a word. "Vivacious."

"Oh, she is." Mrs. Simmon smiles. "Ashley is a regular little hummingbird. She's a lovely girl."

"Well, it's really great of you to be her hosts," I say.

Nobody says anything for a moment. Mrs. Simmon's smile is unwavering.

"Would you mind if we . . . ?" Elza begins, and for a

horrible moment, I think Mrs. Simmon is going to escort us up to Holiday's room herself—denying us the time to search for anything—but she just nods and tells us to find her if we need any help.

They've replaced the carpeting in the hall where Alice poured wine on Elza. I wonder if Holiday got in trouble over that, or if the mass amnesia and brutal cat slaying made some spilled wine irrelevant. Probably the latter. We leave Mrs. Simmon smiling to herself in the downstairs hallway and press on up the stairs, across the landing, through the white-painted door with a golden H nailed to it.

"What was *that*?" Elza hisses the moment the door closes. "Did you see that? She didn't even know how long Ash is supposed to be here! *'She's a lovely girl.'* Just kept saying it! It made my skin crawl."

"It was really weird. She barely seemed to know who you were even talking about."

Elza glares around Holiday's room. "I think we can take about ten minutes in here before it starts to seem suspicious. I'm imagining the white suitcase full of white clothes belongs to Ash?"

"Be kind of a surprise if it doesn't."

Holiday's room is much as I remember it: a neat desk, a bookshelf, a large wall chart with a study schedule highlighted in twelve different colors. Four-poster bed draped with lights, an entire wall plastered with photos of Holiday and Alice and the other popular girls, all standing in those weird posing lines that girls do. Holiday smiles confidently from the center of a thousand different pictures. It's a whole galaxy of frozen smiles. I suppose if things had turned out differently, it would've been me standing next to her in these photos, rather than Mark.

Elza's staring intently at the desk.

"Did you find something?" I ask.

"No," she says, looking away. "Not at all."

She was looking at a framed photo of two girls on the beach, young, maybe eight years old. One of them is blond, the other red-haired and scowling.

"Is that . . ." I begin.

"Yeah, it's me and her," Elza says. "This was so long ago!"

"I always forget you used to be friends."

"I always forget, too. I was sure she had."

"You don't look very happy," I say.

"Second day of a summer in Devon. I was already sunburned. The redhead's curse."

"You used to go on vacation together?"

"Yes. I mean our mums used to be pretty close, too. . . . Anyway, that's over. We're different people now.

I mean, this is so type A!" Elza glances over the rest of the desk with disgust. "Look, she arranges her pencils in order of length . . . and the books are, like, color coded by spine!"

Elza's room looks like a missile strike leveled a library and then someone came and sprinkled tea mugs over the rubble.

The new addition to Holiday's room is a single camp bed, which is unfolded to the right of her four-poster. It's neatly made with white sheets and pillows. There's a white suitcase, which is full of neatly packed white clothes. We rifle through them, growing more and more frustrated. There's an unworn pair of white Converse, two identical white sundresses, a pair of white-framed sunglasses that won't be getting much use in Dunbarrow. A white cardigan, white gloves, a white silk scarf. White jeans, both skinny and straight. White T-shirts, six of them, still wrapped in plastic. White bras, white underwear. Some packs of spearmint gum.

"Who *is* this person?" Elza asks in despair. "Who has a suitcase like this? She can't be human."

Ash is somehow even more of a mystery than before. I don't know what we expected to find, but this wasn't it.

"No occult books?" Elza asks. "No jewelry? Like, a potential sigil or something?"

"Nothing," I say.

"She's going to know we went through this," Elza says. "I can't fold it all up again."

"I didn't think we were worried about that," I say. I put my hands inside the Converse, first the left and then the right, but there's nothing hidden in them. I cast my eyes around Holiday's room, but I can't see anything else that might belong to Ash.

"She could be anyone," Elza says to herself. "Ashley Smith could literally be anyone. Do we know she's even American?"

"It's an impressive accent if it's fake."

"I can't believe this." She sighs.

"What did you think we'd find? A little notebook titled *My Plan to Kill Luke and Elza—Please Don't Read*?"

"Don't be such a jerk," Elza snaps, waving one of Ash's bras around to emphasize her point. "You came up with precisely nothing—"

"What are you doing?"

We both freeze and turn sharply to look at the door, the picture of guilt.

A boy is leaning against the doorframe. He's wearing tracksuit bottoms and a football shirt. He looks about twelve years old. I realize it's Holiday's brother. I remember her talking about him, what seems like a thousand years ago. How she was worried he'd started smoking.

"We're friends of Holiday's," I say.

"Never seen you before," he says.

"We just came by to get a DVD?" Elza says, letting Ash's bra fall to the ground.

"Which one?" he asks.

"Er . . ." I grab the nearest case from Holiday's shelf. "This one. It's mine."

Holiday's brother sniggers.

I'm holding a *Best of Hannah Montana* DVD. Why does Holiday even have this?

"Lame," he says. Then, "What are you doing with Ash's stuff?"

"We thought the DVD might be in there," Elza says. "But it wasn't."

He doesn't say anything.

"We're going to leave now," I say firmly.

We walk toward Holiday's brother, and for a moment I think he's going to block the way and start shouting for his mum or something, but he lets us pass by.

"Are you friends with Ash?" he asks.

"Yeah," I say. "Do you like her?"

"I don't know," he says. "I don't think so."

"She's a lovely girl," Elza says heavily. "Once you get to know her."

I tuck Holiday's DVD into my jacket and we leave, saying a hurried good-bye to Mrs. Simmon. Once we're on the street, we start walking faster, looking around us, half expecting Ash to lunge out of the undergrowth at any moment. The sun is low in the sky, and the trees cast long shadows over the road. There aren't any clouds. It looks like it'll be a cold night.

I say good-bye to Elza in the center of Dunbarrow, and we head our separate ways. I walk back home, stolen DVD still in my coat. I don't know what we were thinking. All we've done is confirm to Ash that we're onto her. We don't know who (or what) she is or what she wants.

About halfway up the hill, I get a call from Holiday's phone. Who knew she still had my number? I don't answer.

I eat dinner, play with Ham. But I just can't get Ash out of my mind. I want to know who she is, what she's doing. We could be in danger. I have to know. So at eleven o'clock, I decide to try something else.

The way it happens is this: I lie on my bed with the door closed. Sometimes it helps to have the radio playing, but not always. I lie on my bed and I look up at the ceiling. I look at the crack in my ceiling and think about not having a body. I look at the crack, a slender dark flaw running through an expanse of perfect white, and forget I have a body. I listen to my breath, to my blood flowing, to the shrill electrical noise that I've come to think of as my nerves singing, and I try to forget I have blood or flesh or bone. I try to hear the silence beyond all these noises.

And when I get it right, become part of that silence, I don't have a body at all.

I'm floating up near the crack, about a finger's length away from the plaster skin of the ceiling. I drift, turn over lazily, like I'm floating in warm salt water. Below, on my bed, my body's eyes are closed. I'm sleeping. Or rather, I'm up here. It's all a bit complicated.

In October, my Host cut my spirit loose from my body and possessed me, drove my body around instead. I managed to get it back from them, but it was a close thing. I'm doing fine, as far as my body is concerned, no adverse effects, but the moorings feel a bit looser now. It seems that after you've left it once, that makes it easier the next time.

The problem with watching people—one of the problems—is it's hard to stay on them all the time. You have to sleep, have to eat, have to piss. Your foot goes dead; you have to lie in the mud; the neighbors call the police because you've been hanging around their cul-de-sac for six hours. Without a body, many of these issues disappear. The only people who'll see me are the ones with second sight, and there aren't many of them in Dunbarrow. Elza and me are the only ones I know of, although for the moment I'm going to assume Ash can see me as well. It's not a perfect way to watch her, but if I stay out of her line of sight, I should be fine.

Anyway, I leave my body safely resting on my bed and fly out through the roof into the night sky. There's a strong wind, silvery clouds rushing past the moon, but without my skin, I don't feel a chill. Dunbarrow from above is a map of orange street lamps, the conical headlights of cars snaking through dark streets. I fly higher, almost touching the lowest clouds, until the town is just a smear of electric light against the dull shapes of the forests and moors. I float there for a moment, looking down at Dunbarrow, at Brackford to the south and Throgdown in the north; then I dive back down, wishing I could feel the wind in my hair as I fall like a hunting bird toward Wight Hill. You don't see a lot of ghosts flying, maybe because they don't accept that they're dead. They're missing out, anyway. It's the best part.

I fly down Holiday's road and come to a halt almost directly above her house. One problem I hadn't thought about is the black-eyed woman. Assuming she does work with Ash somehow, I might dive into the house and come face-to-face with her, which is not something I want to risk. I don't know if Ash herself could hurt me when I'm just a spirit, but that ghost definitely could. If she's hanging around, this will be much more difficult.

I descend in slowly through the attic, homing in on the room where I can hear music. I drift across the landing and lower my head slowly through the floor. For a moment all I can see is the inside of the landing, a horrible blur of darkness; then my face breaks through the ceiling of the room below, and I'm looking down on them all.

They're watching TV: Holiday, Mr. and Mrs. Simmon, and Ash, her vivid white form occupying a beanbag to the right of Holiday's chair. She's wearing white pajamas. There's a game show on. Ash laughs. I wonder why she's putting up this amount of pretense. She doesn't know anybody is watching her, does she? Who is she pretending to be normal for? Maybe it's for herself?

I stay hidden inside the ceiling, with only my face breaking through the plaster. If Ash looks directly upward then she'll see me, but that seems unlikely. Assuming she even has second sight, of course. I watch them for half an hour, and then at midnight the TV goes off.

"Time for bed," Mr. Simmon says, stretching, and then, in a different tone, "Who are you?"

"I'm sorry, dear?" Mrs. Simmon says.

"Who is this person?"

"Dad—"

"No, no! *Who is this?* I've never . . ."

Ash says nothing, just looks at them all with her gray eyes. Holiday's dad gestures at her helplessly as his wife and daughter look on with slight frowns. Nobody gets up from their seat. He clutches at his head and puts the remote down on the coffee table.

"I . . ." Mr. Simmon sounds like he's having trouble breathing. "I don't . . . I think I'll lie down. I must apologize, Ashley. You're a lovely girl. We're glad to have you."

"Sorry about my dad," Holiday groans as he leaves the room. "He gets really stressed out."

"It's fine," Ash says with a wide smile.

There's no way I'm going to leave after that little episode. I keep inside the walls, staying out of Ash's sight, hiding in the insulation foam, lurking beneath the floorboards in the company of spider husks and dust. Holiday and Ash sit on Holiday's bed, talking about the fashion-show rehearsal. Ash does a pretty good impression of Alice Waltham, which would make me laugh if I didn't find Ash the most sinister person on the planet right now.

It's way past midnight by the time Holiday switches the light off and they finally stop talking. They've already tidied the room up from my and Elza's invasion. All of Ash's clothes are folded back into her suitcase. She lies motionless in her foldout bed while Holiday turns over in her bedclothes, snuffling and adjusting pillows. Then there's silence. Holiday's phone is charging under her bed, pulsing orange like the beat of a strange luminous heart. After half an hour, I'm starting to feel like a serious creep. Do I just watch them sleep all night?

Without warning, Ash sits upright.

I dart underneath Holiday's chest of drawers, only the top of my head sticking up through her cream carpet. I see Ash's feet and shadow moving on the floor. She's getting dressed. Silently, she crosses Holiday's room and closes the door behind her.

The chase is on.

I drift out onto the landing, but she's already downstairs. I hear the front door close. I shoot up through the attic and hide behind one of the chimney stacks, peering around it at the moonlit street. Ash is wearing a white overcoat, white leggings, a white wool hat. She's not particularly well hidden, although she moves with an easy silence that I can't help but admire. She makes her way down Wight Hill, seeming unhurried, not bothering to check if she's being followed. I trail her at a cruise, keeping myself behind houses and trees, trying to make sure I'm not crossing any open patches of sky.

Ash strolls down a side street, rustling in her inside pocket for something, then unlocks an old car (surprisingly, it's navy blue) and gets in. How old is she? I know they let you drive earlier in America, but still . . . The car roars to life, coughing exhaust, the headlights illuminating a plastic bag blowing in the road. Ash sits still at the wheel for a few moments, thinking about who-knows-what. Then she pulls out into the road and drives.

She's a good driver, has clearly been doing it awhile, and I have no doubt that if the police pull her over, she's got some plausible-looking license in the glove compartment. This isn't a joyride. Ash does this regularly. She's heading out to the southern side of town, near the motorway, up past the school and out through Kirk's estate, and then farther out, the only car on the road, easily tracked by watching her headlights cut through the trees. There's nothing out here. Where on earth is Ash going? The only thing this far out is the new Pilgrim Grove development, and it's still under construction.

Ash does pull into the development. She drives slowly through the half-built houses, a whole fresh outgrowth of Dunbarrow, two hundred new homes, each with an angled roof and buttery stone walls and geometrically precise garden plots, all half-constructed, windows without glass staring at me like blind eyes. There are yellow construction machines parked here and there, sleeping dinosaurs, monstrous diggers with wheels that look like they should be exploring the surface of the moon. Crates and trucks and barrows and enormous revolving drums of cement. What is she looking for? Her headlights illuminate a mound of gravel, and then a house with half its walls missing, the skeleton of a house, just the idea of a home . . . and then another house that's something more. One of the Pilgrim Grove houses is already finished.

It looks like all the others: sloped orange roof, smooth stone walls, a garage that Ash pulls her car into, a garden that's just churned mud surrounded by a fence, a swinging gate . . . except there's glass in all the windows, a front door, an electric light burning inside; everything but milk bottles on the front step. Ash gets out of her car and fishes for another set of keys, opens the front door, and vanishes inside. I stay where I am, hidden in the shell of the house opposite. Clouds drift in front of the moon. The silvered fields around Pilgrim Grove darken. I hear an owl again, whooping somewhere in the trees. Another light turns on, in the upstairs of the house. Then Ash pulls a curtain across the window.

When I'm certain she's not coming out again, twenty minutes later, I float down to ground level and make my way up to the fence. There's none of the supernatural defenses I've seen in the past: no hazel charms chiming, no undead animals screaming at me from the undergrowth. There doesn't seem to be anything stopping me from gliding right in.

I melt into the house through the wall. I'm in what presumably is meant to be a living room, although it's difficult to tell because there's no furniture. The walls are white; the floor is nondescript polished wood. I can hear Ash moving upstairs. I float into the hallway, which is also empty of anything except a pair of white Converse sneakers by the front door. I move through into another blank room, possibly intended as a dining room. The large bay windows afford a view of a cement mixer, a hollowed-out house, and the moonlit sky. If I had a body, I'd probably have goose bumps right now. I move into the kitchen, which looks slightly more normal. There's a stove, a fridge, a microwave. Someone—Ash, I imagine—has left a package of dried fruit on the counter. At least we've got some proof she eats something. The kitchen loops back around to the front room again. There's a large dark-framed mirror hanging on the far wall, which I didn't notice before.

Being in spirit form isn't making me feel much safer in this place. Is this even the same living room I was in before? I definitely didn't see the mirror last time. I feel like the view from the window may have changed a little as well. Like the moon is in a different place or something. I turn back toward the kitchen and come face-to-face with the one-armed girl ghost.

She's smiling at me.

"Hi," I say.

She replies in gibberish. She is the spitting image of Ash, right down to their voices. She's got the same mouth, same sharp cheeks, same everything. They have to be twins. Her hair is lank and unhealthy-looking, and there's no ring in her nose, but other than that, there are barely any differences at all. Now that I'm looking closer, I realize that this ghost's eyes are a far deeper blue than Ash's colorless eyes.

"Are you Ashley Smith?" I ask her. "What's going on?"

The ghost twin, the one-armed girl, reaches out toward me. I move backward, into the blank living room. I'm extra nervous now, because I'm sure the black-eyed woman can't be too far away. And what's Ash—Ash's body—doing upstairs?

The one-armed girl is pointing behind me. I turn. She seems to be gesturing at the mirror. It's enormous, taking up most of the far wall. I notice we're both reflected in it, which is pretty weird, actually, because mirrors don't normally show reflections of ghosts. . . .

There's a high ringing noise in my ears, and I realize, as the one-armed girl laughs with delight, that I've made a mistake.

When I come back into consciousness, I'm trapped in a strange room. I remember looking myself in the eye, and then suddenly there was no reflection, and everything was chiming like a bell—the sound, I've started to learn, of magic that means business. I'm confined inside a room with black walls, maybe a little larger than your average coffin. There's no space to move, although luckily I don't have muscles that can cramp. The far wall is made of glass, and through it I can see the blank living room in Ash's house. It's empty. The one-armed girl is nowhere to be seen.

The first thing I do is try to fly out, of course, but there's no way. Whatever these walls are made of, it's not stone or wood or metal, and I can't pass through them. I'm trapped here. I don't even know where *here* is.

After a long time, I hear footsteps approaching, and Ash walks through the living room beyond the glass, with her back to me. She doesn't glance in my direction. Is this a window? What am I watching her through?

I must be inside the mirror. I don't know how that's possible, but it's the only view of this room that makes sense.

She clatters about in the kitchen for a few moments, then reemerges carrying a plate of rice cakes, celery, dried fruit. Diet food. She looks me right in the eye, gives a little squeak, and drops the food all over the floor. A rice cake rolls across the blond wood, coming to rest up against the far wall. Ash composes herself.

"How long have you been in there?" she asks, as if we'd just met by accident in the park or something. There doesn't seem much point in lying to her.

"A while," I say.

"Spirit walking . . ." she says to herself. "I should've thought of that." No sign of her permanent questioning lilt. I suppose this is her real voice.

Ash runs a hand through her cropped white hair. She bends down, picks up her plate, puts as much of the food back onto it as she can reach. She leaves the farthest rice cake where it is. I wait silently, still not sure what's going on. Should I be scared?

Ash takes the plate into the kitchen, then comes back without it and walks right up to the mirror. She puts one finger against the glass, frowning. Her nose ring glints in the reflected lamplight. Her eyebrows are as pale as her hair, which is unsettling. I thought she bleached her hair to get it so white, but it seems to grow like that on its own. Ash bites her lip.

"I guess," she says softly, "we have some stuff to talk about."

(ash)

Without saying another word, Ash takes a step back and starts fumbling for something with her left hand in the air, one eye closed, like she's trying to thread an invisible needle. I feel a nasty tug in my chest, and even though I'm outside my body and don't have a stomach, I suddenly want to throw up. I look down, and I see the lifeline that joins my body to my spirit glowing in Ash's hand, as insubstantial as dust lit by a sunbeam. How can she take hold of it?

"I'm sure you know what'll happen if I break this," she says, "but don't worry. I need you alive."

Her American accent seems to be real at least—she hasn't dropped it—but there's a glittering sharpness to her that she's been hiding.

Ash gives my lifeline another sharp tug, like she's trying to reel something in.

"That ought to do it," she says. "Wait here."

"Do I have a choice?" I ask.

Ash smiles, then turns and walks back into the kitchen. I think of shouting after her, but again there doesn't seem much point. She's the one running the show here, for now at least. She comes out with another plate of food, walks back through the living room, ignoring me completely, and disappears upstairs. After maybe half an hour—it's hard to judge time without a clock, with only artificial light—she comes back carrying a white plastic patio chair. She places the chair lightly in the middle of the empty room, facing the mirror, and then, finally spotting the rice cake she dropped, she picks it up and goes back into the kitchen. I'm left looking at white walls, a polished floor, a single white chair. It's like the conceptual-art exhibit Elza dragged me to last month.

After a long while of this, I hear a heavy knock at the front door. So she called someone? I'm going to meet whoever is behind all of this? I knew there had to be someone else pulling the strings. Another necromancer? Ash walks past me again. I hear her open the front door, but no word of greeting, just the sound of a heavy tread in the hallway. Definitely another person. I'm wound tight with fear and anticipation. Who could it be?

Ash comes back into the room holding my hand.

What?

It's my body. No question about it: definitely me. Brown hair, navy polo shirt, familiar face. My jeans and Lacoste shoes are splattered with fresh mud—I must have trekked through the fields to get here. My lifeline pulses between us, thicker and brighter now that the distance between my body and spirit is so much shorter. I had no idea this was possible. My eyes (my body's eyes) are closed. Ash guides me across the room and gently encourages my body to sit down in the patio chair. She runs a hand over my face.

"So really," Ash says, "I can do whatever I like to you. Clear?"

"Perfectly," I say, trying not to show any fear.

"Try anything cute," she says, "anything at all, and you'll wish you hadn't. And whatever I ask you, I want the truth."

Her gray eyes glitter in the harsh light. I'm starting to wonder what exactly happened to Mark Ellsmith.

"Whatever you want to know," I say.

"Great. Let's keep that attitude," she says. She slides one white-socked foot over the smooth wood of the floor. She looks strange and childish as she does it. I'm still finding it hard to match Ash's appearance and mannerisms with the threat she actually poses to me. It's like that picture of the two faces that are also a vase. Picture One: Petite exchange student. Picture Two: Necromancer, possible murderer.

"So," she continues. "Luke Manchett. You're Horatio Manchett's son and heir."

"Yes."

"Horatio died last October," she says.

"He choked on a piece of steak." I confirm.

"So you inherited his Host?"

"I did. There were eight ghosts —"

"I understand how necromancy works, Luke. You inherited his copy of the Book, his sigil, his binding rings, and eight spirits. Where are they now?"

"I got rid of them," I say.

"How?"

"The Manchett Host is broken. They're gone. I sent them back to Deadside."

Ash yanks my body's head back by the hair. "Really?" she yells.

"Yes! Ash! Seriously! Believe me!"

She lets my head roll back into position.

"Don't lie to me," she says.

"Why would I come here myself if I had a Host to do it for me? They're gone!"

"Yes," she says after a pause. "That's what I've been

told. I just didn't quite believe it. So you broke your own family's Host. Banished them. Why?"

"I never wanted them. . . . Necromancy . . . I didn't know . . . I had no idea. They nearly killed me. I had to get rid of them."

"He never told you? Horatio?"

"Never."

"Well." Ash bursts out laughing. I think I preferred it when she was shouting. "That must've been a surprise."

"Yes," I say, unsmiling. "It was."

"Had you ever seen a ghost before?"

"It was kind of a 'deep-end' situation. I had to learn on the job."

"I'm actually impressed," she says. "I know all about Horatio's Host. My father said he was insane to trust Octavius as much as he did. Everyone thought that Host was a disaster waiting to happen."

"Your father . . . ?"

"I don't remember saying this was a conversation," Ash snaps.

"Who are you, really?" I ask.

"I'm Ashley Smith from Marin County, California," she says, but there's this mocking tone to her voice.

"Who's that meant to fool? That's the fakest fake name. It's like saying you're called John Brown."

"There's plenty of people named Ashley Smith. But no, you're right. That's not my name."

"Who are you?" I ask again.

"I'm nobody," she says. "I'm nobody, and I'm asking the questions."

"So ask."

"When did you last see him?" Ash says.

"Dad?" I don't see much use in lying—she might already know the answer, as she seems to know all about me—but I don't want to tell her what happened with him and the Devil last Halloween. "I was six. He was leaving us. He was wearing a red tie with polka dots. He . . . Are you all right?"

Ash is giving me the strangest look.

"It's just very odd," she says. "I've wondered about you for years. What his family was like. Who he loved. Finally meeting you . . ."

I'm seized with sudden inspiration. "He did something bad to you," I say. "Horatio."

"Huh," Ash snorts. "That's hardly a wild guess. He did bad shit to everyone he met, as far as I can tell."

"Me and my mum, too," I say.

Ash doesn't reply. Maybe this is how I get out of here. Play to her sympathy. Show her we're in the same boat. I hope she's not another version of the Shepherd, seeing me and Dad as the same person, hungry for the revenge she can't take on him. . . .

"It sounds like he messed us both up," I say.

"Don't say that!" she screams. "Don't *ever* say that! Don't compare yourself to me! You don't know! Don't you dare tell me that!" She's right up close to the mirror's surface, yelling so loud the glass vibrates.

"Sorry, Ash! I'm sorry! Please!"

She's biting her lip, clearly trying not to cry. She turns away, strides into the kitchen. I hear her banging around. I'm certain she's going to come back with a knife or something and go to work, and I'm frantically trying to pry my spirit fingers into the seam around the mirror's glass, force my way out, but it's just not happening, and then she comes back and all she's holding is a glass of water. She puts some pills in her mouth and takes a gulp.

"Sorry," Ash says absurdly. "I'm sorry. I'm trying to work on my mood and stuff. Be more balanced."

"That's . . . OK, Ash. Let it all out."

I really don't know what to say. She's like the clouds crossing the moon in the night sky outside: cold, distant, constantly changing. She's pacing the pale wood just behind my body's chair. She gestures with the half-empty glass. She's about to say something and doesn't. Ash wants something from me, I think. She wants something from me, but she can't quite come out and ask for it yet.

"It's been ten years for me, too," she says, "since I last saw my father. We were six."

There's something Dad told me nudging at my mind, bumping up against the shore of my memory like a boat at high tide. Something Dad told me . . . last year, that night, Halloween, when I spoke to him and the Devil . . .

He left me and Mum ten years ago. There was a war between necromancers. That was why he needed to summon the Fury, his demon, and why he used . . . why he used my unborn brother for the ritual.

Where does Ash fit in with this?

"The war," I say. "I know about that."

"They were supposed to be on the same side," she says.

The memory isn't a boat bumping against the shore anymore, it's more like a dam bursting. A name flashes into my head.

"Magnus," I say.

"Good," Ash says. "Magnus Ahlgren. And I still remember the last time I saw him."

"You're his—"

"Daughter," she snaps. Ash swallows the last of her water. "I was his daughter. Your father betrayed mine. He sent his Host to our secret house one night and killed my family. My father died. Our family's Host was broken and consumed by Horatio's demon. So you're right, I'm not Ashley Smith. My name is Ashana Ahlgren."

"But you're . . . American? I thought Magnus was Scandinavian."

"We're Swedish. I lived there until I was six, then I lived in a lot of other places. It wasn't safe. But I ended up choosing California when I was twelve, and that's where we've stayed for the last four years. It's beautiful. When we're done here—"

"Done with what?"

She ignores me. She turns the glass around in her hands. She's thinking.

"I'm sorry about your father," I say.

"Don't be. I barely knew him. If we made a noise when he was reading, he'd make us hold a block of ice until it melted. Child-rearing up beyond the Arctic Circle. And Mum had crossed over just after I was born, so."

"Right."

"I loved our Host, though. They're the ones who brought us up. They were kind to me. I barely even spoke to any living people when I was really little. And then, you know, your big dog-headed demon ate them all."

"You always saw ghosts?" I ask. The idea of being brought up by a Host, of loving them, strikes me as totally insane. It's like being brought up by a writhing nest of vipers. The idea of the Shepherd or the Prisoner being my childhood guardian is beyond absurd.

"I've been a member of the Ahlgren Host more or less since I was born. Dad put a sigil minor inside my hand when I was eight days old." Ash holds up her left arm to the mirror. I peer at her hand. There's a tiny white scar, the size of a five-pence piece, on the inside of her wrist.

"There's a sigil inside you? How does that work?"

"Yeah," Ash says carelessly, "it's part of the bone. It's like this little stone charm, and then you do some magic and it fuses into you. Sigil minors are like sigils with training wheels, I suppose. I was going to get a proper sigil when I was eighteen."

"Dad had a black ring. I didn't know sigils could be inside you."

"I know all about those rings. Well, sigils can be anything that's properly worked and prepared. Some of the old necromancers had oaken staves or, like, crowns made of gold, stuff like that. Octavius, your dad's old Shepherd—he had his sigil mark tattooed onto himself. Ahlgrens have always had bone sigils, made part of us, because you can't steal them."

"So you've got a Host?" I ask.

"Sort of. It's complicated. And I'm supposed to be asking *you* questions. . . . So, I know you've read the Book of Eight. Where do you keep it?"

"I got rid of it," I say.

Ash looks me in the eye. "You're a bad liar," she says. "And you're awful at investigating people. Your goth girl-friend? Worst eavesdropper I've ever seen. And coming into Holiday's house like that . . . as if I'd keep anything important there. Honestly."

"Why are you staying there? How did you make the whole exchange story work? Holiday's family?"

"I'm actually discovering that I'm quite fond of the Simmons. Don't worry about them."

"What about Mark Ellsmith?"

"He's in a hotel."

"Would this hotel bear any resemblance to the farm that dogs get sent to when they're really ill?"

Ash snorts. "He's alive, if that's what you mean. I don't just murder people, Luke. He's being paid to live there for a month. I can give you the address if you like."

"I'm hardly in much of a position to check it out if you did. How are you . . . how did you manage all of this?"

"I have my ways. I sort of had some outdated ideas of who you were. I thought you were popular, so I decided I'd just come in at the top and find out what kind of person you were before I asked you for anything. And then I get here and find out you're not invited to anything any-more, and you spend all your time with that one girl . . .

so clearly something had happened with your father's Host. But it was frustrating, and you seemed to be onto me immediately."

"You were hardly subtle. Gliding into school dressed all in white."

"I know." Ash sighs. "I never realized how much I'd stand out in this depressing little place. Ah well."

"And I followed you back here. You didn't expect that."

"No, I didn't. Although you got yourself stuck in a spirit trap. I wouldn't give yourself a pat on the back just yet."

"It's hard to feel smug when you're trapped in a mirror," I admit.

"I don't feel that smug out here," she replies.

"So what do you want from me? Why did you come to find me?"

Ash looks at the floor.

"Actually," she says, "I sort of came here to ask for your help."

I don't know how to respond to this. Usually when people ask for your help, it's assumed you can either agree or turn them down. I don't really feel like I can say no to Ash. She watches me intently, running her right foot back and forth across the floor. Her sock makes a soft sound against the wood.

"Normally people who ask you for help don't have you captured."

"You trapped yourself there. This isn't your house. Nobody invited you."

I don't say anything. Given everything Ash has done in the past few days, I feel totally justified in following her to this house. I'm not about to apologize.

"You seem like someone I can talk to," she says after a pause. "If I let you back into your body, will you promise not to do anything stupid?"

"Of course," I say. Ash barely weighs a hundred pounds. The second she lets me out of here, I'm heading for the door.

She frowns. "Well, you would tell me that. You want me to let you go. You're thinking, *Oh, she's so small and delicate, no way can she keep me here. . . .*"

"I don't hit girls."

"What makes you think you'd get the chance?"

Ash makes a beckoning motion with her left hand. A spirit blinks into existence beside her. The ghost is a tall, dark-skinned woman with long black hair and eyes like pools of oil. She wears a white robe, and a broken spear juts from her chest. The ghost I saw last night. Some of the pieces are coming together.

"This is my retainer," Ash says, "the last of the Ahlgren Host. The Widow."

"We already met," I say.

The black-eyed woman looks from my body to my spirit, trapped in the mirror, and back again.

"What would you have me do?" she asks Ash softly, in a voice like frost forming.

"This is Luke Manchett, Horatio's heir. He will be our guest," Ash says. "He is not to leave without my permission."

"As you wish," the Widow replies.

"When I let you out of the mirror," Ash says, turning to me, "you're to go directly back into your body. If you try and go anywhere else, you'll wish you hadn't. Are we clear?"

"Perfectly," I say, eyeing the Widow. I've got no illusions about my ability to outrun Ash's terrifying servant, and besides, I'd be leaving my body here.

Ash seems satisfied with my answer. She walks up to the mirror and presses her left hand against the glass. A thin, high chime sounds, and the glass of the mirror splits neatly down the middle. The two halves of the mirror swing outward like a set of double doors, and I find myself pushed back into the living room, like a piece of paper caught in a gale. The Widow has one hand resting on the shaft of the spear that sticks from her chest; she's watching me for any sudden movements. I give her what

I hope is a reassuring grin and float toward my body. My head has fallen to one side, and my breathing is light and regular. There's a zit coming through on my left cheek, a deep red hill. I need to shave.

I fall into myself.

I come awake in the white plastic chair, shivering, with a knot of tension halfway down my back. I flex my fingers and toes. The room is absolutely freezing, although I think this has a lot to do with the presence of Ash's servant. The house has that new-paint smell, harsh and artificial.

Ash is facing me, with her back to the mirror. There's no sign of the crack or opening in its surface anymore.

"So you'll behave yourself, Luke?"

"Yeah," I say. My eyes feel gritty. I blink. "I promise, seriously."

"You look cold," Ash says. "Hang on. I have some oversize stuff that might fit." She vanishes into the hall, and I hear her padding up the stairs. I look at myself in the mirror. I don't look good. The Widow is standing behind me, hands resting on the back of my chair. The cold coming from her skin burns. I almost ask if she'd consider backing off a bit, but one look into her tar-pit eyes squashes that idea. Why do her eyes look like that? I'd assumed the Shepherd's eyes were a one-off, just some strange side effect of him being evil, but it seems like there's something more to it than that.

Ash comes back with a white fisherman's sweater. She hands it to me, and I pull it over my head. It's a surprisingly good fit, maybe a bit too tight at the chest. It's clearly made from expensive wool.

Ash fiddles with her nose ring. Neither of us seems quite sure where to go from here.

"Are you hungry?" she asks after an uncomfortably long pause.

"I am, actually."

"Spirit walking, leaving your body vacant, is supposed to speed up your metabolism," she says. "Shamans used to feast for eight days and eight nights before they attempted a journey to the other place."

"How do you know that?"

"I do have Magnus's library," Ash says. "All his books and papers. Your dad stole most of them, but he didn't know about the encrypted backup of the archives. I've been studying them for years."

"Lucky. Dad only left me some random papers."

"I'm not lucky," Ash says.

"Sorry," I say quickly. "I just mean, Horatio only gave me some pages of numbers and stuff."

"And the Book of Eight," Ash says. "Don't forget that. Your demon destroyed my family's copy. Burned it."

"You don't have one?"

"They're not easy to come by. I've read everything ever written *about* it, but I've never seen an actual copy. You're luckier than you realize. Anyway, aren't you hungry?"

She walks past me. I stand up and follow her into the gleaming white kitchen. I lean against the doorframe. I can feel the Widow standing behind me, her deathly cold aura making me shiver even through Ash's sweater. I glance around, accidentally make eye contact with the ghost, and quickly look away. Ash is breezily rummaging through some cupboards, her back turned, but there's nothing I can do. I'm stuck here. She's got me right where she wants me.

Ash makes me a little plate of dried fruit, olives, a cup of yogurt. I sit up on the counter and start to eat. I don't have much of a taste for olives, but the dried apricots are exactly what I needed. The gnawing hunger in my gut quiets down.

"I have Coke in the fridge," Ash says, "if you want some sugar. Or there's tap water. I didn't remember to buy a kettle yet."

"How did you get the electricity connected up here? Whose house are we in?"

"It's mine," Ash says. "I paid for it."

"This development isn't finished until next year."

"I paid five times the market price for this house to be finished by this March, to my exact specifications, and work has been suspended on the other sites for a month."

"That's not possible."

"It's possible," Ash says, "if you have enough money. I needed my own place in Dunbarrow, away from the town. This seemed ideal."

"Are you, like, rich?"

Ash smiles. "We're so rich we're not even on the rich list. The Ahlgrens have been raising the dead for centuries. There's plenty of opportunity to earn in our line of work. Since I'm not eighteen yet, my access is restricted. I can only use some of our fronts and stuff. But I get by."

"The Goodman Foundation?"

"That's one of the ways I move money around."

I remember my own inheritance, the money Berkley tried to tempt me with, the fortune that vanished into thin air when I didn't choose the way he wanted me to. Somehow I suspect Dad's fortune was small compared to the fruits of many centuries of necromancy. When your servants are invisible, intangible, and can kill most people by looking at them the wrong way, it's not hard to see how a necromancer could earn a living.

I swallow the last of my food.

"So what do you want my help with?" I ask Ash.

"I need your copy of the Book of Eight," she says.

"I gave it back."

"To who?"

"The Devil," I say.

"Ah," Ash says, not seeming as impressed as I was hoping, "so that's how you got rid of the Host. Halloween. The Rite of Tears."

"I don't have it anymore."

"Do you think he's lying?" Ash asks the Widow.

"Yes," the ghost replies.

"Now, why would he do something like that?" Ash asks softly.

My stomach lurches. "I don't know what you want with it."

"Fair enough," Ash says. She pinches the bridge of her nose. Breathes in and out. "I didn't want to do this tonight. But you're right. I wouldn't agree to help someone before I knew what they needed help with either."

"Mistress Ahlgren?" the Widow says.

"I want him to want to help us," Ash tells her. "It's the easiest way."

Without another word, Ash turns and walks back through the living room to the hallway and the staircase. I'm clearly expected to follow her, and I do, noticing the lightness in the sky outside the window. We must've been talking all night, although I don't feel tired. My body did sleep, I suppose. Ash must be exhausted. The Widow glides along beside me, her face as blank as the walls.

The stairs are made from the same blond wood, leading at a right angle up onto a large landing. There's a window, affording another view of the dawn's glow rising behind the half-finished estate. There's a bathroom, three doors that are shut, one hanging open. As we pass this door, I can see a bed inside, a desk, a freestanding clothes rack laden with white apparel. Ash's room, I suppose. So she's keeping some things at Holiday's place for show? How much stuff do you need for a month's visit? We stop in front of the farthest door.

"She's in here," Ash tells me softly, and opens it.

This must be the master bedroom—it's big, larger even than the living room downstairs. It's dark, and there's a strong antiseptic smell. I can sense that the room is full of something: large suitcases, or maybe amplifiers? I'm thinking immediately of an audio mixer, because I can see glowing lights and readouts, but that doesn't make sense. Why would Ash be showing me an audio mixer? There's a low metallic rasping noise, like a robot breathing. Ash turns on the light.

There's a bed with a girl lying in it.

The girl is connected to the room's machines. The

room is filled with them; they own the room. It's a room for machines, and it seems like there should be no space for her or anything else that's living. She's got an IV in her arm, tubes in her nose and mouth. Tubes snaking under the white bedsheets. The smell of disinfectant is overpowering, but underneath it I can smell her, the girl, her body's own smell, skin and hair that's gone unwashed. There are machines stacked all around her, banks of lights and dials, a monitor that shows her vital signs: numbers, graphs, an oscillating readout. I see that the master bedroom boasts an impressive array of electric plugs and a sink installed in the far corner.

"She's been on life support for a decade. The machines do everything for her," Ash says to me. "Everything except what makes a life worth living."

I come and stand next to Ash at the foot of the bed. The girl lying there, motionless, is the one-armed girl I saw in the field behind my house. The same girl I saw in Ash's kitchen. Lying here, in human form, I see both her arms are intact. So why is her ghost missing an arm? The girl's hair, long and tangled, is bunched up around her face and neck. She's dressed in a mint-green hospital gown. Her pale feet, sticking out from beneath her bedsheets, are bare. Her face, although difficult to see under the breathing and feeding tubes, is Ash's face.

"You're—"

"Twins," Ash says. "Identical. I'm about an hour older. Her name is Ilana Ahlgren."

Ash brings two chairs through, and we sit at the foot of the bed. It's hard to know where to look. Watching Ilana feels like an intrusion somehow. Ash barely takes her eyes off the monitors.

"I hated to do this," Ash says. "We have private home care in America. Very best. Bringing her over here was the hardest part. But I had to."

"Why?"

"Her spirit wanders at night. You already saw her. There's no way of stopping it. I've tried everything. She's very . . . trusting. She needs the Widow with her, to make sure nothing tries to hurt her. But I needed the Widow here as well, so there really wasn't another way. I couldn't leave Ilana in California."

So the Widow guards Ilana and Ash. I had worked that much out for myself.

"Why did she come to my house?" I ask.

"I don't know. She has strange ideas. Her mind isn't right."

"So you don't have a clue why she might be interested in me?"

"We share a lot of stuff. . . . It's hard to explain. Sometimes I have dreams where I am her. Sometimes she knows things I know without me telling her. I think she knew I wanted to ask you for help. That's why she went to find you."

"Well, I suppose it worked," I say. "In a way, she brought me here."

"I guess so."

"So what happened to her?" I ask. "Why's she in a coma? Why does she climb out of her body at night and wander around?"

"Your father happened to her."

I look at Ilana's face, eyes closed, thin plastic tubes snaking into her nose and mouth. I look at the displays on the machines, pulsing red numbers and oscillating bars, measuring her life out in beats on a screen.

"Horatio didn't even know us," Ash continues. "I doubt he gave me or Ilana a second thought. He sent his demon, the Fury. He was thousands of miles away, back home safe in England with you and your mother."

"I'm sorry, Ash. I never knew."

"So you keep saying," Ash says. She leans forward, looking down at the floor, one hand gripping the rail of Ilana's bed. "That's what makes this worse for me. You grew up without knowing about any of this. You didn't have to run away from home in the middle of the night, six years old, everything on fire behind you. You haven't spent your life looking after Ilana"—she smacks her hand against the bed for emphasis—"moving her from country to country under a fake name. Wondering if Horatio would ever send his Host back to finish us off. I never even cried for the first few years. I couldn't."

"It's not fair," I say.

"No, it wasn't. We'd never hurt anyone. I only remember pieces of that night. The Widow and the Errant woke us up, and there was smoke everywhere. . . . The house was burning, and I didn't know where to go. They wouldn't tell me what was happening. It came up behind us when we were in the courtyard. Nearly winter, snow on the ground. It looked like the smoke at first, rushing at us, and then I saw it had a shape, like a dog . . . a big hungry dog."

"I've seen it as well," I remind her. "It nearly killed me, too." Of all my father's servants, the Fury scared me the most. There was some stiff competition, but at least the Shepherd was human once.

"I think it was after our sigils," Ash continues. "Horatio ordered it to break the Ahlgren Host. Ilana was just behind me. It could've been the other way around. She could be sitting here in this chair, looking at me. It lashed out once with the whip, and it caught her in the arm, the hand with her sigil. Demons' whips, they can't hurt your body, but your spirit . . . they go right through it. She lost that part of her spirit, and your dad's demon ate it right up."

"So that's why her ghost is missing the arm?"

"The Errant flung himself straight at Horatio's demon. It ate him, too, of course, but he saved us. I barely remember anything after that . . . just Ilana screaming and the Widow carrying us through the snow. Ilana went the next day. Fell asleep. She hasn't woken up properly since."

Ash falls silent. Her eyes are closed, and she's gripping the end of the bed. I have this urge to hold her, but I can't bring myself to do it. She clenches her jaw. The muscles in her neck tense. After a long silence, Ash shakes her head and opens her eyes again.

"Sorry," she says.

"Do you need time alone?"

"It's hard to remember anything about that night," she says. "It's hard for me."

"My dad was a real bastard. I'm glad he's gone."

"Me too. But it's not enough."

I want to ask Ash what would be enough, what exactly she wants from me, what she's going to do with the Book of Eight, but she sighs and stands up. I realize Ilana is standing to the right of the bed. Or rather, her body is still in bed. Her spirit stands beside it, one-armed, smiling at me and Ash. She says something in her strange language.

Ash answers in the same singsong voice.

"What language is that?" I ask.

"We had our own way of talking," Ash says. "Twin-speak. We grew up together. . . . Magnus kept us hidden away. We only had each other to learn from, a lot of the time. We spoke English and Swedish, too, and we got some Latin from our Host, but this was our special way to talk. After the demon cut away a part of her spirit, she started to lose her mind as well. Our twin language is the only one she remembers now."

Ilana chirps to Ash again.

Ash responds, then turns to me. "She's hungry."

"What do you mean, hungry? I didn't know spirits got hungry."

"It's best if you see this. So you understand."

Ash calls out to Ilana in twin-speak, and Ilana smiles broadly. She glides across the bedroom, straight through her own body and the hospital bed, and stops right in front of Ash. They link their hands, each a warped reflection of the other, white-haired girl and one-armed ghost. Ilana moves even closer to Ash, brings her lips to her sister's. Ash breathes something out, like solid light, a shimmering white mist, and Ilana drinks it in.

It goes on for a while. I'm standing by my chair, not sure how to react, poised to move quickly away from them if it seems necessary. Ilana is pulling something out of Ash, the same kind of light I've seen linking my body and soul when I spirit-walk.

Eventually Ash pulls back, breaking the connection. Ilana chirps and tries to lean back in, but Ash stops her, snapping at her twin. Ilana protests, then turns and sees me. With a wide smile, the ghost glides across the room, holding out her single hand. Ash yells something in twin-speak. Ilana doesn't listen. I'm pressed up against the wall, with the ghost's smiling white face right in front of me. Her hand strokes my head, sending waves of cold through my face and neck. I can't move. I can't turn away from her.

"Please . . ." I say, barely managing a whisper.

Ilana's blue eyes shine with happiness. She dips her mouth to mine.

There's a flash of searing light, and the ghost shrieks and flies up through the ceiling. Ash is in front of me, left hand outstretched, breathing hard.

"Sorry," she says. "Sorry. I've told her again and again . . . it's only for her and me. Nobody else."

"What was happening?"

"You saw her wound," Ash says. She sits back down in her chair, looking at her sister's body, the machines threaded into it and around it. "The demon's whip took her left arm, but only in spirit. That wound can't be healed. She's losing herself, day by day. Her essence is leaking out.

It's like a loose thread in a sweater. She's unraveling—she has been for ten years. The only way I can keep her alive at all, keep her from disintegrating completely, is by giving her my own life force. I used to share it once a year, on our birthday. That kept her going. Then it was once every six months. Then every three months, then every full moon. Now it's once a week. This past week, it's been more than that. She asks me every night. It's killing me, Luke."

"Then don't do it," I say.

Ash doesn't respond.

"You shouldn't have to kill yourself to let her live. Not like this. If she properly understood what she was costing you, she wouldn't do it. You've done more than anyone could ask from you."

"She's not just my sister," Ash says softly. "She's me. She's my other half. We came into the world together. We're one person. What would you give for someone you love? I can't live without her. I love her. I'll do whatever it takes."

I think of Mum, Elza, even Ham. The people I love. I can't say how far I'd go to save them, keep them alive. I hope I'll never have to find out.

"I understand," I say.

I look at Ash, slumped in her chair, and Ilana, her body asleep in the bed. Two broken things, clinging together as best they can. My father did this to them. He tore their lives apart and probably never thought about them again. He never even mentioned them to me. I wonder if he even knew that Ashana and Ilana Ahlgren existed when he ordered the attack. Does that make it better or worse, if he didn't know? Ilana's heart rate rises briefly, and then returns to normal. I look down at my muddy shoes, then back at the girls. They haven't moved. Ash doesn't look frightening anymore, just lost and scared.

"My hair started growing in white a year ago," Ash says. "My eyes are gray and they're supposed to be blue. I love my sister, but she's killing me."

"So what do you want me to do about that?" I ask.

"I need the Book of Eight. There's a way to heal Ilana, make her whole again. I know it exists. But only the Book itself will give me the knowledge I need to perform the rite."

I consider this.

"I'd need an afternoon with it," Ash says. "That's all. I have reading equipment, page sequences, everything else. I just need to know how I can save her. I want you to want to help us. I'm asking you. Begging you."

"I do want to help you," I say.

Ash looks at me.

"I know you're a good person," she says. "I can tell."

"You'd only need to read it once," I say.

"There's no other way. That's all I'm asking. I know the Book of Eight is dangerous. That's why I'm not asking you to read it. I'll take the risk."

I close my eyes. This has been one of the longest, strangest days of my life. It must be dawn by now, Wednesday morning. It's the first of April. I've been in this house all night. In a few hours it'll be time for school. I need to get home before Mum knows I've been gone.

If I've got a chance to fix even one thing my dad broke, wouldn't that make everything that's happened to me worth it? If there's a chance the Book of Eight could do someone some good, I'd like to take it.

"I'll help you," I say.

Ash engulfs me in a hug. Her white hair is surprisingly soft against my neck and chin. She breathes into my chest.

"Thank you," Ash says. "Thank you so much."

It's dawn when we leave Ash's strange, empty house. The sky is a watercolor wash of pink and yellow, the sparse clouds tinged with peach. The air has a bite to it, although the sweater Ash gave me is thick and warm. I stash my hands deep in my pockets. The menace that clung to the building site at night has faded with the darkness. Ash leads me to her car, and we climb in. The inside smells stale and old, and the passenger seat sags when I put my weight on it. She must've gotten this third- or fourth-hand. She could afford something much better, I'm sure, but the thing about this car is nobody would look twice at it.

Ash starts the ignition and backs out of the garage. I was right to think she's done this a lot. She could easily pass her driving test if she were seventeen. I've managed to convince Mum to let me back the car out of our driveway a few times, no more than that.

"How are you allowed to drive?" I ask as we pass by the half-built houses.

"I've got a U.K. license," Ash says.

"But you're not old enough."

"My license says different."

"So it's fake."

"There are still people out there who respect my family name," Ash says quietly, and I decide to leave it at that. We pull out onto a main road, no real traffic at this time of day. I'm wondering how stealthy my body was about leaving Wormwood Drive. If Mum realizes I've been gone, I'll be in deep trouble. Did it lock the door behind it? Maybe Ham got out. These are all minor concerns compared to what could've happened to me, but they're concerns nonetheless. Ash slows the car as a black cat darts out of the hedgerow and across the road, out on some early-morning mission.

"How did you get my body to come to the house?" I ask her after a while.

"Oh," Ash says, "that's simple. As long as you can find the link, it's easy to summon an earthly vessel. I've never done it in real life before, but I knew the theory."

"What would happen if someone did that to Ilana?"

We're driving through Kirk's estate now. We just went past his house. We used to be best friends, and we haven't said a word to each other in months. Maybe I shouldn't have asked Ash about her sister. She's looking at the road ahead, hands clamped on the wheel.

"Ilana doesn't have a proper link to her body, so it wouldn't work. That's her main problem: the bond between her animus and soma is almost totally broken."

"But I thought when it broke—"

"You die, yes. What happened to us doesn't seem to have ever happened before, or at least I can't find records of it. Ilana should've died years ago. My life force is keeping her here. The Ahlgren Host was broken, destroyed. Magnus was the Host's necromancer and he died, but his sigil and our family's Book of Eight were destroyed as well. Neither of us can inherit. The Host is gone. But he'd already made us minor masters of his Host, and that binding wasn't fully broken, so . . . I don't know. We're like a wheel without a hub. It's unstable."

"What is a minor master?"

"I suppose it's like a sublet. You give someone limited authority over your Host. Most necromancers wouldn't even dream of it, but it's perfectly possible. It's old magic, blood magic. Usually works best if you extend it to family members."

"So you're both bound to the Widow? She takes your orders."

"Yes. But I can't summon or bind new spirits. I wouldn't try it even if I had the Book of Eight. Ilana's situation is so precarious . . . even trying to summon a new member of our Host might tip her over the edge into death. She was a minor master, like me, but her sigil was destroyed. . . . It's complex."

Despite never having read the Book, Ash seems to understand far more of the theory behind necromancy than me.

"I thought Hosts were eight ghosts," I say.

"Yes," she says. "Hosts are made from nine spirits. Eight dead servants, one living master. That's always been the way. The master can assign others as minor masters, but their authority is limited in some ways. And most necromancers don't do it at all, because it can unbalance the Host if you have too many masters."

Is that why Dad never gave me a minor sigil? I suppose I could always track him down and ask him.

"That does seem complicated," I say.

"I can give you some reading if you like. There's this great treatise from fifteenth-century Germany that outlines most of the theory—"

"I think I'm all right."

We drive through the estate. We pass a milk van, stopped outside one of the identical redbrick houses, engine still running, pumping out a gray haze of exhaust. The sun is peeking over the horizon. Birds crowd the telephone lines. We drive past Dunbarrow High, school gates still padlocked. There's a single jogger making her way uphill, struggling along in black-and-pink sneakers, panting out white billows of breath as she runs in the cold. I look at her face as we pass her, but she's fixated on some point on the horizon.

"And Mark's in a hotel," I say.

"Luke," Ash says, "we're not going to get anywhere if you don't trust me. Why would I hurt him? Where would that get me? He's in a hotel in Brackford. He's being paid."

"He agreed to this?"

"He thinks he's consumer-testing the place."

"And why does he think that? How do you . . . I mean, why did everyone think you're an exchange student? Are you, like, a hypnotist? How does that work?"

"By magic," Ash says, which I suppose is a pretty obvious answer. "And I'll give you Mark's room number and check-in date if you don't believe me. You can go talk to him if you like. But you're going to have to start trusting me sometime."

We drive through town and climb the long hill toward Wormwood Drive in silence. Ash knows which house is mine without being told, which is unsettling but not surprising. We come to a halt just shy of the entrance to our driveway. The street is deserted. I unclip my seat belt.

"Well, it's been an interesting night," I say.

"Likewise," Ash replies.

"I suppose I'll see you at school."

"I guess so."

She taps her hands on the steering wheel, biting her lip, then cuts the engine.

"Can I see it now?" she asks.

"See what?"

"The Book of Eight."

Her gray eyes search mine.

"No." I shake my head. "Absolutely not. It's, like, five thirty in the morning. How's it going to look when Mum wakes up and finds you in the house?"

"All right." She looks away. "Sorry."

"Look. Come by tonight, after school."

"I will," she says.

The street's stillness is complete and total. You could believe that time had stopped, that we'd be here in Ash's car forever, the sun never rising or falling, the sky stuck in its strange tropical blend of pink and blue. Inside their houses, my neighbors will be asleep, waiting for the shrilling of their alarms. Ash is facing ahead, breathing lightly, not seeming to look at anything in particular. I wonder what she's thinking. I think about my neighbors, immobile in their darkened beds, and the dead, lying in their dark graves.

Ash restarts the engine, breaking the spell. I reach for the door handle.

"Hey, do you want your sweater back?" I ask.

"Keep it," she says. "It fits you better than me."

I get out of the car, shut the door behind me. I walk around to our gate and look back at Ash, still parked, watching me. I'm not sure what's appropriate. Are we friends now? I'm helping her with something important, but I'm still not even sure if we like each other. She trusts me. I'm trusting her, too, come to think of it.

In the end I give her a little wave, but she's already driving away.

(a glass darkly)

I wake up in my clothes, my alarm chirping, Ham
scratching at my door. Seven thirty. I got maybe an hour
of sleep. An hour later and I'm in my uniform, sitting on
the damp wall of a crumbling mausoleum, drinking coffee
out of a thermos. My yawns stretch out my jaw like I'm a
snake swallowing eggs.

Elza pushes her way through the gap in the fence,
wearing her dad's old leather jacket over her school clothes.
She makes her way across the graveyard, boots shiny with
dew. "Are you all right?" she asks. "What happened?"

"You should probably sit down," I say.

"You look grim," she says.

"I didn't really sleep."

Elza wraps her arms around me. I return her embrace,
but I feel awful. I'm going to have to tell her a lot of stuff

I've been keeping secret, and I don't think she'll take it that well.

"Did you have another fit?" she asks.

"No. Look, sit down. I need to talk to you."

"All right." Elza sits beside me, folds one leg over the other. She winds a strand of hair in her fingers as I talk.

I give her the whole story, from us parting ways last night to me being dropped off at my house by Ash this morning. I tell her about Ilana and the Widow, Magnus Ahlgren, and my promise to Ash. She listens without saying a word. Halfway through, she takes out a cigarette.

". . . so she's coming by tonight to read the Book," I conclude. "Or that's what I told her, anyway. I don't know. It was strange."

Elza lets smoke leak from her mouth.

"Can you say something?" I ask.

"Honestly? I don't even know where to begin."

"Are you angry?"

"Am. I. Angry?" The words come out staccato.

"I'm really sorry that I didn't tell you—"

"About what? What are you sorry about?"

"Elza, I'm really sorry I didn't tell you about the Book of Eight. I shouldn't have kept that a secret from you."

"Berkley came back to Dunbarrow? He came to your house and you didn't even mention this?"

"I . . . look, I—"

"Oh, just . . . save it. Seriously. So you've had it buried in the field behind your house this entire time. You can walk out of your own body and you didn't think I needed to know about that, either? And then you just go flying up to this horrible house. Ash could've killed you—"

"I don't think she would."

"You don't know her! We don't even know she's a person at all!"

"She is," I say. "And she needs my help."

"Well, at least I know how to get you to trust me!" Elza snaps. "Keep you prisoner inside a mirror! Because apparently you're totally OK with sharing your every secret with someone who does *that* to you."

"Elza, I do trust you."

Her voice is like ice. "You know what hurts about this, Luke?"

"Elza—"

"What hurts is I thought we trusted each other. I thought I'd finally met someone I could share everything with. Someone else who saw ghosts. Someone else who knows more about what happens when you die than anyone might reasonably want to know. I've always been honest with you. And it really hurts that you've been keeping stuff from me."

I don't know what to say to her. She's right. I should've told her. I don't really know why I didn't. I could tell her

I wanted us to be as happy as we could, didn't want to bring up the dark parts of my life if I didn't have to, but that's not totally true. Maybe I just wanted to pretend I was still normal, even if it was just to myself. Maybe I wanted to pretend it was entirely my decision to spend all my days hanging out with Elza in a graveyard while all my old friends avert their eyes when I walk past or do impressions of me having a seizure? I wanted to pretend there wasn't some big dark anchor tied to my foot, pulling me away from them. It's not that I don't love her. I do. But sometimes it doesn't feel like I ever had a choice about being with her.

"I'm sorry," I say after a while.

Elza stamps her cigarette out in the wet grass. I want to take her hand, kiss her, but her expression stops me from moving. I just want to wrap my arms around her and go back to bed.

"I need you," I say. "I can't deal with this alone."

"I'm very pissed off with you," she says.

"I know."

"I haven't decided exactly how pissed off I am. But you're on thin ice."

"Elza—"

"Just don't, all right? We've got other things to worry about right now. Whoever, whatever, Ash is, you told her you'd help her. Whatever that's going to mean, we don't know. But you're giving her free rein this evening with the Book of Eight."

"I never said 'free rein'—"

"Luke . . . She. Is. *Dangerous*. She's got a bound spirit, this Widow. You said this ghost knocked you down like you were hit by a car. She's powerful. What do we have? Some hazel charms? Your dad's rings?"

"I don't think Ash will hurt us," I say. Elza didn't sit by Ilana's bedside. It wasn't Elza's dad who broke Ash's world apart, put her sister in a coma. Elza's dad is an IT professional whose greatest pleasure in life is looking at birds through a pair of binoculars. He's never come close to killing anybody, except perhaps by inadvertently inducing lethal boredom at a dinner party. Elza doesn't have the kind of family you need to atone for.

"Well, I'm coming to your house tonight as well. I think it's best if we both supervise her, don't you? Since you apparently believe anything she says as long as she flutters her eyelashes at you."

"Elza, that's not fair."

"Yeah, it's not nice, is it? When someone treats you unfairly."

The graveyard's grass ripples in the wind.

"Look," Elza says, "I'll see you tonight."

She walks away at a pace that doesn't invite me to follow her. A few sulky spits of rain darken the gravestones.

I put my thermos in my backpack, pull my hood over my head. That went about as well as I expected. I slip out of Saint Jude's the way we came in, through the gap in the fence, pushing on into the school grounds.

Holiday, Ash, and Alice are standing just inside the school gates. When they spot me, they forge a path straight toward me.

"See? I said they'd be in their graveyard," Alice is saying.

"Luke," Holiday says, "I want to talk to you. Is Elza around?"

"You just missed her."

Ash says nothing. She looks as exhausted as me.

Holiday gives me a brittle smile. "So when I got home from rehearsal, my mum told me you and Elza came to our house and went through my room and Ash's stuff?"

"You know that's, like, totally illegal?" Alice asks us.

"I've always stuck up for you, Luke," Holiday says, glaring at me. "People say horrible things about you, and I always tell them to leave you alone."

"Well, thanks," I say.

Ash is fiddling with her nose ring, her face a perfect mask of boredom. She's a good actress.

"Look, I don't know if this was your idea of a joke or what, but it isn't funny. It's weird. Tell your girlfriend that, too. I've told my mum that if you come over again, she shouldn't let you in, all right?"

"Sure," I say.

"You're such a total creep," Alice says.

"I know you've got"—Holiday's smile is stretched about as thin as I've ever seen it—"*mental health problems.* I'm sure it's hard. I don't want to cause more trouble for you."

"I'm glad to hear you're so concerned about my mental health problems," I say.

"If you could give my DVD back, I'd appreciate it," Holiday says.

"It's in my bag."

I rummage in my backpack. I wonder what Holiday would do if I told her the truth about Ash. It's a moot point, I suppose. Holiday doesn't have the mental framework to even begin to understand the truth about her new friend.

I pass Holiday her *Best of Hannah Montana* DVD, and she tucks it into her handbag with as much dignity as she can muster.

"Well, I hope this was at least funny for you," Holiday says.

I don't say anything. Ash's gray eyes are boring into me, hungry, almost seeming to shine. Is Elza right? Do I trust her only because she's a pretty girl? I remember thinking the Vassal was evil because he had some kind of skin condition, and he was actually the kindest of all my dad's ghosts. I suppose it's too late. I made a promise to her, and there's no way she's going to leave me alone now.

Holiday tosses her hair and walks away without another word. Ash and Alice flank her, making their way to homeroom. I look up at the sky: pale blue, dappled with high gray clouds. It might rain later, or then again, maybe not. It's one of those spring days. Everything's up in the air.

I meet Elza again after school, and together we make the walk up to Wormwood Drive in chilly silence. The clouds have clotted into a tumorous ceiling, a layering of grays and whites with occasional hazy glimpses of blue, like a half-remembered dream. The wind is high and cold, and the trees that are coming into bud seem misguided.

When I come in, Mum's on the sofa with Ham, watching TV. He gets up when he sees me and rushes right at me and past me, going out into the hall to nose at Elza, who's still untying her boots. Mum looks guilty.

"You're always telling me not to let him up there," I say.

"I know," Mum says. "He just has such sad eyes, though, doesn't he?"

"He's got nothing to be sad about," I say. "We treat him like a king."

"He's a good dog," Mum says, and then her face lights up as Elza walks into the room. "Elza! Hello! How are you?"

"Oh," Elza says, "I'm fine, Persephone. Just came by to do some studying. Mum's working tonight"—her mum's a nurse—"but she can pick me up later, after her shift, if that's OK?"

"You can stay over if you like," Mum says. "Save her making a trip after work."

Ham butts and snorts at Elza while she scratches his furry shoulders. I'm left standing in the doorway as Elza makes her way into the room, my mum and my dog hanging on her every word. Sometimes I wonder if my family wouldn't secretly like it if Elza were the one who lived here, and I just came by to visit sometimes.

"We've got an owl living out back," Mum's telling Elza, who smiles as if it were the best news anyone had ever given her. "Haven't you heard it, Luke? The last few nights?"

"Yeah," I say, remembering the field past midnight, the first time I met Ilana and the Widow. I shudder. "I've heard it a few times."

"I'll have to tell Dad," Elza says. "I'm sure he could identify it by the hoot alone."

"It's a lonely sound," Mum says.

"I don't think I'd mind being an owl," Elza says absently, stroking Ham's snout.

"Me either," Mum says.

"They're beautiful creatures," Elza says.

"Drifting through the night," Mum says. "Sitting under the moon."

"Eating small mammals whole," I say. "Spitting up dry little pellets of bones and skin."

Elza, Mum, and Ham all look at me with naked disgust.

"Does anyone want tea?" I ask.

They do, and I take the excuse to vanish into the kitchen. Elza still hasn't spoken to me directly since this morning. Exactly how angry she is, I can't tell. We have arguments, of course. We're different people in a lot of ways. Elza likes sitting still with a book; I like running around with a ball. Elza likes movies in black and white, preferably with subtitles, and I like movies where as many things as possible explode at the end. I think Elza is too quick to brand people she doesn't even know as "stupid" or "dull." Elza thinks I get far too emotionally invested in local soccer teams. She really hates that I wear polo shirts. I really hate that she smokes. She can't stand trance, and I think most punk bands need to learn how to play their instruments. Elza encourages me to grow my hair and will sometimes try and coax me into buying some old cords or a moth-eaten tweed jacket while she's rooting around in a thrift store, and for my own part, I wonder if she really has to put on black lipstick and a spiked dog collar just to go out and buy a quart of milk. You get the picture. At our core, though, we've always been an unshakable team. My Host saw to that. Elza saved my life, and had several near-death experiences herself along the way, and the bond we formed seemed to be unbreakable.

That is, until today.

Mum has chai; Elza favors Earl Grey. I'm still suffering from my lack of sleep last night, and I'm brewing up a big strong pot of coffee for myself when there's a sharp knock at the front door. I make my way into the hall and open up to find Ash standing on the front step. She's wearing a white backpack and carrying what looks like a brief-case made of dark polished wood, an unexpected palette change. It has a leather strap that hangs from one of her shoulders. She smiles.

"Hello, Luke. I'm here to work on our project?"

Her charming greeting is slightly spoiled by the presence of the Widow, white-robed and glaring, stranded just at the end of our drive, beyond the protective influence of Elza's hazel charms. It's possible for Elza to grant Ash's servant entry to my house, but I'm not about to ask her to do it.

"Your friend has to stay outside," I say in a low voice.

Ash frowns. "I was hoping—"

"No," I say. "Just you."

"She was a Priestess of Osiris. She knows the Book. I might need her opinion on some passages."

"You can go to the end of my drive and ask her, then. She's not coming in."

Ash looks back at her ghost and makes a small motion with her left hand. The Widow bows and then blinks out of existence.

"You still don't trust me, do you?" Ash asks.

"Not quite."

"Fair enough. Still," she says, laying her wooden case down in my hallway, "I'm trusting you. Without her, I'm totally defenseless."

"What's in the box?"

"My father's reading equipment," she says.

I never knew you needed equipment to read the Book of Eight. I just opened it up and used my dad's number sequence, which even now I can't say I totally understand. I think his notes are still at Elza's house, actually. I should have thought to bring them over. What was it Dad called them? *The sequence.* I wonder if Ash has a sequence inside her wooden case.

"You should probably meet my mum," I say. "Elza's in there, too."

Ash raises her eyebrows, a gesture I find difficult to

interpret in this particular context, and moves on ahead of me into my living room. Elza looks up at her with suspicion and hostility, Mum with drowsy welcome, and Ham with crazed joy. He rushes up to Ash and buries his head into the space between her knees, grunting like a wild hog. He nearly knocks her over. Ash falls back against the wall and, laughing, scrubs at his back with one hand. Ham is usually pretty good at judging character. He was afraid of the Host from the start, but seeing him so relaxed and friendly with Ashana Ahlgren seems like a good omen. Elza remains suspicious, hunched up in one corner of our sofa.

"He's so big," Ash says cheerfully. Her public voice is much more dizzily Californian than her real one, a voice honeyed with the sound of beaches and palm trees and wide, dazzling oceans.

"Ham's a deerhound," Elza replies in a voice as cold as the damp foggy moors around Dunbarrow. "They're known for being pretty sizable."

"Mum," I say, "this is Ashley Smith. We're working with her on a project. Ash, this is my mum, Persephone Cusp. And you already know Elza."

"Persephone," Ash says with a warm smile, "so great to meet you!"

"It's always nice to meet one of Luke's friends," Mum says. "Are you American?"

"Yup—I come from Marin County, just north of San Francisco. I'm here on an exchange program."

"It must be very beautiful out there," Mum says.

"Oh, sure," Ash says, "but I like it here, too. It's bleak, y'know, but also beautiful?"

Mum nods at this, seeming pleased, like Ash just told her something enormously important. Maybe my family could just adopt Elza, and Ash as well.

"Would you like some tea, Ash?" I ask.

"Oh, no, thank you. I'm really eager to get started on our work," she replies.

"Enthusiasm is a great gift," Mum says. "What are you working on?"

"Old documents," Ash says.

"Math," I say at the same moment.

"We're doing a project on the arithmetic of ancient hieroglyphs," Elza says after a pause, getting up, giving me a cold look.

"That sounds very interesting," Mum says. "I really think there's a lot we can learn from looking at ancient civilizations and how they lived. What kind of hieroglyphs?"

I'm a little bit surprised at this question. The old version of Mum wouldn't have asked any more questions. She'd have waved her hand and smiled. I like that she's getting her life back on track, but she's becoming dangerously interested in what I'm up to.

"Early period," Elza says firmly, heading for the door.

"Yeah," I say. "Really early."

We head upstairs to my room, Ash leading the way, even though she doesn't actually know where we're going. The wooden case thumps against her shin. I push past her once we're on the landing, close enough to smell the faint tropical hint of her shampoo, and then lead us into my bedroom. Looking around, I find myself wishing I'd had time to straighten the place up. It's not as bad as Elza's room, but there are dirty clothes all over the floor, three cereal bowls with muck congealing in the bottom of them, a few pairs of boxer shorts drying on the radiator. My bedsheets haven't been changed for a while, and there's a stuffy smell to the whole place. It's a long way from Ash's sparsely furnished house. She stands in the middle of my room, still holding her wooden case, looking at the black-and-white photos Elza took of me back in January. I'm out on the moors with Ham, snow turning everything white around us. Elza developed the prints herself. Ham and me are far away, about to vanish behind a snowcapped boulder, just two little figures in a huge blank landscape.

"These are great," Ash says.

Elza flings herself down on my bed.

"Thanks," she says.

"Did you take them?" Ash asks, sounding amazed. "You're *so good*."

"We're not friends," Elza says flatly. "I don't know what you want with Luke. But I don't like it, and I don't like you."

"OK. I understand," Ash says. She doesn't seem hurt; more thoughtful, like she's seriously considering Elza's point.

"And flattering me, telling me just how much you *love* my photography," Elza continues, "isn't going to change my opinion of you one bit. Are we clear? I'm not Holiday. I know you're a necromancer. I know you're trouble."

"So about the Book . . ." I say.

"It's all right," Ash says. "She's not Holiday. I get the message."

Ash walks over to my desk and sweeps my papers into a pile at one edge. She puts her wooden case down in the center, next to my laptop and my French-to-English dictionary.

"Say what you want about Holiday," Ash continues, offhand, "but at least she's not in denial about the whole 'hair spray and leather' thing being played out."

"What's *that* supposed to mean?" Elza spits. "You look like someone who's just been deprogrammed from a cult. What is with your clothes?"

"It's my family color," Ash says. She doesn't seem particularly angry.

"Please," I say.

"What?" Elza snaps, looking like she wants to fight me now as well.

"Can we just do what we need to? You asked to be here, Elza."

"Someone needs to keep an eye on her," Elza says.

"I'm just here to look at the Book," Ash tells Elza. "I want to help my sister. I presume Luke has filled you in that far."

"It's down here," I say. I need to give us something else to do, or these two are going to bicker all night. I kneel down and take out the bottom drawer of my wardrobe. Buried under a mound of socks and underwear is the toolbox that I originally hid both the Book and my dad's rings in, still with scraps of mud clinging to it from the excavation. I open the latch and take out the Book of Eight.

It's small and thick, about the same size as a pocket dictionary, with a pale-green leather cover and pages the color of a smoker's teeth. There's an eight-pointed star embossed in gold on the front cover, and the Book is sealed shut with silvery clasps. I haven't touched it since the day I buried it. The leather feels cold and smooth under my fingers. The Book's size and weight belie the depth of information concealed within it. The pages are endless, inscribed with symbols of the utmost magical power. The Book of Eight is a dizzying monster that took over my mind, and I'd hoped I'd never have to look at it again.

Ash can't take her eyes off it.

"This is Octavius's edition, isn't it?" Ash asks.

"Who?"

"Octavius. Your father's Shepherd. He made this copy himself."

"Did he?" I ask. I try to spend as little time thinking about that black-eyed bastard as possible. "He never mentioned it."

"Seems unusually modest of him," Elza says.

"It's definitely his," Ash says. "I've read descriptions of it. Supposedly he had it bound in his father's skin."

"Er . . ."

I gesture energetically for Ash to take the Book from my hands, but she turns back to my desk and unlocks her wooden case. Elza sits up with a look of astonishment on her face as the case opens up. I can't see what's inside—Ash's body is between me and the desk—so, still holding the Book of Eight, I move closer to Ash, peering over her shoulder. Her reading equipment turns out to be something remarkable.

The case opens like a normal briefcase, but what's inside is a strange, intricate network of clockwork and mirrors and slender strips of brass that unfold upward with a gentle creaking sound. It looks a little bit like the interior of a typewriter—lots of thin strips of metal and ribbons of black silk. It must have been made by hand.

Ash seems awkward and hesitant about using the device, and she spends a long time adjusting various gears and runners, carefully encouraging different bits of the device to rest in their proper places. At one point she takes out a small bottle of oil and dabs a few droplets onto a joint that's refusing to extend properly. Me and Elza don't say a word. When Ash is done, she steps back, one eye closed as she examines every part of the machine. When she's satisfied, she reaches into her bag and takes out a large piece of black cloth.

The finished device is difficult to describe, part typewriter and part clockwork and part tower of mirrors. It's made of old brass and polished wood, and although it was originally compacted flat inside the case, it's now expanded upward a considerable distance. The device seems to be supporting a periscope of some description, which is aimed downward at an angled wooden surface. There's a smell of old metal and oil and dust.

"What on earth is that?" Elza asks.

"As I said," Ash replies, draping her black cloth around the highest part of the periscope, "this is my reading equipment. My great-great-grandfather made this."

"For reading the Book of Eight?" I say.

"Yes," Ash says. "It's for the Book. My family discovered a way of reading it without risking some of the more dangerous side effects. If viewed through eight mirrored wards, the Book has considerably less power over the reader. And the clockwork page-turning mechanism makes entering long sequences quicker and less exhausting."

She gestures at the typewriter part of the device. I see that there are eighteen keys: nine white keys with numbers on them, and nine black keys with the numbers inverted. I think I'm beginning to understand.

"So you put the Book of Eight into this thing?"

"Yes," Ash says in a tone that suggests she'd like to get on with exactly that.

"How does it run?" Elza asks, her earlier hostility fading now that we're faced with something that interests her.

"Clockwork, with a hint of magic. It draws power from my sigil," Ash says. "Luke, do you want to open up the Book?"

"All right," I say. I walk over to my door, take the raincoat off its peg. My dad's sigil—focus of his, and my, power—is still in the inside pocket. I slip it onto my right ring finger. It feels heavy and cold. I haven't worn it since last Halloween. I don't like how it feels, having it back on my finger.

I move over to the desk and, trying not to think about the unusual provenance of the Book's binding, stroke the green cover with my right hand. The clasps on the cover respond to the sigil's power at once, snapping open, the Book of Eight rippling and moving, pages turning, coming to rest on a blank double spread in the exact center of the volume. Appearances are deceptive when it comes to this Book: the pages are infinite, and so any given point of the Book is its center. Ash reaches out a trembling hand and turns one of the pages. We're still in the center of the Book, still on a blank spread.

Ash lets out a long breath.

"This is really it," she says.

Elza is frowning again. Last time I read the Book of Eight, I was trapped in some kind of trance state for days, and it clearly has had lasting effects on my mind. She's scared of the Book, for good reasons. I don't think she even likes to see me in the same room with it. She's winding and unwinding a strand of hair in her fingers.

Reverently, Ash picks up the Book of Eight and slots it into her reading device. It rests on the wooden lectern in the middle of the machine. Ash then gently arranges various spokes and levers, placing them in between the pages of the Book. There are nine on the left-hand side, nine on the right. When she's done, they're slotted in between the pages of the Book, for nine pages on each side. Ash presses the first of the white keys. There's a smooth mechanical click, and the levers turn the Book's pages one to the right. She presses a black key, and the pages turn one backward, toward the front cover. Ash grins.

"Still runs like a dream," she says.

"So you just type?" I ask.

"Yeah," Ash says. "This is how you input sequences. He got the idea when he first saw a typewriter, obviously. He was a clever guy."

"What are sequences, exactly?" I ask. "I never understood that."

"Mapped paths through the Book. They're usually pretty reliable. There are variants, of course, some paths that split into several different useful routes. Or you can just go rogue, hope you find something useful . . . hope the Book doesn't kill you."

"The Book can kill you?" Elza asks.

"Oh, easily," Ash says with a grimace. "It eats your mind. Nasty. My dad lost an aunt that way."

"That's rough," I say uneasily, thinking of the symbols I drew on Monday. Is that what's happening to me?

"He wasn't that bothered," Ash says. "Magnus wasn't especially sentimental about anyone. I think you've met her, actually."

"We have?"

"She was Horatio's Oracle. A gift from my father."

"Oh," I say. I think of the Oracle: white dress, white veil, bare white feet. I never saw her face, so I have no idea if she resembled Ash.

"Your dad gave his own dead aunt to Luke's father as a servant? I thought they were enemies," Elza says.

"They were friends first," Ash says, in a way that suggests she'd like to move along to another subject.

"How long will this take you?" I ask her.

"I really don't know. A few hours, maybe. It's hard to say."

"So what are you actually looking at?" I ask.

"You view the book through mirrors and treated panes of glass." Ash gestures at the viewer. "You put your head under the cloth and peer into the viewing pane."

"And you've never done this before?" Elza asks.

"No," Ash says. "I know the theory, though."

"What if something goes wrong?" Elza says.

"Well, then I'm in a lot of trouble. But I'm not doing this for me."

Elza doesn't say anything. Ash looks over at me.

"Just do what you need to," I say. "We'll be right here."

"Thanks," Ash says. She looks scared and excited. She rubs her temples, then sits down at my desk. She drapes the black cloth around her head and stares into the viewing pane. She starts to tap at the keys. I presume she has memorized the sequence she needs. The machine turns the Book's pages, back and forth, and Ash starts to type faster and faster. Soon her tapping has reached a frantic pace, and when I ask if she's all right, she doesn't answer. Elza looks at Ash and shrugs.

"She's gone," Elza says.

I sit down on the floor. Elza's still on my bed. I want to talk, but I don't know what to say. I don't know if Ash can still hear us. It's a creepy situation, being in the room with someone who's there but not. I think about what Elza went through last year, hiding me in her spare room for three days, not sure if I'd ever snap out of it. When I look over at her, I know that she's remembering those days, too. Despite our argument, I can see she wants me closer. I sit up next to her on the bed, and her hand intertwines with mine.

Ash ends up reading the Book of Eight for just under two hours, nowhere close to my record. The noise of typing suddenly stops, and she sits bolt upright, throwing the black cloth off her head.

"Are you all right?" I ask. I'm doing homework; Elza is reading a paperback.

Ash's eyes are wild, and her pale face is tinged with green.

"What happened?"

"Ash—" Elza says.

Ash tries to talk, then gulps and crams one hand over her mouth. She pushes past me and rushes out of the room. I follow her, not sure what's going on, and hear her retching in the bathroom. I press my head against the door.

"Ash! Are you all right?"

I hear her spluttering. Wet sounds.

"Ash?"

"I'm fine," she says, muffled.

"Do you need some air?"

"That might be good," she says.

Elza is at the doorway to my room, her eyes narrowed.

"What's up with her?" Elza asks.

"I don't know," I say, then, "Ash, are you really all right?"

Ash unlocks the door. She's dabbing at her mouth with toilet paper. She gives us a sheepish smile.

"Interesting book," she says lightly.

"What happened?"

"I just came out of it funny," Ash says, without meeting our eyes. "It's no big deal."

"If you're sure."

"Did you get what you needed?" Elza asks.

"I did."

Ash doesn't seem like she's about to say anything else. There's an awkward pause. What exactly did she see in the Book? She's holding something back; anyone can see that.

"So what do you have to do?"

"Let's go and get some air," Ash says. "I could do with a look at the sky."

"All right," I say. "Sure."

Me and Ash go downstairs. Elza stays behind to hide the reading machine and Book, in case Mum pokes her head in. Ash doesn't say a word to me, keeps mouthing something to herself, under her breath. I get Ham's leash and fasten him up, and then we set off into the back-yard. It's getting dark now, with just a slim band of navy blue left at the horizon. The clouds have melted away. Overhead I can see a thin scattering of stars, the hard glint of satellites.

When we reach the stone wall, I stop to wait for Elza. Ash leans on the wall, looking out over the fields at the inky black bulk of the hills and forest beyond them. I've got some treats for Ham in a zipped pocket of my coat, but he can smell them and keeps nosing at that side of my body, trying to nibble his way through. I fend him off as best I can.

"This is a nice place," Ash says, gesturing back at my house.

"It is," I say.

"You should see our house in Marin sometime," Ash says. "We're right by the ocean. It's gorgeous. The sunsets in California are unbelievable."

"Right," I say, unsure if this is a serious invitation or just one of those things people say to pass the time. I still don't quite know how to feel about Ash. I look at the

"It cut part of her soul away and ate it," Ash says. Her face is creased, and I know she's remembering that night again.

"Sorry," Elza says.

"What happens to spirits who've been eaten by a demon?" Ash asks us.

I look at the dark garden, the house, the stars. I still have trouble believing what's happening to me sometimes. *What happens to spirits who've been eaten by a demon?* It's like someone coming up to you and asking what flavor of sky is your favorite. The question makes no sense.

"I don't know," I say, but my mind runs backward through time to the night when I stood on a distant gray shore and spoke to the Devil and my father. I remember the Vassal vanishing into the Fury's white-hot gullet. I remember asking the Devil about the Vassal, my only loyal servant, and what the Devil told me in response. He compared the Vassal to clay being baked into a pot. *The process of being fired, in the kiln, has changed it forever.*

"They become something else," I say. "The demon . . . it doesn't just *look* like a furnace. It *is* one. They turn spirits into something different."

"Yes," Ash says.

"So the demon eats them," Elza says, "and then what?"

"It consumes them. They become part of the demon's

spirit flesh. All the sin and greed and guilt, the lust and anger and envy of the spirit, it all becomes part of the demon. Makes it bigger."

"So they're gone?" I ask.

"Not quite," Ash says. "Not entirely. See, everyone— every human being—has a part of them that's good. That's worth something. Some have a small part. In some people it's nearly invisible, the size of a grain of sand. But everyone has it, and demons can't feed on that part of a ghost. They can't digest it. So it sits inside them. It collects. The goodness, the virtue of these spirits, it just sits there and builds up over the centuries."

"Like a pearl," Elza says.

"Just like a pearl," Ash says, nodding. "It's a kind of spirit pearl, I suppose, made up of the best parts of every person the demon ever ate. It's more than a pearl. It's the most fantastic object in creation, according to people who've seen one. It's called the nonpareil."

"The none-parry-what?" I ask.

"*Nonpareil*," Elza says. "It's a French word. It means 'without equal.' "

"Sorry I spoke," I mutter. How does she always know this stuff?

"And if we get this nonpareil," Elza continues, "you can fix your sister? Ilana?"

"Yes," Ash says. "The Widow and I have suspected for

years that this would be the method. And now I know for certain. I know the rituals and incantations that will make it possible. But I need your help."

"To do what?" Elza asks.

Ash swallows. "To resurrect my sister, it is not enough that we obtain *a* nonpareil, and trust me when I say that would be hard enough. We need the *exact* nonpareil that her spirit has become part of. We must hunt down your father's demon, the Fury, and remove the nonpareil from its body."

I somehow knew this was coming. I knew and didn't know. I close my eyes, remember the Fury: the eighth and greatest of my father's servants, a towering black shadow with infernal hollows for eyes. A mouth like a volcanic rift. Hands like tormented roots dipped in tar. I can't imagine a more dangerous spirit to pit ourselves against.

"How?" I ask.

"The Fury was yours," Ash says in a low voice. "It was part of your Host, Luke. The Fury was bound to you, and although you broke the binding, a trace of the bond remains still."

Ham is rooting in the compost heap. He's a dim gray shape in the darkness.

"There is a rite," Ash continues, "the Rite of Return. If you perform this rite at a passing place, you may summon any of your freed servants. It is your privilege as their old master. They must attend to you, if they are able. The demon will answer to you. We can call it up from the darkness where it lives and bind it, and then we can kill it."

"No," Elza says.

"Elza—" I begin.

"No," she says louder, turning to Ash. "Are you crazy? No. Absolutely not. Luke said you could read the Book of Eight, and you have. You know what you need to know. We're done."

"I was afraid you might feel this way," Ash says.

"That thing nearly killed both of us," Elza snaps. "It nearly killed me twice. It *did* kill Luke. It went inside his mother and made her stab him to death. It's a monster. It's a living black cloud of misery and rage. You have no idea what the two of us went through, what Luke had to do to get rid of this thing. You want to invite it *back* to Dunbarrow? Give it a one-way ticket into Liveside? Are you serious?"

"Yes," Ash says coldly. "I'm serious."

"Do you understand what that demon is capable of? Do you—"

"Yes!" Ash screams. "*Yes! I do!* I was six years old! It ate my family! It ate my *sister*! It's a monster! I feel sick just thinking about it, and I'm still prepared to face it again!"

The girls are face-to-face. Ash, a head shorter than Elza, still looks ready to tear her apart. Ham is hiding behind the shed, peering around the corner at us. I see that the Widow has her hand on the shaft of her spear, although what she intends to do with it, I don't know. Ash is trembling.

"I know what I'm asking," she hisses, staring Elza right in the eye. "I know."

"Then you'll know why we can't possibly help you," Elza snaps.

"You have to."

"Why?" I ask. "I'm with Elza. I don't want to see that thing ever again. If you want to kill it, you summon it. I don't see why I have to help you."

Ash's face is tense, unhappy. I look her in the eye.

"I'm sorry," I say gently, "but what you're asking is too much. I can't do this."

"I see," she says, looking from Elza to me and back again. "I see."

"Summon it, cut it open, do whatever you want," Elza says. "Just not here. Not around us."

"How many demons do you imagine there are?" Ash asks me.

"I don't know," I reply.

"There is one for every page in the Book of Eight, or so they say. There's an infinite number of demons. How easily do you think I would find the demon that carries Ilana's spirit in its belly?"

"I don't see how—"

"It could take more years than our universe has existed for," Ash says to me. "If you perform the Rite of Return at a passing place, your demon will return to you. The demon bound as Horatio's Fury. The one we want. It will take you moments. You'll save Ilana's life, and mine. And you won't help me?"

"The risk—" Elza begins.

"My sister will die. There's nothing I wouldn't risk to save her. Nothing." Ash seems close to tears. She composes herself. "Still, I see you won't help me without there being something in it for you."

"That's not what we're saying," I tell her.

"No, no, no," Ash says. "You clearly want something out of this for yourself, so . . . how does a hundred thousand pounds sound? Each."

"Well . . ." I say.

"No," Elza says.

"Hey," I say to her, "can't we talk about this? A hundred grand *each*—"

"No, Luke. I'm not letting that thing back into Liveside. No way. Not for a hundred million."

"All right," I say, seeing the look in Elza's eyes. "No deal, Ash. Sorry."

Ash sighs. She shakes her head slowly, like she's embarrassed it came to this.

"You've been having dreams, haven't you?" she asks me. "Sigils, stars, magic circles? I saw you writing on the board the first day we met. The same thing happened to my great-aunt. Before she died."

"What are you saying?" I ask.

"Your mind is going," Ash says. Her gray eyes bore into me. "Day by day. Hour by hour. The Book of Eight is inside you, and it's eating you alive. You're going to go mad and die, Luke Manchett. I know this for sure."

"What . . . ?" Elza says.

I look up at the sky. Try to breathe. My legs are shaking.

"Of course, it doesn't have to happen like that," Ash says.

"You can help me?" I ask.

"Oh, so now we're talking about *helping* people?" she sneers.

"How can you help him?" Elza asks her.

Ash doesn't reply. Instead she turns to the Widow and makes a motion with her left hand. The ghost reaches inside her white robe and draws out a dim object. She holds it out for us to see. I lean over the wall, squint in the darkness. The Widow is holding a cup made from gray stone. It's an old cup, the kind of thing you'd probably call a goblet or chalice.

"Water from the River Lethe," the Widow pronounces.

"The what, now?" I ask.

"It's one of the rivers that flow through the under-world," Ash says. "The River of Oblivion. The waters help the dead who drink there forget their lives."

"So how does that help us?" Elza asks her.

"When used on living beings, the water can have milder effects," Ash says. "How do you think I could just move into Holiday's house?"

"Their memories," I say. "They remember inviting you . . . but it never happened."

"As I said," Ash replies, "I have my ways."

"And this helps Luke how?" Elza asks.

"If Luke summons his Fury back into the living world, I'll give him a drink from the chalice. With the Widow's guidance and the Lethe's water combined, I know that the Book of Eight's pages can be forgotten. He'll have his mind back." Ash fiddles with her nose ring again. "I was going to do this for you anyway, once we'd gotten hold of the nonpareil, but since you won't help me willingly, I'm making this my price."

"So you—" I begin.

"Your life for my sister's life," Ash says. "That's the deal. Take it or leave it."

I look up at the stars, the bright sliver of moon. I close my eyes, and maybe it's just because Ash was scaring me, but I find I can see the contents of the Book crawling over the insides of my eyelids: thin jagged lines, crescent moons

and eight-pointed stars, magic circles and sigils and dia-
grams of stranger shapes I can't even name. I try to will
them away, but they flare even brighter. I imagine them
like locusts, swarming through my synapses, devouring
the words and images and the memories I keep there. I
want them out of me.

I open my eyes. I can still see the symbols, faintly,
swimming in the darkness. They blend with the night
sky, monstrous constellations, flaring and dancing in the
spaces between the stars. The moon itself seems branded
with a vast sigil, a symbol of power, blaring out across the
universe. I shake my head and they're gone.

"I'll do it," I say.

Elza doesn't say anything.

"I need both of you," Ash says.

"Why?" Elza snaps. "What could I possibly do to help
you?"

"I need you to kill the demon," Ash says to her.

"What on earth are you talking about?"

Ash slowly reaches into her white jacket and takes out
a knife. Clearly she was never as defenseless as she made
out to be. I should have patted her down or something
before I invited her inside. She lets the weapon balance on
her right hand, holds it out so we can see it. I move closer.

The knife isn't made of metal. The blade is only a few
inches long, made from strange white stone, and the hilt is

silver. I can see symbols, runes of some kind, cut into the pommel. I rest my hand on the knife's blade. It's smooth and cool.

"What is this?" I ask Ash.

"An heirloom," she replies. "It's an old witch blade. It's made from one of my ancestors."

"Why are you showing us this?" Elza asks.

"The knife was carved from a necromancer's thigh bone. It was made by the Daughters of Lilith to destroy demons. In the hands of someone with Lilith's blood, it will kill the Fury and cut out the nonpareil."

"What are you talking about now?" Elza asks her. She sounds almost panicked.

"You have her blood," the Widow says.

"Who? Lilith? She's a myth," Elza says.

"She lived and breathed," the Widow says. "Her blood is in your veins."

"Did I just miss something?" I ask them.

"Lilith was the first witch," Ash says. "Adam's first wife as well, if you believe that part of the story. Which I don't."

"You said yourself," I remind Elza, "when we first met. You said there might be witch blood in your family."

"I said there *might be*," she says, voice trembling. "I wasn't sure. Besides . . . *Lilith*. It's like saying you're descended from King Arthur or something." She takes a final drag on her cigarette and drops the butt into the long grass, grinding it out with her boot. "You're absolutely certain about this?" she asks Ash.

"The Widow is," Ash says. "She felt it in you."

"The line is weak," the Widow says. "Her blood is thin within you. Such is the way now. But Lilith's daughter you remain. This knife will know your touch."

I'm remembering other things about Elza, too. The way the Shepherd called her *witchlet*. I never asked him exactly what he meant by it.

"And she was real?" Elza's asking them.

"Real as you or me," Ash replies. "So. Will you help us, Lilith's daughter?"

"If you'll save Luke," Elza says, "I'll do it."

"When we have the nonpareil, I will give Luke a draft of the Lethe's waters. The pages of the Book will be forgotten. I swear."

"I swear it, too" comes the Widow's cold voice.

"And we can trust you?" Elza asks them.

Ash holds out the knife to her, hilt first. Elza reaches out and takes the silver handle. She raises the witch blade up to her face, turning it over in the moonlight, frowning down at the markings carved into the bone.

"I'm defenseless," Ash says in a whisper. She tilts her

head up to the night sky, exposing her neck. "I left my guard outside this house. I've given you my only weapon. Either you trust me, or you can open my throat right now."

Elza snorts.

"Kill me, then," Ash suddenly screams. "Do it! Either help me or kill me!"

We both take a step back, scared, even though Elza has the knife. Ham starts barking.

"Ash, my mum'll hear us—" I say.

"I'm not going to murder someone in Luke's yard," Elza says.

Ash's face is horrible.

"We want to help you," I say. "We really do."

Elza, still pointing the knife at Ash, gives me a look.

Ash calms as quickly as she did last night when I was trapped in the mirror, but what I saw in her face was real desperation and terror. This seems like her last chance.

Ham butts at my thigh.

"It's all right," I tell him.

I notice that Mum is still looking at us through the kitchen window. I don't think she can see the knife, but it's probably worth playing it safe.

"Let's go inside," I say. "And keep calm."

We work out the rest of the details back up in my room. The Rite of Return isn't linked to any particular day or lunar phase, so we agree to perform it tomorrow night.

We end up agreeing that we'll keep the witch blade, and Ash can keep the Book of Eight—which Elza had already packed up inside the reading machine, folded away into a compartment within the wooden case—until tomorrow night, as a gesture of mutual trust. I'm hesitant, but Elza seems remarkably relaxed about the exchange. Maybe she's hoping Ash really will steal the Book, so there'll be no chance of me using it again.

It's past ten o'clock when Ash finally leaves. Mum's gone to bed. I watch from the end of our driveway as Ash recedes into the darkened street, a small white figure, walking silently into the shadows beneath the trees. Wind rustles their branches. A cloud covers the moon.

After Ash is gone, I lie with Elza on the beanbag chair in my bedroom. There's a DVD playing, but we're barely watching it. Ham lies at our feet. It's harder to feel angry with each other now that we know what we have to do. Elza's head rests on my shoulder. Her finger traces infinity signs on the back of my hand. The witch blade lies on the floor beside me.

"Are you afraid?" Elza asks.

"Now, is that any way for a Daughter of Lilith to be talking?"

"Don't call me that," she says, with the first smile I've

seen out of her in a while. I press on with the joke, trying to feed my anxiety into it.

"I'm not sure if I can keep dating you now. You've got distinguished blood."

"Yeah, you're right. You're only a necromancer, Luke? I don't think so."

"Maybe I need to date someone from my world. A lady necromancer. A beautiful lady necromancer, with beautiful white hair—"

"Oh, just *stop* it!" Elza's laughing now. "She's not even that good-looking! Her face is, like, completely flat, and those gray eyes are just spooky."

"I don't think jealousy is very becoming to a Daughter of Lilith."

"Luke, I will slap you! I'm serious! Stop calling me that!"

"A million apologies, my dark lady—"

"I hate you," she says, still grinning. "Honestly. It's so *embarrassing*. Daughter of Lilith . . . It's, like, a great name for an all-girl metal band or something. I can just imagine it embroidered on a denim vest. . . . But OK, seriously, are you afraid?"

"Of the Fury?"

"Of Ash."

"I don't know," I say. "I don't think she wants to hurt us."

"No," Elza says. "But I think she would if she had to."

I think back to Ilana's bedside. The way Ash's face looked when she sat there with her sister. I remember Ash breathing out white light, her twin drinking it into herself.

"She's got her reasons," I say.

"People die," Elza says. "You need to let go of them. They move on to other places."

"So you think she should let her sister go?"

"Maybe."

"I don't think she can."

"I mean, what we're going to do? This is madness. Summoning Horatio's demon back from Deadside? I'm supposed to cut it open? Take the most perfect object in creation out of its belly? It's insane. What she's asking of us is beyond crazy."

"I don't want to go mad and die, Elza. I don't think we have a lot of choice."

"Can we not . . ." Elza starts to say something, then bites it back.

"Can we not what?"

"Is there some other way we could get hold of that chalice? Do we have to help her?"

"You think we should steal it from the Widow? Do we even know if that's possible?"

"I mean, we can just borrow—if all you need is a draft . . ."

"I don't think so, Elza."

She sighs, tugs at her hair.

"I don't see how we could," I continue. "I mean, could we steal that spear from her? Isn't it, like, part of her, somehow? And it wouldn't be right."

"No," Elza's saying. "I was thinking the same thing."

"So tomorrow night, then," I say. "Devil's Footsteps. We follow Ash's plan."

"Seems like it."

"I don't see what else we can do," I reply.

"Ash must really love Ilana," Elza says.

Ham grumbles and turns over in his sleep. I look out the window at the dark sky. The moon looks back at me, bright and white.

"If I died, Luke . . ." Elza's saying.

"If you what?"

"If I died before you," she says again, talking slow and low, like she's half asleep, "I wouldn't want you messing around with stuff like this. Just let me go."

She nestles closer against me.

"Elza . . . why are you saying this?"

"I just . . . I hate seeing Ash trying to tear the world apart to bring someone back to her. It's not . . . healthy. You can see it in her. She's too hungry. She wants to put the world back to how it was before. And she can't. It's not possible."

"Neither of us is going to die," I say. "Not for a long time yet."

"Of course not," she says.

We watch the DVD.

"But if," Elza says again, later. "If I do. Just let me go. Do you promise?"

"This is getting kind of intense, Elza. Can we, like, drop it?"

"Sorry," she says. "Being around Ash puts me in a funny mood."

We lie together on the beanbag, Elza's breath tickling down my neck, and somewhere along the line we fall asleep.

(our mutual fiend)

Thursday passes with the jangling queasy feeling you get from standing on a high-dive board. We meet with Ash after school in the place we agreed, the parking lot of the supermarket in the middle of Dunbarrow. My stomach is a writhing sack of insects. I see pigeons squabbling over a crust in the dirt. I see my own face distorted in an oily puddle. A chips bag flails in the branches of a nearby tree.

Ash is waiting by her car, wearing a white overcoat, white jeans, what has to be one of the only pairs of white hiking boots in existence. The wind ruffles her white hair as we approach her. She doesn't look quite real.

"How's everyone feeling?" Ash asks as we draw near. I feel like she's exaggerating her accent again, chirping like some peppy cheerleader before the big game. I remember last night, how she bared her throat to Elza, told us to kill her. I remind myself what lies under her surface.

"All right," I say. "Do we have everything?"

"Sure. I got the paint. We've got the Book of Eight in the reading machine in case we need it. You brought your sigil. Elza has the witch blade. Right?"

Elza pats the front of her leather jacket.

"So that's everything?" I ask, holding up my hand so Ash can see the sigil ring.

"I think so," Ash says. "The rite itself isn't complicated. Once the demon is summoned, we should be able to bind it inside a devil trap."

"What's that?" Elza asks.

"Well, I only have one," Ash says. "It's an old mirror. Luke already tried it out. It will be kind of heavy and awkward to lug out there, but it's the best way, I think."

"And I'm not binding the demon to me?" I ask.

"We went through this," Ash says. "You're allowed to summon it into the living world. You still have that right. But the demon won't be part of your Host. You broke that bond. You don't have a Host anymore."

"So it can kill me this time."

"Yes," Ash says. "It can. You don't have any protection. It can kill all of us. So no mistakes."

"I couldn't agree more," Elza says.

We get into the car. I sit passenger side. Elza crams

herself into the backseat next to the case with the reading device. I can see the mirror Ash trapped me inside propped up in the back, half-wrapped in cloth.

"How did Holiday take the news?" I ask.

"Oh, that I'm missing her charity fashion show? She was heartbroken," Ash says. "So was I, actually. I was really looking forward to strutting my stuff."

I laugh despite myself. You can almost imagine that we're all friends, heading off on a road trip somewhere exciting. We pull out of the parking lot, heading through town, past the main street and over the bridge on the river, uphill, heading out of Dunbarrow. It's nearly six o'clock, and the roads are full of people coming back from work in Brackford or Throgdown. The Devil's Footsteps is pretty close to the high school, but you have to walk across the playing fields and then quite a way uphill through woodland. There's no way we're going to carry Ash's mirror all the way up there. There is a more direct path, but finding where it joins up with the roads is difficult. We leave Dunbarrow as though heading for Brackford, then loop back around, looking for the entrance to the trail. After half an hour of arguing and jostling with the map—Elza is a backseat driver extraordinaire—we manage to find it, the National Trust road sign obscured by an overgrown hedge.

We drive down the lane for a few miles, the farmland

turning to forest around us, trees thickening and darkening, the hedges pressing in like the shaggy flanks of
an ungroomed monster. The road becomes muddy and
rutted, and there are several points where I think we'll
end up getting out and carrying our equipment on foot.
Eventually we round a familiar bend, and I recognize the
tree I found Mum's yellow car parked underneath, back
on that morning in October. I remember not being sure
I'd ever see Elza again, then her getting out of the car, the
dawn light streaking her face. I think that was one of the
best moments of my life.

"This is it," I say, and Ash pulls to a halt.

We get out without much ceremony, dividing everything we need to carry between us. I take the mirror, Elza
lugs the reading machine (although the idea of assembling
the contraption and carefully arranging its spokes while
we battle the Fury is funny, in a black, hopeless kind of
way), and Ash carries the paint. We make our way down
the path, turning off beside the rotten birch tree, climbing a shallow stony ridge and down the other side again,
through dead orange bracken and the green exploratory
shoots of this year's growth. Before I know it, we've come
out into the clearing, and I can see the Devil's Footsteps.

The stone circle hasn't changed since the last time
I saw it. There are three standing stones: one tall and
upright, maybe seven feet high, accompanied by two

smaller, rounder stones, the lowest of which is almost like an angled table. If they weren't set in the exact center of the clearing, you might think they were natural. We walk over spongy moss and clumps of needle-thin reeds. The ground is boggy, and some of the clearing's hollows are half-full of stagnant water. The whole scene is overshadowed by a canopy of enormous ancient oak trees.

Ash puts the paint can down, gives a low whistle.

"Now, *this* is a passing place," she says.

"Dunbarrow's finest," I grunt, resting the mirror faceup on the moss.

"How old do you think these are?" Ash asks us. "Iron Age? Older than that?"

"They're supposed to predate metal tools, I think. The carvings are very crude," Elza says.

"Do the standing stones make it a passing place?" I ask Ash. "I never understood that part."

"Sometimes you can create a passing place. Sometimes they just happen on their own. But I'll tell you one thing—" Ash pauses, seems to be listening to something in the air. "Whoever made these stones, I don't think they were trying to get a doorway open. I think they wanted to keep one shut."

"What makes you say that?"

Ash shrugs. "Just a hunch. There's tension here. It's easy to feel. I think this gateway to the other place was wider, long ago. Passage was granted more frequently. Whoever put the standing stones here was trying to choke the path off. Keep traffic more manageable."

"Should we even be using them?" Elza asks.

"It won't make a difference," Ash says. "You can never keep a place like this entirely closed, but the gateway is more like a crack now. Bringing one spirit through won't change that."

"If you're sure," I say. There is something about this clearing, now that Ash has pointed it out. It's hard to say what it is. It's like a sound just beyond your range of hearing, something about to be said that never quite will be. It's not that the stone circle feels evil, exactly, although some inarguably bad things happened to me here. It's more that it feels uncomfortable, out of balance. You feel like you might look through the stones and see something else on the other side of them. Last time we came here it was midnight, and we were in a hurry, and I didn't have much time to drink in the ambience. In the light of late evening, as the shadows lengthen, I feel like you can almost taste the world beyond the stones.

Setting up doesn't take us long. Using a can of white aerosol paint, Ash draws a neat circle around the standing stones, walking backward and bent double. It looks uncomfortable, but she doesn't complain. Once she's done with the major circle, she adds a smaller one, just outside the main circle, a few feet in diameter, and then links them with a double line of spray paint.

"The circle's done," Ash says.

I make my way into the middle of the big circle, in the midst of the standing stones, and take a ring from my pocket. It's not Dad's sigil—I've still got that on my finger. This is one of his other rings, a golden band studded with red rubies. Elza and me missed a few tricks back in October, but Ash set us straight. I inherited nine rings from my father: a black-stoned sigil and eight binding rings. Each member of the Host had their own ring, and Dad would keep the spirits inside them when they weren't needed. I don't know why we never figured out what the other rings were for. I thought Elza was going to spit blood last night when Ash casually explained it to her.

This ring, gold with red stones, was the Fury's binding ring. Ash told me I'd be able to feel which spirit had been inside which ring, the same way you know where your body is, even when you close your eyes. They were my Host, and I was linked to them; my spirit merged a little with theirs, and I found that I can still feel their presence in the binding rings. I place the ring on the moss in the middle of the Devil's Footsteps. It ought to act a little like a fishhook, or maybe a magnet. I get confused sometimes, trying to compare magic with the real world.

Anyway, Ash says we'll get a faster result if I use the ring as the focus of the rite. I'm not entirely sure I want a fast result—part of me is really hoping the Rite of Return just won't work—but it's Ash's show, and she calls the shots.

I make my way out between the standing stones and take my position in the smaller magic circle. My stomach is churning like a washing machine.

"OK," Ash says loudly. I turn to look at her, standing beneath an oak tree, reading machine and mirror set next to her. "Let's run through the safety basics again."

"Yes, let's," Elza says.

"Luke remains inside his magic circle until the rite is complete and the demon has been bound inside the mirror. As long as Luke stays in the small circle and nobody crosses the boundary of the larger circle, we should be fine."

"And if something does go wrong?" Elza says.

"I can summon the Widow. She'll arrive within a few seconds."

"And we all scatter," I say.

"Do you think the Widow will be much good against that monster?" Elza asks Ash.

"They've fought before," Ash says.

I grimace, remembering the Fury leaping on my Vassal, a fight so one-sided it barely seemed worthy of the name. My entire Host was terrified of the creature. Ash's servant seems powerful, but when the chips are down, I have my money on the ravenous, merciless, soul-consuming demon.

"Her spear isn't for show," Ash tells me, obviously sensing my unease, "and demons aren't invulnerable."

"And if she can't beat it?" Elza asks. "What then? We'll have this thing loose in Dunbarrow, completely unconstrained."

"There are other measures," Ash says.

"Like what?"

"Nothing is going to go wrong," Ash replies. "It's a simple procedure."

"Luke," Elza says, "I changed my mind. This is—"

"Sorry, Elza," I say. "Sorry. We have to do this. I can't . . . I don't want to go crazy. I just can't."

"We already agreed," Ash says, hard-faced.

"Yes," Elza says. "I suppose we did."

"Let's just get this over with," I tell them.

Before I can think twice about the rite, I turn away from the girls and face the stone circle. I take a deep breath, like I'm about to dive down under the water, and raise my right hand, pointing my sigil toward the binding ring.

"What once I was, I will again be. By the stone and the hand and the ravendark tree, I beg my Fury: return to me."

The leaves of the oak trees rustle.

The sigil is growing cold on my finger.

I speak again:

"What once we were, we will again be. By the river and the eye and the everburning tree, I beseech my Fury: return to me." The sigil is sending waves of power through my arm, up into my head, my teeth, my tongue, and now my voice is as loud and cold as the crash of Arctic waves.

"What once I was, I will again be! By the lake and the heart and the barrenwhite tree, I bid my Fury: RETURN TO ME!" I finish the last words of the Rite of Return in an echoing yell. There's a moment of perfect silence, stillness, and I feel amazing; the ritual feels important, like you're important and you matter and just in this moment, the universe can hear your voice, dances to your tune, and the ring of stones seems like an invitation, a message written in a language you could read if you only looked closer—

"Luke!"

I come back into myself. One foot is poised to walk toward the Devil's Footsteps and cross the line of my protective circle. I withdraw it and stand totally still.

My sigil is pulsing with cold, like a frozen heart.

"Are you all right?" Elza's shouting.

"I'm fine," I say. "It's OK, really."

"Did it work?" Ash asks me.

"Yes," I say.

For a moment, nothing does seem to be happening. I'd almost think I got it wrong, except I know I didn't, the way you sometimes know you'll score a goal even before your foot touches the ball. The rite worked.

Then, silently, the golden ring lying in the middle of the Footsteps seems to explode, like someone struck oil under the mud and moss. Black smoke boils up out of the ground, and I see the hungry orange glint of flame. A screaming noise is building, a sound beyond the human and beyond even the animal, a cry of elemental rage. It builds and builds until the stones of the circle themselves must be vibrating, and I've got my ears plugged with my fingers as the black mass within the circle surges and grows. It shoots out tendrils of shadow, probing the boundaries of the magic circle like an ink-dark jellyfish searching for a crack in a bottle.

The probing lasts only a few moments, and then the demon contracts, molding itself into a pillar of dark smoke maybe nine feet tall, higher even than the largest stone. The top of its mass congeals into a familiar jackal-like head, with two blazing pinpoints of flame where the eyes would be. The thing looks at me, then turns its head to take in Elza and Ash as well.

The Fury opens its volcanic jaws and treats us all to a deafening bellow.

Being careful not to move so much as an inch toward

the boundary of my circle, I turn to look at the girls. Elza looks anxious, disgusted, one hand cradling the knife inside her jacket.

Ash's face is impossible to describe.

She walks toward me, her gray eyes fixed on the stone circle, on the demon trapped inside. She approaches until she's standing nearly beside me, and then gets even closer. She's right beside the flattest stone, looking over it at the Fury. The demon stares back, leaning its awful black jackal head toward her, but she doesn't shy away an inch. The white-haired girl and the beast of pure shadow take each other in.

"You don't remember me, do you?" Ash asks it.

The Fury gives no response at all.

"We were six," Ash tells it. "We were little girls. I don't suppose it matters to you how old I was. I don't even know what you are, what it's like to be you. Whether you feel afraid, if you feel anything at all."

Ash's white hands are clenched into fists.

"Afraid or not," she says to the demon, "sorry or not. I'm still going to kill you. We're going to break you apart. There'll be nothing left."

The Fury still hasn't said a word. It's impossible to read emotion in those burning eyes, the strange sculpted smoke of its body. It has as much reaction to Ash's speech as the stones around it.

"If you're waiting for it to beg," I tell her, "we might be here a long time."

Ash doesn't reply.

"Let's put it in the mirror," I say. "It doesn't have anything to say to us."

"Don't tell me what to do!" Ash screams at me.

"Ash! Can we just—"

"You don't know! You have no idea!"

"Ash!" Elza yells.

"And you!" Ash shouts at her. *"Both of you—"*

"Ash!" Elza screams back. "There's someone here!"

"What?" Ash asks. Her anger is gone, like it was never there.

I follow her gaze. Ilana is standing at the edge of the clearing—long, dirty hair, mint-green hospital gown, her left arm missing. She's staring at Ash and the demon.

Elza is backing away from the ghost. "Is that your twin?" she asks Ash.

"What's she doing here?" I ask.

"I don't . . . She must have followed us. . . ." Ash says. She calls out to Ilana in their twin-speak, but the spirit doesn't respond. She's still looking at the demon.

Just as I'm wondering what on earth Ilana is thinking about, she starts to scream. The scream is high and brittle and seems to split the clearing in half.

The Fury opens its mouth and screams in response, a deafening choir of agonized voices.

"Ash!" I'm yelling. "Get the mirror! Seal it away!"

Ilana is making noises that actually beat the demon for volume. Elza is cringing on the ground, hands clapped against her head. Ash can't hear me; she's pelting headlong at her sister, shouting in their shared language.

"Ash! The mirror! Ash!"

Ash reaches out to Ilana, and her one-armed twin grabs at her and, still screaming, lowers her mouth to Ash's. Ash lashes out with her sigil hand, but Ilana ignores it. White light is streaming from Ash's nose and mouth into Ilana. It's more than last time, much more.

"Elza!"

I still can't move from the magic circle. All I can do is watch.

"What can I do?" she yells. "Is that her *sister*?"

"Get Ilana off her! She's going to kill Ash!"

"How?" Elza asks.

"Use your knife! Do something!"

Elza pulls the pale knife from her jacket, and at the sight of it, the Fury cringes, the first emotion I've seen from the thing since we summoned it. The demon isn't scared of us, but it knows what that blade means.

Elza steps toward the twins. Ash is lying on the moss,

eyes open, not moving, and Ilana, no longer screaming, is sucking long, greedy drafts of white light out of Ash's mouth.

As Elza approaches them, witch blade held toward Ilana, something comes rocketing out of the trees, striking the twins with enormous force. Elza gasps as Ilana is literally sent shooting right through her, twirling high into the air and drifting down to earth as though she were made of feathers.

The Widow stands over Ash, spear held in her right hand. She bellows at Ilana in twin-speak, and Ilana screams back. The one-armed girl turns and flies away into the woods.

"Help us!" I shout.

The Widow doesn't reply. She rockets off after Ilana, ignoring me, Elza, and the demon.

"Yeah, thanks so much!" I yell as the ghost vanishes into the trees.

Elza leans down over Ash.

"Is she alive?" I ask.

"I think so. She looks . . . old."

"How do you mean?"

"She's gotten wrinkles. It's bizarre."

"Well, what do we do now?" I wave my arms. "I'm stuck in this circle! We've got the Fury here and . . . Elza, the mirror! Get the mirror!"

"How do we use it?"

"I . . . I don't know! Ash didn't explain that part."

I look helplessly back toward the demon. The Fury is floating in the middle of the standing stones. The creature is just waiting for me to break my circle, I realize, and then it'll be free as well. I can't mess this up.

"So we don't know how to bind it?" Elza asks.

"No! Not until Ash comes around."

"Oh, fantastic," Elza says. "So we can just sit up here all night, then."

She slumps down next to Ash, knife still held in her right hand.

"It could be worse," I say, sitting down as well, slowly and carefully. The magic circle gives me room to sit cross-legged, but sleeping isn't going to happen.

Elza rests a hand against Ash's neck.

"Heart's beating," Elza says, "but who knows when she'll come around?"

"What a mess," I say.

"Her twin . . . What on earth was happening?"

"I think Ilana got upset," I reply, "because she saw the demon. I don't think she really knew what she was doing. She just wanted the thing that makes her feel better."

"Ash's life," Elza says, running a finger over the knife blade. "Yuck."

We sit in silence for a few minutes. The clearing is

darkening rapidly. I don't know if we brought flashlights. I think there's one in the car. It doesn't seem too cold, at least.

When I glance over at the demon, I see that it has contracted into an orb of shadow, swirling and twisting like a gas giant. It's strangely beautiful, something I never expected to say about the Fury.

There's something I haven't thought of.

The Book.

"Elza," I say, "the Book of Eight! It's still inside the reading machine."

"I don't want you looking at it again," Elza says sharply.

"Come on! Ash could be gone for hours! And I've got the reading machine this time—"

"No, Luke. We don't know what it'll do to you. What if you go into a fit and break your circle? What if me passing it into the circle counts as breaking it?"

"Point," I say.

"Besides," Elza says, "the Book is—" She cuts herself off and gets to her feet, putting the witch blade back inside her jacket.

"There's people," she says.

"What?"

"Voices," Elza says. "People are coming up here."

"No," I say, looking from the magic circles to the

demon to Ash, lying unconscious on the damp moss. Just when it seemed like things couldn't get worse.

Because Elza's right. I can hear voices now, a girl's laughter, coming this way. And through the dark trees, I can see the searching glare of a flashlight.

I'm willing them to choose somewhere else, but the light comes closer and closer. I can hear voices now, two of them, male and female.

"Hide!" I hiss at Elza, but she shakes her head.

"What's the point?" she asks me. It's true; I can hardly go anywhere. Ash is still laid out on the wet moss, unconscious. I think of telling Elza to drag her somewhere at least, into the bushes, but there's no time. The Fury still seems to be sleeping, or waiting, whatever it's doing. It hangs silently in the middle of the Devil's Footsteps, expanding and contracting slowly, occasionally letting a tendril of blackness escape its main body in order to probe the edge of the circle. It looks like ink dropped into a glass of water.

The voices are audible now, a boy and a girl.

"—telling you, it's creepy up here."

"I'm terrified," the girl's saying, but in a teasing voice.

"Really," the guy says, "it's spooky. It's some pagan stuff. They say *the Devil* put the stones here."

"I can't believe it's so near the school," the girl says.

I think I recognize the voices.

"Yeah. Well, better than Holiday's thing, I'm telling you."

"I can't believe she would say *that* to me. I mean, I worked so hard on this fashion show with her. It was my idea, basically, and then she says *Emily* can go before me—"

"Harsh," the guy says. "Well, we can have some fun, right?"

"Yeah." The girl laughs.

Elza looks over at me with panic. The couple are right on top of us, just coming through the bushes at the far end of the clearing.

"I'm telling you," the guy says, "they used to have human sacrifices—" The flashlight's beam sweeps over me, the light searing my eyes.

"What the *hell*?" the girl shrieks.

"Hello," I say, palms open, making sure to stay inside the circle.

The Fury has formed back into the dog-headed human shape it likes to take and is watching the new arrivals with unpleasant interest.

"Is that Luke?" the guy asks.

"Yeah, mate," I say. "It's me. Hey, Kirk. Hey, Alice."

"What are you doing here?" Kirk Danknott asks.

"Oh, my *god!*" Alice Waltham shrieks. "His dog's here, too!"

At first I think she means Ham, that Ham's followed us somehow, and then I realize Kirk is pointing the flashlight at Elza. With the light off my face, I can see the pair of them in the dimness: Kirk in a gray tracksuit and neon-orange sneakers, Alice dressed in jeans and a hooded red Adidas jacket. She's holding a big bottle of beer.

"What are you doing?" Kirk asks me.

"There's someone on the ground!" Alice says. "Kirk! There's someone on the ground! It's Ashley!"

Oh, great.

"Look, if we can all calm down—" I begin.

"They're *sacrificing* her!" Alice screams. "They're trying to sacrifice Ash! I said they were, like, satanists! I told you!"

"We haven't hurt her," Elza says as calmly as possible under the circumstances. She's squinting in the flashlight beam.

"Oh, yeah?" Kirk says. "Looks pretty hurt to me."

"She's . . . asleep," I say lamely.

Alice gets her phone out and waves it at me like she's holding a gun.

"I'm going to call the police!" she says. "I'm calling them now!"

"There's no signal here," Elza says.

From the way Alice is frowning, I imagine Elza's right.

"Look," I say, "you should really just go. This isn't a safe place."

"Why?" Alice snaps at me. "What are you two freaks doing?"

"They're psychos," Kirk says. "Let's just go."

"What? And just leave Ashley?" Alice sneers. "Are you *scared* of them?"

I remember Kirk in the park, watching my body eating an entire dead bird. I think he's pretty scared of me.

"We're not going to hurt anyone," Elza says. "But you really should leave."

"Or you'll what?" Alice asks. "You'll put a spell on me?"

"No," Elza says sharply, "of course not."

Alice turns to me.

"This is your idea, isn't it, Luke? You're playing a game? You think you're magic?"

"Yeah," I say, "it's a stupid game."

"Come over here," Alice says. "Help us with Ash. Your game's not funny. She needs a doctor or something."

"I can't," I say.

"Oh," Alice laughs. "You've got to stay in your magical circle. Is that the game?"

"No," I say.

"So come here and help me with Ash."

I don't move.

Alice Waltham stalks over to me. She's grinning.

"You're really messed up, aren't you?" she says.

"You don't know what you're doing," I say to her.

"Alice, seriously," Kirk says.

"Run away," she says to Kirk. Alice turns back to me. "What if I go in your magic circle?" she asks.

"You'll die," I say, staring at her, trying to convince her with my expression.

Alice just laughs.

She takes a step toward the rim of the circle, the big one, the circle binding the Fury. The demon is pressed up against the magic barrier, as close to her as it can get. One of its long black hands is nearly touching her shoulder. Alice turns to me again.

"You're ridiculous," she says.

"Alice!" Elza runs toward her, trying to drag her back, but Kirk blocks her with his body. Elza screams at him and draws out the witch blade. Kirk leaps out of the way, but it's too late.

"You need to get this into your weirdo heads. There's no such thing"—Alice steps across the spray-painted white line, into the middle of the Devil's Footsteps—"as magic."

She turns to look at us, grinning, and the Fury pushes one of its spidery black hands into her face, through her eye.

Alice is still smiling, but she's frozen in place, like a statue. The Fury, seeming to find what it was looking for, slips into Alice's face, dividing into strands of living black smoke that crawl into her body through her ears, her eyes, her mouth, her nostrils, and the pores of her skin. Within a second, the demon is completely inside her. She's still facing us. Her mouth is smiling, but her eyes look desperate. They roll in their sockets, as if she's trying to move her body and can't. Then they close.

I'm moving backward, breaking my magic circle (what does it matter now?), backing away toward Elza and Kirk, who's looking from Alice to the knife in Elza's hand as though he doesn't know which to be more frightened of. Alice's eyes are still closed. Her mouth is open as if she's screaming, but no sound is coming out.

"What?" Kirk gasps. "What?"

"Shut up," Elza says. "She's being possessed."

I point my sigil toward Alice, and Elza takes her place beside me, holding the bone knife out toward the stone circle. Kirk is still whining to us.

"What the hell do you mean, she's possessed? That's

not real. You're nuts. I'm gonna get the police, mate. This is, like, a human-rights abuse—"

"Be quiet!" Elza snarls.

Alice's eyes snap open. Her mouth is drawn out into a pained-looking smile.

Before any of us can say anything, she lets out a shrill scream and turns away from us, vanishing into the undergrowth on the far side of the clearing. She's gone before I can even let out my breath. Kirk's flashlight illuminates an empty stone circle.

"What just happened?" he breathes.

"She's been possessed by a demon," I tell him.

Kirk looks at us with the panicked eyes of someone who's been told the plane is going down and there aren't any parachutes.

"Mate," he says, "are you . . . are you, like, magic?"

"Yes!" Elza shouts. "We're, *like, magic*! And we're all in big, big trouble!"

"Kirk," I say, "thanks to you and Alice, there's an evil spirit loose in Dunbarrow. I hope you're happy."

"I've got human rights," he repeats.

"This thing isn't human!" Elza yells.

"Well, what did you bring it here for?" he asks us.

"Excellent question! Kirk bloody Danknott hits the nail right on the head!" Elza shouts. Why did we bring it here, Luke?"

"What we're going to do," I tell Kirk, "is go and kill it. You—" I point at him, letting him see my sigil, in the vain hope it might confer on me some kind of authority over the living as well—"are going to stay here. And you are going to make sure she"—I point down at Ash—"is OK. And if she wakes up, tell her Alice Waltham is possessed and she went toward the school. Are you clear?"

He doesn't look at all clear.

"Sit down!" Elza snaps in a schoolteacher tone. "Look after Ash!"

Kirk sits down. He looks like he's going to cry. He scratches his stubbly head.

"I'm going to sue both of you," he says. "This is, like, emotional abuse."

"I look forward to hearing from your lawyer," Elza says. "Luke, we have to go!"

I give Kirk one last look, and then I turn and rush off into the forest. We'll just have to hope he stays put. Alice has a head start, but I can clearly hear her crashing through the undergrowth downhill. The demon is covering ground fast, trying to get out of the woods. Elza has taken Kirk's flashlight, and the beam casts crazy roiling shadows over the landscape as she runs. I'm already breathing hard; I haven't been training properly since I got kicked off the school rugby team. I slip in mud, get my jeans caught in brambles.

I can hear Alice ahead of us, and at one point the light illuminates a flash of her red Adidas top in the distance. I think we're gaining on the demon. What I don't understand is why it's running.

"Where is it taking us?" I yell to Elza.

"I think it's afraid of the knife!"

"How do we get it out of Alice?"

"I don't *know*, Luke!"

Hurtling downhill in the dark takes its toll. I fall twice, scrambling in the wet earth, pulling myself up and running on without even thinking about it. My Lacostes are going to be completely ruined. Branches clutch at my face and slap my arms; stinging nettles brush my hands and cause patches of welts to rise on the back of my fingers. We keep running.

We break out of the woods, into the empty lot that separates them from the school playing fields. It's full dark now, with a big white moon hanging above the rugby grounds and Dunbarrow High.

There's a small silhouette sprinting across the moonlit grass, heading for the school.

"I can't believe this," Elza gasps beside me.

"Bad luck," I say.

"I knew this was stupid! I said so!"

"Yeah," I say, watching Alice recede across the school grounds, "you did. Come on, we have to follow her."

Elza is flagging.

"It's the cigarettes," I say. "Clog up your lungs. I'm always telling you."

"Shut up," she rasps, "just shut up and run."

The possessed have the advantage of endless stamina, as far as I can tell. We manage a pained half-jog across the playing fields, and by the time we reach Dunbarrow High, the demon-ridden girl is nowhere to be seen. Elza has to stop and lean against a wall to catch her breath.

"Where do you think it went?" I ask.

"I'm not sure. . . ." Elza huffs. "I think those doors that are wrenched off their hinges might be a good clue."

Sure enough, the doors that lead into the school from the main yard have been smashed open. We make our way across the yard, crunching as we step in the broken glass around the doors.

Alice Waltham is lying in the entrance hall, facedown.

We approach her, Elza first, holding out the witch blade.

Alice groans. "Who's that?"

"It's Elza and Luke," Elza says. "Can you move?"

"I cut my hands," she says.

"Elza," I say, "is that her? Where is it?"

Elza reaches down and rolls Alice onto her back. There's no frantic grin on Alice's face anymore. Her eyes look up at us, sad and empty. Her face and hands were cut by the glass, and there's blood on the tiles.

"What the . . . what did you do to me?" she asks.

"We didn't do anything," Elza says.

"It's somewhere else," I say. "It isn't in her. It's somewhere else in the building."

"What are you talking about?" Alice whimpers.

"The thing that hurt you," Elza says. "We have to take care of it. Stay here."

"Holiday's fashion show," I say to Alice, "the charity show. Is it still happening?"

"Yes . . ." Alice says, confused.

I look at Elza. She nods, and we leave Alice behind, hurrying off into the darkened corridors of the school. We make our way to the main hall, heading for the sound of applause.

We open the double doors as quietly as possible, slipping into the back of the room. The school auditorium has been transformed for the big event. There's a catwalk protruding out into the middle of the room, surrounded by circular tables draped with white cloths. The tables are ringed with parents, grandparents, brothers and sisters. I don't think anyone is here who isn't related to the girls who organized the show. Holiday is raising money for a charity that supplies clean water to African villages. There have been several announcements about this in assembly.

"I never thought I'd say this," Elza whispers, "but I feel bad leaving Alice like that."

"We don't have a choice."

"Can't we tell a teacher she's there?"

"And then what? They'll ask us how we knew, and what we're doing here anyway. She won't die."

"I suppose you're right," Elza says. "I'm so angry with her. I could've strangled her after what she did up at the Footsteps."

A few people at the nearest tables are looking over at us. I realize how we look: scared, breathless, covered in mud. Elza has twigs stuck in her hair. I wave uneasily at someone's mum, and she looks away in a hurry. I scan the faces in the crowd, looking for someone holding their smile a little too long, someone with something other than joy in their grin. This is a nightmare, with so many potential hosts for the demon to hide inside.

Holiday is up onstage, holding a microphone. "Next we have Evelyn," she says, her voice echoing through the PA system, "modeling an exciting spring look."

Evelyn Elkhart, one of Holiday's courtiers, saunters down the catwalk. Her exciting spring look seems to be some kind of military jumpsuit, paired with neon-pink boots. She strikes a pose, to muted applause.

"This thing could've gone anywhere," Elza hisses.

"I know. Let's just keep moving."

I press on, smiling apologetically as we block people's view. Holiday frowns when she sees us crossing the space in front of the catwalk, but her cheerful commentary doesn't miss a beat. Evelyn has been replaced by Maddy, who's wearing a polka-dot dress and some kind of vest made of fur. We've made it across the school auditorium, and I duck behind a long blue curtain that hangs at the side of the stage. Nobody's around; we're backstage, out of sight. Applause ripples through the hall behind us. This is eerie. If it was going to attack us anywhere, it would be here. There's a doorway that leads into some rooms I've never been in before, which seem to be the school kitchens. We turn in the opposite direction, heading for an unmarked fire door.

"Where are we going?" Elza asks.

"Who knows?" I reply, swinging the door open.

I'm faced with a bedlam of half-dressed girls, racks of clothes, mounds of shoes. This seems to be where the "models" are changing in between their walks. Before I can so much as open my mouth to apologize, one of them spots me, and chaos breaks out: screaming, swearing, several girls throwing shoes in the direction of the door, which seems a bit much. I narrowly avoid having my eye taken out by a six-inch silver stiletto.

"Yeah, not that way," I tell Elza, slamming the door. "What do we do now?"

"I have no idea, Luke!" Elza pinches the bridge of her nose. "I don't know! The Fury could be anywhere! It might not even be in the school anymore! I just . . . How are we supposed to find it?"

"When Ash—"

"Oh, Ash doesn't know what she's doing! None of us do! This was so *stupid!*"

"Look, let's just keep calm." I rub Elza's shoulder. "We can deal with this. We dealt with the Fury before."

"Luke Manchett?" comes a voice behind us. "Elza Moss?"

I turn around. Mr. Hallow is standing behind us. It seems like he's just come out of the kitchens. I nearly jump out of my skin, but my math teacher makes no move to attack us. He stares at us with an odd expression.

"I've been looking for the pair of you. I found a girl in bad shape in the southern hallway—very upset. Alice Waltham. She says you are responsible."

Shit.

"We, er . . ." I start to say, gesturing in the air.

"The thing is—" Elza begins, smiling innocently.

The fire door behind us slams open, and a girl stands there, hair tangled, wearing a tie-dye jacket. "Mr. Hallow," she begins, "Luke just came in and looked at us all changing—"

"I'm dealing with it, Stephanie," he says. "Thank you."

"—and he was taking pictures on his phone," she continues.

"I was not!" I protest.

Stephanie doesn't even argue with me. She just gives me and Elza a chilly android expression of contempt.

"Stephanie, I'll speak to you later," Mr. Hallow says.

Stephanie nods and closes the fire door again.

"This is very serious," the teacher continues once she's gone. "The police have been called." His mouth twitches. For a moment there he almost looked amused. Some teachers like nothing better than to exercise their authority, I guess.

Elza bites her lip.

Where did the demon get to? How are we supposed to find it if we get locked up for assault?

"I need you to come to the receptionist's office," Hallow tells me, leaving no question that we're supposed to follow him. Elza's still got the witch blade in her jacket; that's going to look bad if they search us. Mr. Hallow leads us back out through the main hall, into the darkened corridors of the school.

How are we going to get out of this? What did Alice tell him? Is she safe? What's happened to the demon? I feel like we're going to the gallows. We could not have screwed this up worse than we did. Ash is probably still unconscious in the forest, under the dubious care of Kirk. We're both going to get expelled. Elza should ditch the knife somewhere . . . but how? Hallow's watching us. What did Alice tell him? Did she say she found us trying to sacrifice Ash?

We pass halls of locked classrooms and round a corner, and we're in the main entrance hall of the school, receptionist's office on the left. There's nobody else here.

I turn to look at Mr. Hallow for the first time since we started walking, hoping maybe I can find some excuse for Elza to go to the bathroom or give him the slip or something. He's standing in the dark doorway, staring at the two of us. His face, normally slightly irritated-looking, like there's a bad smell somewhere in the room, has twisted into an expression of ferocious joy.

Elza's first reaction is to scream, which I think is pretty sensible. My first reaction is to aim my sigil hand at Mr. Hallow, with the vague hope that something might happen. The ring refuses to oblige me. Elza's second reaction is to grab at my sleeve, pulling me backward and off-balance. I stumble and fall hard on the linoleum tiling of the school hall.

The demon was inside him the whole time! Stupid, stupid, stupid. I should've noticed, should've thought . . . but the demon had never spoken to us before. It must have learned more about how to control people's bodies. I should've been more alert, and now we're right where the demon wants us—alone.

He advances toward us, his shoes clacking on the tiles. The hall is lit by the glow of street lamps out in the parking lot. The demon-possessed Mr. Hallow is between us and any plausible exit. Behind us is the empty entrance hall and the large front doors of Dunbarrow High, which, since it's after hours, are locked. Elza screams again, but we're about as far from the fashion show in the auditorium as you can get; I doubt anyone is going to hear her.

Mr. Hallow shrieks like a bird of prey, a mockery of Elza's own cries, and lunges for her. Elza's boots leave scuff marks on the floor as she twists, waving the witch blade at him, unwilling to actually strike. I can't imagine it'll help us much if she does stab Mr. Hallow, since the demon can leave his body anytime it wants to. Knifing a teacher to death after hours seems like it would have a pretty severe effect on your college choices.

The demon knows this, too. Mr. Hallow lunges at Elza again, heedless of her blade, and knocks her down onto the floor. Elza's struggling, trying to get free, but he's got her trapped tight by the hair, fist crunched into a death grip right at the crown of her head. She's shrieking like a banshee. Hallow's smile is unchanged. He gets Elza's throat in his other hand and starts to squeeze. I try to pull him off her, but his body is like a statue, immovable.

I punch Mr. Hallow as hard as I can in the face. He doesn't even look at me.

He's got Elza's knife hand trapped now.

She can't breathe.

What do I —

I need to knock him out. The demon can't use Hallow's body if he's unconscious.

The fire extinguisher. There's a fire extinguisher in the corner of the hallway. I'll hit Hallow with it and —

There's an explosion of cold, like an icy wave breaking over us, and Mr. Hallow goes limp, his body collapsing forward. Elza wrenches his hand from her throat, gasping. Mr. Hallow falls onto her like a man-size rag doll. I pull him off her.

The whole thing happened in moments.

"You're OK," I say. "You're OK."

Elza is gasping. At least she can breathe.

I look up to see what's happened to the demon.

The Widow, her bare feet tensed against the floor, is holding her broken spear with both hands. The spear is stuck into a writhing mass of black shadows that I realize is the Fury—she hit the demon so hard, it was knocked clean out of Mr. Hallow's body. The Widow seems to be trying to force the demon flatter into the ground, both arms tensed against the spear, but the demon's body flows out and around the spear point, and the black mass forms back into the humanoid shape I'm all too familiar with, jackal-headed and furnace-mouthed. The Fury roars and unfurls its whip of flame. The whip is a thin lash of brilliant orange fire, which the demon uses to take unfortunate spirits apart. The Widow takes a step back, keeping perfect poise, never once taking her eyes off the whip.

The Fury sends the lash curling toward the Widow, who jumps nimbly aside and strikes out with her spear, catching the Fury in the shoulder. The blow doesn't seem to do any lasting damage, but the demon doesn't like it. The Fury bellows and answers with a flurry of blows from the whip, sending the flames coiling in impossible contortions toward the Widow, who somehow avoids every blow. The demon is clearly becoming frustrated. The Widow bends backward, almost double, to avoid a horizontal swipe—she moves with the frightening grace of a leopard—and yells to us, "Ashana is coming!"

"Where?" Elza screams, her voice back, and she's answered by a sudden flash of white light all around us. I turn and see light flowing in through the main doors of

Dunbarrow High, accompanied by a tremendous noise. I barely have time to register the light as coming from a car's headlights when Ash rams the double doors, breaking them open.

The doors don't explode like they might in a movie; they just collapse inward. Ash reverses her car, which is still running fine, even though the front is now crumpled like a half-finished origami, the car apparently being one of those invincible ancient models that could probably survive a nuclear blast. Me and Elza rush out through the broken doors into the staff parking lot. Ash has brought her car to a halt and is already out of it, running around to the back.

"It's in there!" I shout. "With the Widow!"

"I know!" Ash says.

"The alarms!" Elza's saying. "The alarms!"

"The what?" I ask her.

"Burglar alarms!" Elza screams at me. "You don't think anyone will notice we just ram-raided Dunbarrow High? And Hallow already said he called the police! We need to go! Now!"

"Not yet," Ash says. She opens the trunk of her car and is struggling with the mirror. I rush to help her. We heft it down onto the asphalt of the parking lot. Ash tears the wrapping off it, inspects the mirror for damage.

"*Ash!*" Elza yells.

I turn to look. The Widow is falling back, dancing through the broken double doors, jabbing this way and that with her spear. Her long black hair flows as she dodges and pirouettes. I have the greatest respect for her grace and skill, and I've never seen any other spirit go up against this thing and stand even the slightest chance, but she's clearly in trouble. As it comes after her, into the parking lot, the Fury seems bigger than ever, longer and lither and thinner, like a sketch of someone's nightmare that they scribbled down as they were waking. The demon is clearly a match for Ash's servant, and the flaming whip is coming closer and closer to its target. As I watch, the Widow ducks a fraction of a second too slow, and the demon's whip shears into her trailing hair, causing the ghost to cry out.

"Help her!" I say to Ash.

"It's OK," Ash says to us, smiling. "We've got it."

She taps the mirror with her left hand and says a word I don't understand. The mirror flares with white light, brighter than the headlights of her car, so bright I have to cover my eyes with my hands. There's a high ringing tone, like a bell. The Fury roars in response, seeming to realize too late what's going on.

A wind starts to blow, air being sucked into the surface of the mirror. Through my fingers I can see the demon frantically trying to escape, Widow forgotten, flying as fast as it can away from the parking lot, trying to get back into the school. The demon manages to make it a few paces toward the broken front doors, but the force emanating from Ash's mirror becomes stronger still. The scene is beyond surreal, the whole parking lot and front of the school floodlit by the incredible radiance coming out of the mirror. Despite the Fury's efforts, it can't move any farther away from us. The Fury expends more and more energy just to keep itself in the same place, and then, as the ringing of the bell becomes louder and higher, the demon is drawn back toward the surface of the mirror. It shrieks and struggles, becoming longer and thinner, scrabbling at the asphalt with frantic fingers, but the ground might as well be made of ice for all the purchase the Fury can gain on it. With a final squeal of rage, the demon is drawn out as flat and long as a black ribbon, stretching an impossible distance, and then, like smoke being pulled into an extractor fan, the demon's body is sucked into the surface of the mirror.

The shrilling bell fades. The light cuts out, and I take my hands away from my face, my vision streaked with those purple-and-green afterimages you get if you look at the sun. Elza looks equally dazed. My ears are still ringing.

"Well," Ash says, "that could totally have gone worse."

(nonpareil)

We make as clean a getaway as we can under the circumstances. I help Ash load the mirror, demon freshly trapped within it, into the back of her car. Ash looks awful. There are blue traceries of veins in her neck and face that weren't visible before, like her skin's made of paper. I can see wrinkles at the corners of her eyes and mouth. It's like looking at an old woman's face surfacing from under a teenage girl's skin. She's covered in mud and soaked with water, her overcoat clearly unsalvageable. Her white boots are now black.

"What about Mr. Hallow?" Elza's asking us. There are red marks on her neck where he was crushing it.

"The Widow can deal with him," Ash says, covering the mirror with cloth again.

I go back into the entrance hall of the school. The Widow is kneeling beside Mr. Hallow, holding the chalice of Lethe water. She's got one hand supporting his head, and the other is tilting the cup, making him drink. He doesn't seem to be awake.

The Widow sees me watching her.

"Were there others?" she asks me.

"What?"

"Others the demon used as a vessel?"

"Alice Waltham," I say. "Blond girl, red jacket. She was lying in the hallway by the main yard. I don't know where she is now. Nurse's office? She's got cuts and stuff." I make a gesture in the direction of the back part of the school. The Widow nods.

"She will forget," the ghost says. She lays Mr. Hallow's head back down on the tiles gently. "I will attend to her now."

"Luke!" Elza shouts behind me.

"What?"

"Get in! The police are coming, remember? We have to leave!"

Ash's car is parked right outside the ruined doors, engine idling. We're lucky it still works at all. Turning away from the Widow, I rush out into the parking lot and get in by the passenger-side door.

As soon as I close the door, Ash guns the engine and we speed away, narrowly missing a street lamp. It's only now, sitting down, that I realize how fast my heart is going.

My throat is dry, my spine bubbling like fresh-popped champagne. Ash heads toward the Pilgrim Grove development.

"What happened to you?" I'm asking Ash.

"Ilana had a moment, I guess," she says flatly. "It was bad timing. Sorry."

"We can talk about that later," I say.

"I woke up under a tree, and there was that gross boy with the shaved head. Kurt? He spent about five minutes telling me you'd gone chasing after Alice down to the school, and she was 'smiling all crazy' and that you were both magic. I knew more or less where to go. He won't remember any of what happened, so don't worry."

"Where's Ilana now?" I ask.

"Asleep," Ash says. Her face looks really bad; the irises of her eyes are almost transparent.

"Hello," Elza says. "I'd like an ambulance, please."

Me and Ash whirl around to look at her.

"What are you—"

"Elza?"

She puts one hand over the speaker of her phone.

"There are two people back there in terrible condition," Elza hisses at us. "Were you just going to wipe their memories and leave them?" She speaks into the phone again. "Hello. Sorry. There's been an accident. Dunbarrow High. A girl and one of the teachers."

"Well, sure," Ash says, almost to herself, "do what you think is best."

After another ten minutes or so, we pull up in front of Ash's house in Pilgrim Grove and she cuts the engine. Elza is looking at the house with trepidation. I've already described the house to her of course, but there's something about the strangeness in this place that you can't convey with words.

Our first task is to carefully transport the mirror into the house. Elza does a double take when she sees the empty living room. Me and Ash carry the trapped demon upstairs and take the mirror into a spare bedroom that I didn't see the inside of last time. There's a symbol drawn on the floor, a magic circle with a triangle inside it. We lay the mirror in the middle of the magic circle. I look down into the mirror. At first all you can see is your reflection — unflattering, since it's from below — and then the blank white ceiling above you. But if you have second sight, and you look at the mirror in just the right way, you can see the black-walled room inside it, can see the demon beating itself against the glass, screaming at you with inaudible fury. It's like watching a wasp in a bottle.

"Are we going to kill it now?" I ask Ash.

"No," she says, "sunrise is the best time. Strike it with the dawn on our blade."

"So I'm waiting for dawn?" Elza asks.

"Yes. I've got a spare bed for you both. You can stay here tonight. We'll need to be up and ready for six thirty-two a.m."

"You never said anything about that," Elza says.

"I'm telling you now," Ash says mildly.

"So what's all this for?" I gesture at the magic circle.

"Oh," Ash says, "that's for security. Don't want to take chances."

She steps back out of the magic circle to join us and makes a gesture with her left hand. The Widow insinuates herself into the room the way ghosts do.

"Mistress Ashana," the Widow says. "Luke, Elza."

"Did you give all witnesses the Lethe's draft?" Ash asks.

"I did," the Widow replies. "They will not remember the night's excitements. The student and the teacher are receiving emergency attention. There are police present as well. Nobody knows what happened."

"So we got away with it?" Ash asks.

"There were several recording devices in the parking area and school building. I have ensured these videos are unusable."

"Excellent," Ash says. "So what's left? Just the car, I guess."

"I will dispose of the vehicle," the Widow announces.

I'm starting to appreciate the advantages of a well-behaved Host.

"And Ilana?" Ash asks.

"She sleeps."

"All right. Get rid of the car, then I want you to guard the demon's prison."

"I obey," the Widow says to Ash, and vanishes.

"So we're here until sunrise?" Elza asks again.

"You don't have to stay," Ash says. "I'm not going to make you. But I'm not using that car again, and we'll need to be up by five to get ready. So unless you want to walk back to your house by yourself, get an hour's sleep, then walk right back, I think staying here is the better option."

"Yes." Elza sighs. "I suppose it is. I'll have to phone my mum, tell her I'm staying out. It'll be OK since it's a holiday tomorrow. You too, Luke."

"Do you want to meet Ilana?" Ash asks her.

Elza says she does, although her eyes say different. Ash doesn't pick up on her reluctance—or pretends not to, in any case—and leads us across the landing and into the master bedroom. Nothing's changed. Ilana is still lying in the same position, eyes closed. The same tubes run into her mouth and nose. I don't think her body has moved at all. The numbers on her life-support machines pulse in steady rhythms. You can hear the soft hum of batteries, a faint noise that might be liquid flowing through a tube.

"Hello, Ilana," Elza says quietly. "It's nice to meet you properly."

She rests her hands on the rail at the end of the bed. Looks for a long time into Ilana's sleeping face.

"I'm very grateful," Ash says to Elza. "This means so much to me. To us."

"And the nonpareil will bring her back?" Elza replies, not taking her eyes from Ilana.

"Yes," Ash says, "yes. It will. You'll bring her back. You and Luke. I can really be with my sister again. I can't . . . You're so kind."

There are tears in the corners of Ash's gray eyes. Slowly, not quite sure what to do, I move over to her, wrap my arms around her. She starts to sob, crying into my chest. Elza puts her arms around her as well.

"Thank you," Ash keeps saying, "thank you. I'm so happy. Thank you. I know she'll say thank you, too. You're amazing. Thank you."

And it's easy to feel, the three of us standing there in one another's arms, in the bedroom of the girl whose life we're helping to save, like we're going to make a difference. To feel like we're good people. Like we're doing something, for once, that's inarguably good.

o o o

You can't embrace and cry all night, of course, and Ash's tears pass almost as quickly as they arrived. We leave Ilana upstairs and head down to the empty living room. Elza asks why Ash didn't bother to order some furniture, and she just laughs and says she "basically forgot." She goes back upstairs and slides her big double mattress down the stairs, and we lay it out flat in the living room. Ash gets a stereo from her room, a bottle of wine, plastic cups. She changes out of her dirty clothes into a new white T-shirt, white jeans, a white denim jacket. She looks, once again, like she just got beamed down from another planet.

We end up having a sort of victory dinner party, just the three of us, sitting on the double mattress in the middle of a blank wood floor. Ash makes us a weird supper of crackers and salmon and a wheel of what tastes like pretty expensive cheese. She barely eats, just crunches on a succession of celery sticks. Ash's taste in music turns out to be pretty much exclusively pop-punk groups from the early 2000s, which irritates Elza like there's sand in her eye.

"Can we not just listen to some *actual* punk, please?" Elza whines.

"Ash likes what she likes," I say. "You can enjoy music just because you enjoy it. It doesn't have to pass the Five Tests of True Punk."

"This"—Elza gestures at the stereo—"is trash, and I'm

sorry, Ash. It's barely music. It's cookie-cutter corporate-sponsored faux-rebellion without a soul or brain. It's political commentary—"

"Political commentary that comes from a paint-by-numbers kit," I say.

Elza frowns. "Have I said that before?"

"You say that about twice a week," I tell her affectionately.

"I think this album is fun," Ash says, completely unfazed. She takes a crisp little bite of her celery stick. "So how long have you guys been a thing?"

"A thing?" we both ask her.

Ash grins. "As in, finishing each other's sentences and stuff. It's cute."

I catch Elza's eye, and amazingly, she's actually blushing. Our relationship is quite a private thing, so far. It's not something we're used to being asked about. We're pretty separated from the rest of Dunbarrow High, for obvious reasons, and my mum seemed to accept Elza coming into our lives the same way she greets most things that happen to her: with unfocused good will. I haven't had any kind of "talk" with Mum about Elza and me and whether she can stay over or not. She just refers to Elza as my "friend" and that's it. Elza's parents have been pretty welcoming, although sometimes I catch her mum giving me the kind of look you'd give a toddler that you saw carrying a priceless Ming vase around its playpen, bewildered that I ended up being given something so valuable, and totally mistrustful that I know how to take proper care of it. Her dad's a bearded nonentity, as meek as the two Moss women are forthcoming. He's crazy about bird-watching and about programming ancient computers, and I think he likes having someone else around to watch rugby with.

"Since October last year," I tell Ash.

"Oh," Ash says, "so tell me more. How did you meet?"

"He kicked a ball at me," Elza says.

"Romantic."

"Kirk kicked it!" I protest. "I didn't kick anything at you."

"OK," Elza says, "your best mate kicked one at me, and then you all laughed about it."

"I wasn't laughing!"

"I can really see why you were drawn to him," Ash says to Elza, straight-faced.

"It was because of his Host," Elza says. "I've always had second sight. He just developed it once he signed for them. Once I realized what was happening to him . . . well, I had to do something."

Ash looks like she might cry again, but she stops herself.

"Tell me about your Host," she says to me. "What happened with them?"

I've talked a bit about what happened last Halloween with Elza, but not with anyone else, and although it feels strange explaining everything to a third party, it's actually quite interesting trying to arrange it all in a way that makes sense. I tell Ash about my meeting with Dad's lawyer, Mr. Berkley, and the contract I signed, about him giving me the Book of Eight and Dad's rings, the first night when the window blew open and Mum was so sick she didn't even notice. I tell her about seeing the Vassal and the Judge on the bus, about meeting the Heretic and the Prisoner and the Shepherd, about the Oracle and the Innocent, and of course the Fury.

Elza takes over at certain points, explaining what happened to her when she left Holiday's party, filling in some of the gaps, talking about hiding me from her mum during the three days I spent reading the Book of Eight. In about an hour of drinking and talking, I've taken Ash all the way up to the night before Halloween, the Rite of Tears at the Devil's Footsteps.

Maybe it's the drink, maybe it's the company, maybe it's the sense, like I said before, that I did something good and I've got nothing today to be ashamed of. But I start to talk more, take them further than I thought I would. The wine is good and strong. I tell Elza and Ash how it felt when Mum stabbed me with a kitchen knife. I tell them about Deadside, about Mr. Berkley when I met him the second time. The beast's shape, billowing up out of the man's. I tell them about meeting my dad on that gray lonely beach and the conversation we had.

Ash is particularly interested in what it feels like to walk around in Deadside, and I spend a while talking about the mist and the grayness and the strange otherness of the place. I take a drink and then I tell them about the Fury and the Innocent, how my dad stopped my brother from being born, something I've never said before out loud. I tell them about the choice the Devil gave me, the deal he wanted me to make.

I stop talking. My throat's gone dry. I finish my wine, pour out some more.

"So what did you do?" Ash asks me.

I look her dead in the eye.

"What do you think I did? I sent that piece of shit to Hell."

Ash grins.

"You've made me very happy," she tells me. "Does anyone want more wine?" She stands up, almost falls off the mattress onto the floor. "Whoops."

"I'm not sure we need any more," Elza says. She's still holding my hand tightly, but it's hard to read her expression.

"Nonsense," Ash says, and she lurches off the mattress

and into the kitchen, while me and Elza sit together in silence, listening to her rummaging in the fridge.

A short time later, Ash—who seems pretty drunk—says she's going to spend some time with Ilana, and if we want to go to sleep, we're welcome to. I'm lying on my back at this point, the white ceiling spinning slowly, slyly, denying that it's actually spinning if I focus really hard, and then starting to rotate again when I relax. Ash turns the light off and stumbles upstairs, and I'm left alone with Elza. I rest my hand on her hip. I hear Ash moving overhead.

"Well, she's happy," I say.

Elza doesn't answer.

"I'm sorry I never told you before," I say.

Silence.

"Are you pissed at me?"

"I don't know what to tell you," Elza says quietly.

"It's not like I was lying to you. It's just hard, you know? With Dad and my . . . with my brother. It's not an easy thing to bring up."

"I know," she says. "I'm not angry."

"You sound angry."

"I shouldn't be."

"So that means you *are* angry."

No answer.

"I didn't send him to Hell," I say after a while. "I just told Ash that. I set him free. The Devil says I owe him for it. But I don't know what he wants."

"Yeah, I knew that," Elza says.

"What do you mean?"

"Well, not the 'I owe the Devil something' part. But I knew you'd let Horatio go. I can tell when you're lying, Luke. The way you were speaking to Ash, it was like someone saying a movie line. I knew you wouldn't send your father to Hell."

"Do you think Ash knows?"

"I think sometimes people want to hear certain things, and you told her what she wants to hear."

"So you think she believes me?"

"I think she'll be happier if she does believe you, and she knows that, too. For Ash, he's in eternal torment, and that's enough for her."

My stomach is churning. I wish I hadn't eaten so much salmon.

"It wasn't something I found easy to talk about. I was going to tell you."

"When?" Elza asks me.

"When it seemed right."

"So when it seems right is when Ash asks you? Like it did with the Book—you told her you still had it before you told me."

"That had nothing to do with it."

"Sure," she says.

"Look, I don't know what you're implying. But it's dumb."

"Sorry," Elza says. "But first not telling me about the Book and now this . . . I just thought we trusted each other. I trusted you. I tell you everything."

"I do trust you, Elza. It's not like I don't trust you."

"I know," she says. She sniffs. "I'm sorry. I'm drunk. It was a shock."

We lie there in the dark.

"And the Devil?"

"Yeah. He said I owed him. Something worth as much as my father."

"So a pile of dog shit," Elza says in the darkness.

"I wish. He wants something from me."

"And when were you going to tell me about *that*?"

"When I needed to. I didn't want you to worry."

"I see," Elza says.

My hand is still resting on Elza's hip. I can smell her hair spray, her leather jacket, all mixed up with the strange clean smell of the fresh paint on the walls.

"Can you take that ring off?" she asks.

"What?"

"The sigil. I can feel it touching me. It's cold."

"Sure," I say. I take the ring off my finger and slide it

into the smallest pocket in my jeans. I put my hand back on her hip.

"So are you angry with me?" I ask.

She doesn't answer.

Ash wakes us up at five thirty in the morning, like she promised. I have a headache with a pulse, and my teeth are furry. She flicks the lights on and stomps across the wooden floor, waving to me cheerfully. Elza groans.

"I have a kettle now," Ash says from the kitchen, "if anyone would like coffee."

"Black, please," I say.

"Elza?" Ash asks.

"No, thank you," she says quietly. Her thundercloud hair is all flattened to one side where she slept on it. She runs a hand through it.

"Are you all right?" I ask her in a whisper.

"Sure," Elza says. She gives me a real-enough-looking smile. "We can just talk later, OK?"

"I mean, if you're sure, though."

"Luke," she says, "I'm sure. Really. Don't worry. Let's get this demon-slaying done with, and then we can get the Book out of your brain once and for all, right?"

"Yeah."

"So, shower's upstairs," Ash says over the sound of the kettle boiling, "and if you want some of my clean clothes, Elza, I'm happy to lend you them."

Elza makes a vomiting face.

"I think I'm all right," she calls.

I can smell the coffee brewing in the kitchen, and it's enough to make me get out of bed. I stand up, head pounding, and make my way across the living room. Friday the third. Good Friday. It's still dark outside, with just a hint of dawn approaching. Ash is wearing a white tracksuit, her hair wet from the shower. She turns to smile at me, and I'm surprised to feel actual affection for her. She looks more alive than she did last night, although her wrinkles are still there, creasing the corners of her mouth.

"Here," she says, holding a mug out to me. I take the coffee. It's still too hot to drink. Ash is making scrambled eggs, and she's put toast on as well.

"So dawn, then?" I say.

"Yeah," Ash says, "we've got about forty minutes now."

"And she's going to what? Stab the demon?"

"There's a short incantation," Ash says, scraping egg into a bowl, "and then she plunges the knife into the surface of the mirror. The Fury will be destroyed, and only the nonpareil will remain."

"And it's totally safe?"

"Oh, of course. We don't even have to let it out of the mirror. Very safe."

She holds my gaze without blinking.

"All right," I say.

We eat eggs and toast, sitting up on the counter with our plates, and I'm done by the time Elza reappears, her hair wet and hanging over her shoulders.

"Eggs?" I ask.

"Maybe not," she says. "I feel a bit sick."

"Do you want some milk or something?" Ash asks.

There's a silence. I watch steam coiling from the spout of the kettle. The horizon has blushed vivid pink. Sunrise can't be long.

"Just some water," Elza says at last.

Ash nods and turns to the sink.

I take a shower, and then we make our way outside to wait for sunrise. Ash leads us through the back garden of her blank house, and into the fields beyond Pilgrim Grove. The mirror is propped against one of Ash's white patio chairs, pointed toward the eastern horizon. The Widow is waiting beside it. She gives me a shallow bow.

I look into the mirror's surface. The Fury is just beneath it, floating like an oil spill, watching us all through the glass. I remember it eating the Vassal, cutting him apart with its whip and swallowing his spirit down. I remember it hiding in my body, chasing Elza, trying to make me kill her with my own hands. I remember my mother sliding a knife into my chest. The world will be better off without this particular spirit; I'm sure of that.

I raise my hand and, making sure the demon is watching, wave good-bye.

The creature doesn't react.

Dawn is close now. The sky is lightening by the minute, a wash of purples and pinks, with a seam of gold behind the trees. I watch a pair of rabbits cavorting at the other end of the field. There are birds singing in the forest. Nobody says anything. Elza's hair is still soaking wet, and she looks strange without it fluffed up by hair spray.

I've got way too bad a headache for a ritual like this.

"I think it should be time," Ash says, looking at her phone.

"All right," Elza says.

"You remember the incantation?" Ash asks her.

"Of course. It's hardly complex. You remember what you've promised to do for Luke? The Lethe waters?"

"You have our word," the Widow says.

"Just making sure we're all on the same page," Elza says. She takes the witch blade out of her pocket and steps up to the mirror. Her reflection and the demon's black form occupy the same surface area, fighting each other to be seen.

"About a minute now," Ash says.

Elza raises the knife above her head. The Fury watches us all, expression unchanging. If the demon feels a trace of fear, it doesn't show.

The sunrise flows along the knife, turning the white bone to gold.

"Now," Ash says.

"*Let the dawn's light be the end of this darkness,*" Elza says, and brings the witch blade down into the center of the mirror.

There's a ringing sound, like crystal being struck with a hammer. My head starts to throb even harder. The surface of the mirror allows the witch blade to pass through, burying itself up to the silver hilt. Then the knife sinks deeper, and Elza's arm sinks with it. She turns to look at me.

"Luke—"

"Is this . . . what?"

Elza's right arm is stuck elbow-deep into the mirror.

Her eyes widen.

"It hurts!" she says.

"Elza!" I try to reach out to her, but I can't move.

My body feels ice-cold.

I look down, and there's a spear sticking out of the middle of my chest.

"Hush, boy," the Widow says, just by my ear. "Be still."

"No," I say, "Elza . . . you . . ."

Elza tries to pull her hand back out of the mirror. She's terrified. *"It hurts . . . Luke . . . !"* She shrieks like a siren.

I can't look away. I try to pull the spear out of my chest, but my hands go through it.

Bloodred fire, hungry fire, explodes from the surface of the mirror. Elza is wreathed in flames. She screams and tries to pull away, but she's stuck.

She turns to Ash. "You piece of shit!" Elza snarls, fire coursing over her face. "You—"

Ash doesn't say a word.

Elza screams again, and the flame spouts up out of her mouth and eyes, a fountain of demon fire.

My body feels like ice. I'm so heavy—

Elza falls to the ground. She's crumpled on the grass in front of the mirror. Blood-colored flames are oozing over her skin.

I try to reach out to her, but I can't.

"Be still," the Widow hisses. "This must be."

Ash looks down at Elza's burning body, her expression unreadable. Elza's hand came out of the mirror as she fell, but the witch blade is still stuck into the mirror's surface. Ash takes hold of the silver hilt and pulls. The knife comes free, sliding from the surface of the mirror as if it were water, and with it comes the nonpareil.

The nonpareil is the size of a grapefruit or an orange, and at first I think it *is* a fruit, although that word doesn't seem to do it justice. It's like a fruit, or maybe a beautiful egg, some kind of seed bursting with potential and promise. It has a sheen to it, like a pearl, and it changes color as I look at it, like the coating that crow feathers have. At first I think it's mainly white, like fresh snow, and then I become certain that the nonpareil is green, the green of summer grass, but that leads me to see the blues in it, blues like the most perfect tropical ocean you ever saw. I see the silvery scales of a fish, the smooth cool black of finely worked onyx. I see the red of ripe apples and a yellow that makes me think of hay bales, of the sun itself. The nonpareil looks like sunlight hitting fresh water. It looks like someone took your favorite song and gave it a shape.

I think the best way to describe the nonpareil is this: While Ash is holding it in her hands, I completely forget that Elza is lying on the ground in flames. I forget the Widow just stuck a spear through me. I forget my own name.

Ash pulls the witch blade out of the nonpareil and tucks the knife back into her coat, then carefully wraps the nonpareil in a dark cloth. As its light is extinguished, my fear and pain and grief come washing back like a lead-gray wave. The Widow twists her spear in my chest, and I fall to the ground. I feel like my heart is stopping. My arms and legs won't work.

"Elza," I say. The Widow looks down at me, her face impassive. Her black eyes have no pity in them. They're like empty graves.

Ashana Ahlgren leans over me. I want to tear her throat out with my teeth. I can't even blink. She doesn't look happy. I want to strangle her.

"Sorry," Ash says.

I manage a gurgle.

Ash reaches down and gently closes first one of my eyes and then the other.

I wake up inside the mirror. I suppose I'm alive, suppose that my body is alive somewhere, because I still have a life cord sticking out of my chest. I have that much to be thankful for. It's the same black space I was in before, barely bigger than a coffin, with the far wall transparent, so I can see what's outside the mirror. Of the previous prisoner, the Fury, there's no trace at all.

I'm out in the forest somewhere. There are no landmarks I can see, just pine trees. It must be around midday. I can see new bracken, tree trunks, some rocks. I can see a cardboard sign leaning against the tree opposite my mirror prison. It reads:

SORRY

NO CHOICE

YOU WERE GOOD TO ME

There's no signature. It hardly needs one.

I feel sick just looking at the sign.

Sorry? You're sorry?

Say that to Elza. Say that to her while she's screaming, with flames —

No. I don't want to think about that.

I don't know what to think about.

You know the worst part? I was actually starting to like Ash. Despite myself.

No, the worst part is that I didn't see this coming.

It was so obvious.

Was it obvious? I cast my mind back over the past few days: Ash smiling at us, Ash begging us for help, Ash crying as she looked at her comatose sister. Ash handing me a fresh cup of coffee. The way she asked us, *So how long have you guys been a thing?* With a cheeky little smile, like she cared about us. Like she didn't know that Elza would —

That Elza would get hurt.

She must have known. I don't want to believe she did. But she must have.

I remember Ash's face after she read the Book of Eight. I remember her throwing up in my bathroom.

She knew. Ash knew what would happen to Elza.

Flattering her. Elza said she wasn't going to be won over by Ash praising her photographs, but when someone gives you a fancy magic knife and tells you you're descended from Lilith . . .

Was that how Ash got her?

Ash got us both through me. The Book of Eight. I didn't want to go crazy.

I don't think that's unreasonable.

Elza is still alive. I'm sure of it.

It was just a burst of demon fire. I'm sure she'll be all right.

I wonder where she is.

I can't believe that Ash —

That Ash what? That Ash lied to us?

I knew she was a liar. It was right there from the start.

"Ashley Smith."

"The William Goodman Foundation."

She was a liar in plain sight and she showed me her sister and told me how sick her sister was and how hard their lives were and I couldn't wait to fall for it.

I was just being a good person.

YOU WERE GOOD TO ME.

I was, and look where it's gotten me. Stuck inside a mirror, no idea if Elza is even alive, no idea what time it is, what day it is . . .

I remember hugging Ash in Ilana's room, me and Elza hugging her, and the whole time her secret was inside her like a worm in an apple—*she knew she knew she knew.* Ash knew she was going to betray us.

She knew for days.

Maybe that's why she was crying.

No, she was crying for Ilana. That's all Ash cares about.

I saw that from the start, too.

Me and Elza were both just a means to an end for her.

Now she doesn't need us anymore.

What even happened to Elza? It looked like the demon attacked her somehow . . . but then it must've died, since the nonpareil . . .

I should've asked Ash exactly what would happen.

I did ask her. She told us it was safe.

Why did I believe her?

I trusted her.

I'm sorry, Elza. I'm so sorry.

YOU WERE GOOD TO ME.

NO CHOICE.

I can't take this anymore.

I just want to see Elza again.

I just . . . Is that Ham?

It is Ham. How can that be Ham? I left him at my house. . . .

There's no mistaking the identity of the beast approaching through the trees. Long-bodied, long-limbed, a noble head topped with a ridiculous tuft of fluff. It's undeniably Ham. He's trotting along with uncommon purpose, heading straight for the mirror. There's nobody with him. I can see he's wearing his collar, the name tag jingling as he lopes through the undergrowth. He makes his way right up to the tree my mirror is propped against.

His big shaggy head looks into the mirror, his marmalade eyes wide and sad.

"Hello, boy," I say.

Ham whines.

"How on earth did you get out here?" I ask.

No answer.

"Ham, you need to rescue me. Go and fetch . . ."

Who on earth can Ham fetch? Mum? She'd just see a mirror.

Can Ham even hear me? He can definitely see me.

"Where's Elza, eh, Ham?" I ask.

Ham whimpers again.

I need someone to smash this mirror for me.

"Look, go and find some bored little boys who like vandalizing stuff."

Nothing.

I'm really starting to wish we'd gotten a super-dog, the type that rescues people from wells and burning barns. Where do you buy those dogs?

"Seriously, how did you find me?" I ask. "I'm in a tough spot, Ham. I need some help."

Ham leans right into the mirror and presses his snout against it. He starts to breathe in and out. The surface of the mirror mists over around his wet black nose. The skin of his lip is pulled upward, revealing his weird little Dracula teeth.

"What on earth are you doing, boy?"

He whimpers and breathes in again, deeper, and I feel a slight breeze inside the mirror.

Ham's breathing through the glass somehow.

He sucks air into his nose again, and I feel the air of this prison stir.

I went into Ham's body once before, to cross a magical barrier that I couldn't pass on my own. It seems I'm being invited back.

On his next inbreath I'm ready, and I slip out of the mirror, through the glass, carried by his breath, flowing up into Ham's snout and then into his head.

o o o

Am Ham. Am Luke. Am sad. Sad sad sad. Girl hurt. Hurt very bad. Love girl. Find girl. Ham run. Run run run. Hello fields. Hello trees. Hello bad rabbit. Want to chase rabbit. Will catch rabbit. Make him squeal.

No Ham. Bad Ham. Am Luke. Find girl. Run run. Busy beast. Must run. Sad sad. White hair girl bad. White hair girl very bad. Must bite. Want to bite.

Through stream. Splash splash. Nice stream. Paws wet. Through woods. Am Ham. Sun bright. Nice woods. Through bushes. Scrape scrape. Rustle rustle. Smell bad deer. Hear her in woods. Naughty deer. Run deer run. Is gone now. Will catch one day. Ham love to chase.

Am Luke. Get deer later.

Run field. Wet field. Jump wall. Small wall. Jump over. Love to jump. Ham run. Run run run. Mud in field. Mud go spoosh. Jump wall.

Now sheep. Bad sheep. Lots of sheep. Want to chase. Tractor man shout at Ham. *Get out!* Not want to get out. Ham like sheep.

Man stop tractor. Time to run. Run run.

Go fast Ham. Am Ham. Run run run. Find nice girl. Am sad. Miss girl. Where is girl? Nice girl. Will kiss girl. Am Ham. Ham run. Run run. Very fast. Busy beast. Find girl. Girl hurt. Girl burnt. Very bad. Must find.

More field. Big long field. No sheep. No rabbit. No nothing.

Bad place. Unplace. Unplace very close.

Bad house. Bad bad place. Am Ham. Ham brave. Am brave. Want to go back. Big brave Ham. Must go on. Am brave Ham. Unplace. Fog all over. Unfog. Bad fog.

Am scared!

Am Ham. Am Luke. Am bravest. Unplace bad. Unfield.

Unpeople.

Bad bad bad.

I come out of Ham's body in a rush. I didn't mean to stay in there as long as I did, but there's something intoxicating about being a dog on a sunny day. My worry and fear felt far away, like they'd happened to someone else. That lasted until we came within visible distance of the Pilgrim Grove housing development, and then Ham got scared himself. There's something wrong here.

Although it's a bright afternoon, the field is dimmed by gray fog. The fog sits like a giant amoeba over the whole building site and doesn't seem to be moving with the wind. I've seen fog like this once before, in Deadside.

"That was some good familiar-ing," I say to Ham. "Good boy."

Ham whines anxiously.

I glide across the wet grass, Ham following behind me at an uneasy trot. The fog oozes around us. We reach the edge of the new housing development, and we make our way through half-finished houses, past fog-shrouded cement mixers and the dull-yellow dinosaur shapes of backhoes. The day grows even dimmer as we approach the site of Ash's blank house. The fog is thickest here, dirty-linen white, bloated like a growth of spectral fungus. The house itself is invisible. I turn to Ham.

"Wait here," I say, and plunge into the white fog, heading for the house.

The fog grows thicker still, and there's a strange ringing, a high-pitched chime. The fog is so thick, I can't even see my hands anymore; all I can see is white, and then, bizarrely, I get a flash of a black sky above me, filled with glittering cold stars. I move farther, faster, rocketing through the blank white void . . . and find myself face-to-face with Ham. I'm in the exact spot I started from.

"What happened?" I ask him. He whines.

I turn and plunge into the fog again, heading for where I know the front door of Ash's house would be, but as soon as I get to the place where the front yard should start, everything vanishes. There's no ground, no sky, no wind, nothing but fog. On a whim I plunge downward, finding no earth to sink into, just bleak endless void, and then, at a depth that should be far underground, another glimpse of a dark sky, stars. The chime sounds, the fog thickens, and I find myself flying right at Ham again. I come to a halt.

Where has Ash's house gone?

I make my way in a circle around the site. The fog is emanating from the exact spot where the house used to stand. Everything else seems to be in place, and it's only the house that's missing. I can even find part of the wall that separated Ash's backyard from the fields beyond, but past this wall, the fog congeals into its thickest state and nothing beyond it is visible. Is this a ward, like the line of glowing blood the Fury drew around my house? It's clearly magic of some type.

When I loop back around to Ham a third time, there are human figures standing next to him in the fog. If I had skin, I would jump out of it, but Ham doesn't seem afraid, and as I get closer, they resolve into shapes I recognize. Three boys, a little older than me, with wet-gelled hair and bleached jeans, white sneakers. The tallest one is wearing a pink polo shirt.

"Oh, look who it is," he says.

"Hello, lads," I say.

These three are some of the town ghosts, residents of Dunbarrow. They died in a car crash a few years ago, and they've been hanging around ever since. Their names are Jack, Ryan, and Andy.

"Thought that was your dog," Andy says.

"Yeah," I say. "Listen, I'm in a bit of trouble. You lads seen my body anywhere?"

"You lost it again?" Jack grins.

"To lose your body once is an accident," Ryan says. "To lose it twice starts to look careless."

"I'm not really in a joking mood," I say.

"All right, mate," Ryan says, "no hassle. We haven't seen it."

"OK," I say. "What are you doing here?"

"Heard there was a gateway opened up," Andy says. "Always wanted to see one."

"Gateway?"

"Yeah, mate," Jack says, "to Deadside."

"That's what this is?" I ask.

"It's a passing place."

"But . . ." I gather my thoughts. "The Devil's Footsteps is the only passing place in Dunbarrow."

"New one got made, mate. It's big magic. Everyone's talking about it." Andy shrugs. "Don't look like much to me, if I'm honest. Bunch of fog."

"What d'you expect?" Jack sneers. "A bloody big door with fire coming out of it?"

"Maybe," Andy says. "Maybe."

So Ash created a new passing place? A huge one, by the look of it. If the entire house turned into a gateway, then that's far larger than the stone circle. What on earth would Ash do that for? Is this to do with the nonpareil?

Has she gone to Deadside?

I remember telling her the story of what happened last Halloween, how interested Ash was in hearing what Deadside was like. She must have known she was about to cross over. . . .

"Is there a way to go through the gate?" I ask the ghosts.

"Nah," Ryan says.

"Not here," Jack agrees. "We were thinking of having a peek through. Dunbarrow's been getting a bit old. But this passing place here isn't public access."

What am I going to do? I don't know where Elza is, if she's OK. . . . Did Ash take her and Ilana into Deadside? What about my body? If she kept it in her house and took it over to the other side with her, then I'm in serious trouble.

"Can you help me look around this place?" I ask the ghosts. "See if my body's around?"

"Follow your lifeline," Jack says.

"That works?" I ask.

"Should," he replies.

Embarrassed that I didn't think of it myself, I look down at my chest, searching around in the air until I find the slender thread of light that connects me with my body.

Trying to grab hold of it is difficult—like trying to guess where something is by looking at it through the surface of water—but eventually I manage it, and hold my lifeline in both hands. It feels like sunlight on my palms.

I tug on the line, like I'm pulling myself up a mountain, and there's a tightness in my chest. The lifeline goes taut, and then I start to glide, pulled toward my body. The other ghosts and Ham follow beside me. To my relief, the line doesn't lead me into the thick fog where Ash's house used to be, but away from the house, back across the field, into the woodland beyond. The fog has faded here, and we drift in between sunlit trees, floating over a carpet of moss and brown leaves, Ham scampering ahead of me.

Even though it's my lifeline and my body, it's Ham who finds the right spot. He's rooting under fallen leaves and branches when I arrive, scratching at the edge of a plastic tarpaulin. Someone tried to hide it, covering it with debris from the forest floor. Ham takes one corner in his mouth and drags the covering off the two bodies.

We're lying next to each other, my body still breathing, asleep, with my faint glowing lifeline sticking out of its chest.

Elza is dead.

She's lying there, still in her dad's leather jacket, jeans, with her eyes open, leaves and twigs stuck in her hair.

I remember sitting with Ash by Ilana's bedside that

night I followed her to their house. Remember her saying to me, *I can't live without her. I love her. I'll do whatever it takes.*

Ham is whining and scrabbling at Elza, trying to get her to wake up.

"Stop that," I say to Ham. "STOP IT!"

He jumps back, whimpering.

"She's gone, you stupid dog!" For a moment everything is still. The Dunbarrow ghosts, Ryan and the rest of them, stand silent a little way from us. Ham is trembling. Elza's still dead.

"Sorry," I say, and I'm not sure who I'm apologizing to.

(opener of the gate)

I rejoin with my body and wake up flat on my back, the sun shining low through the trees and into my eyes, making me wince. I feel shivery and stiff, and my head aches.

Elza lies beside me. I reach out with one hand and close her eyes. Her face is cold and feels strange. She's really gone.

What am I going to do?

"Sorry about this, mate," Ryan says.

"Yeah. We'll take care of her, don't worry."

"What do you mean 'take care of her'?" I ask.

"Well," Andy says, "she's dead now, right? One of the town ghosts."

"No," I say. "She's not—"

"Look," Jack says, "she's gone, Luke, mate. Crossed over. She'll be around somewhere. Don't worry, it ain't so bad. We're all used to it."

"She won't have to get used to it," I say. "I can bring her back."

Ham licks my hand.

"How you gonna do that?" Ryan asks.

"The nonpareil," I say. "Ash said it could resurrect people if they were killed by the demon. I just need to find where Ash is and get the nonpareil from her, and then—"

"You've lost me, mate," Ryan says.

"No, see, Ash went into Deadside, so I just need to follow her—"

My sigil. Where's my sigil?

It was on my finger, but I took it off last night. I start to search my pockets. Ham and the ghosts look at me, bemused. At last I find something cold and round in my smallest jeans pocket, and I pull out the black ring. Ash clearly didn't search me, or she would have taken it. Even though I don't know what her plan is now, she must be in a hurry.

"See!" I'm saying. "I have this. I still have power. I just need the Book and . . ."

Ash has the Book of Eight. It's still inside her reading machine, which was in her house. It's gone over to Deadside with her. I'm so stupid. . . . How did I ever trust her? She's been leading us right where she wants us this entire time . . . and she has the Book.

I almost throw up.

Without the Book of Eight, I'm powerless. If they've gone to Deadside, then I have to follow Ash there, but I've no idea how to do that. I know the Devil's Footsteps is supposed to be a place you can cross over, but how is it done? I doubt you just walk up to the stone circle and say "Open sesame." My only chance to follow them, to fight Ash in any effective way, was in the Book.

This is it. I've lost Elza.

"No," I'm saying, "no, no, no . . ."

She's gone, really gone. There's no coming back from this. I'll never see her again. The last time I ever saw her, she was in pain and I couldn't help her. . . .

"Luke," one of the ghosts says, "it's all right, mate. We'll look after her."

"No!" I shout. "You won't! Shut up! You don't even know what you're talking about! Bunch of ghouls who died in a car crash! Go away! I don't need your help!"

I glare at them, my eyes clouded with tears.

"We can see you're very upset," Andy says after a pause. "We'll see you around, mate."

The three ghosts turn and glide away into the trees, leaving me with Ham and Elza's corpse.

"Sorry, Elza," I say. "Sorry. I don't know what to do."

Ham whines.

"She's gone, mate," I say. "She's gone."

She's still lying there, in the same position we found her, head fallen to one side and her arms lying at strange angles. Leaves in her black hair. Mud on her jeans and combat boots.

There's nothing I can do. Everything we went through together, and this is the end of it. Ash wins. All my magic, everything I've learned about death, and I can't save her.

I hug Ham and sob.

When my tears have ebbed away, I feel strangely calm, numb. I can't sit out here with her all afternoon. I need to do something, go somewhere. If someone sees me leaving the woods where the dead body of my girlfriend is found, I'll be in even more serious trouble. I need to get back home, work out what I'll say.

I pull the plastic sheet back over her body, make it as inconspicuous as I can. I leave the forest and press straight into the fog that coats the field, hiding myself from view. I make my way through the foggy gray building site, and when I come out the other side, with Ham trotting at my heels, the late sun on my face seems like an insult. How can it be sunny when she's dead? How can birds still be chirping and wheeling above the trees? We pass an old man walking his terrier, and he smiles at me and I want to punch him. How can anyone smile at me now?

We reach Wormwood Drive, and I try to compose myself. Mum knows me well, and she'll know something isn't right, but I can't give too much away. I'm scared she'll look me in the eye and see Elza's death somehow, see my guilt. I stand on our front step for five full minutes, digging my fingernails into my palms, trying to make myself feel normal, until I worry one of the neighbors will see me out here and say something. I quietly open the front door.

"Luke?" Mum's voice comes immediately from the kitchen. "Is that you?"

"Yeah," I say.

"Can you come through here? I've got some bad news."

"What?" I ask, walking into the kitchen.

"I'm afraid Ham's gone missing, love. He ran away."

"He's with me," I say, trying to sound cheerful. She must see something's wrong.

"Is he?"

Right on cue, Ham comes bowling into the kitchen after me, leaping up at Mum.

"Where did you find him?" Mum asks, astonished.

"He came to find me."

"Well, you could have called me! I've been ringing you all day. It kept going to voice mail. . . . I've been worried sick! He leaped over the garden wall this morning and ran away! Where have you been?"

"My phone battery died," I say, then wince at my choice of words. "Sorry. I was with Elza, I thought I said."

"Are you all right, love?" she asks, petting Ham, looking at me properly for the first time.

"I'm fine," I say quickly.

"You don't look well, love."

"I'm just tired."

"Are you sure you're feeling all right?" Mum asks, frowning. "You haven't been getting any flashes or anything, have you? No headaches? You look very poorly. Would you like some herbal tea?"

"No, thanks."

"Some dinner?"

"No, I've already eaten," I say, but I'm not sure if she believes me.

"You haven't had another fit, have you?"

"No, Mum."

If I stand here another second, I'm going to start bawling again.

"You're still having a scan at the hospital on Monday, don't forget. And if something happens in the meantime, please tell me, won't you, love?"

"I'm just tired," I repeat. "I'm going upstairs to lie down."

"Are things all right with Elza?" Mum asks.

"Fine."

"You know you can talk to me if something's wrong, don't you?"

"I'm OK," I say. "I'm just going to my room."

I take the stairs three at a time so she won't see me crying. I walk into my room and see the impression on the beanbag from where we slept that night, the impression of her body, and that makes it worse. I don't want to touch the beanbag. I want to keep that impression there forever. I lie down on my bed. The photograph of her, one I took with her camera, smiles at me from its place on the wardrobe door.

I'm sorry, Elza. I'm sorry.

I remember that night on the beanbag, her voice, whispering against my neck.

Just let me go.

I can't. How can you ask that?

"How, Elza?" I'm saying. "How?"

I need to watch out.

Talking to myself.

Shit!

I punch the bed as hard as I can. I don't feel much better. I punch it again, and there's a solid thump as my fist hits something under the pillow.

That's weird. Why would there be something under my pillow?

I move the pillow aside. To my disbelief, I see a book.

A green book, a book bound in green leather, with silvery clasps and a golden eight-pointed star on the cover.

How?

Is this . . . ?

I pick it up. It really is the Book of Eight. How on earth can it be in my bedroom?

It really is here. I run my finger over the cold clasps.

Elza.

Elza was sitting here, on my bed, Wednesday night. When Ash had the Book in her reading device . . . I run through the night in my head. Ash went to throw up, and then we went downstairs, outside . . . and Elza followed later. She was alone up here with the Book of Eight. She hid it under my pillow . . . and when we came back upstairs, the reading machine was already closed up, ready to be carried away. We thought the Book was inside, but Ash never actually looked. . . .

"You genius," I whisper to the photograph of Elza. "I love you. You genius."

Ash thought she had the Book of Eight when she crossed over, but she didn't. Elza didn't trust her with it.

It's right here.

I can get her back. I know it. I can follow Ash to wherever she's gone. I get up and lock the door to my bedroom. Then I walk back over to my bed, slipping Dad's sigil ring onto my finger.

Without fear or hesitation, I stroke my finger along the Book's green spine. The clasps open with a muted click. I look at the blank pages. Now that I've read the Book before, the path seems clearer somehow. I remember the start of Dad's sequence. . . .

Seven. I turn seven pages to the right. *One reversed.* I flip one page back, toward the front cover. *Four, three reversed, seven, five, four, nine* . . . I turn the pages, and they flow beneath my touch, the Book responding to its true owner. I see the pages begin to fill with sigils, marks of power.

And soon I'm not in the room at all.

When I come back into myself, the room is dark, the sky barely dawn-lit. For a moment my heart nearly stops, thinking I've been reading the Book for days, weeks, but I was only under for about eight hours. It could've been much worse. I snap the Book shut. I close my eyes, and sigils flow unbidden across my eyelids. I may be destroying my brain, but right now I don't care. Elza's all I care about. And there is a way to get her back. I know it.

One who wishes to tread the paths of the dead would be advised to bring a guide. I haven't read that, not those exact words, but that's how I remember what the Book told me. *Those rare spirits who have journeyed deep into death and returned are gifted with eyes that have the aspect of liquid darkness.* The Widow's been to Deadside before, and she'll be helping Ash, guiding her in whatever they're doing there. I can't face them on my own. But I know someone who might be able to help me.

It's the stupidest plan I've ever made, but I don't see another option.

I take the Book, my sigil, and one of Dad's rings, a silver band set with jade. I leave the house quietly, locking the door behind me, and walk alone through Dunbarrow, too late for the milk vans and too early for anyone else. The town sleeps. I walk across the bridge, past the park, up the hill to our school and beyond. I walk through the forest, feeling drawn on, like I'm a leaf in a raging river. Nothing could make me turn back.

Just let me go.

I can't. I won't.

The magic circle is still drawn around the Devil's Footsteps, white lines of paint. The golden binding ring we used to summon the Fury is still lying in the center of the circle. I check that the lines are unbroken, and then I remove the golden ring and leave the jade ring in its place. I take my own position in the smaller circle. I raise my sigil, feel cold run through my body. I say the words, the names. I perform the Rite of Return.

I don't have long to wait. Within moments, there's a

ghost standing inside the ring of stones; the ghost wears an old-fashioned black suit, black boots, a wide-brimmed black hat. He wears a white shirt fastened at the collar with a strange silver pin. His hair is gray, hanging down over his shoulders. He has a long beard and a waxy face that looks half-molten. His fingers are slender and white, with cobwebs of wispy hair at each knuckle. His eyes, those oil-black eyes, are hidden behind mirrored glasses.

The Shepherd paces around the magic circle, looking for breaks or imperfections. Having satisfied himself that he's properly bound and imprisoned, the ghost turns to me.

"To what do I owe this pleasure?" he asks.

"I can have you return to me if I want to," I reply. "It's my right."

"You may swallow boiling lead if you please," the Shepherd says. The look on his face suggests he'd enjoy seeing me do it. "That is your right, too. But I do not believe you would do so. Why have you called upon me?"

"I need your help," I say, keeping my voice level. Now that I'm face-to-face with him, I don't know how I imagined this would work, but I have to try. I need a guide.

The Shepherd throws back his head and laughs, the only time I've heard him do it. It's a nasty sound, like a crow having a heart attack.

"I will never help you," he says. "You have clearly lost your mind, Luke Manchett."

"Where did the Devil take you?" I ask.

"It took me to the darkness," the Shepherd spits. "And I have suffered. I suffered and suffered and suffered. Exactly as you intended. So I congratulate you."

"Where are you now?" I ask him.

The Shepherd looks around us at the standing stones and the oak trees and the moss and the reeds. He looks at the bracken and the stony bank behind me.

"We appear to be at the Devil's Footsteps. The site of your previous victory over me."

"And where are you not?" I ask.

"I am currently not in a great many places," the Shepherd says. "Say what you mean or keep your tongue still. I do not deal in riddles."

"You're not in Hell."

"True," the Shepherd says.

"I can send you back there whenever I want," I say. I raise my right hand so he can see my sigil. "I say the words, and you're right back in the darkness. You know I can do it."

He swallows.

"You can," he says.

"So, given that while I'm talking"—I gesture around

at the stone circle—"you'll be here, in Dunbarrow, on earth, do you not think it might be worth listening to what I have to say?"

The Shepherd says nothing.

"Well," I say. "That's a shame. I'll have to try someone else."

I raise my sigil to dismiss him.

"Wait!" he snaps. "Wait. Perhaps I have been . . . hasty."

"Perhaps," I say.

"What is it that you need from me, exactly?" he asks me.

I explain what's happened in the past week. I tell him about Ash, Ilana, the Widow. I describe the witch blade, the magic mirror, our summoning of the Fury. I tell him about the ritual yesterday at dawn, Elza screaming in pain as spirit fire spewed from her mouth and eyes. That Ash's house is gone, and there's a passing place where it used to be. I tell him as much as I can as fast as I can, and he listens without saying a word.

When I'm done, the Shepherd bursts out laughing a second time. He cackles like a hyena, slapping his bony knees with his palms.

"You fool," he says. "You blind, trusting fool!"

"Look—" I say.

"She is a fool as well," he says, still chuckling. "How the years fly by! I remember Ashana when she was knee-high. Magnus Ahlgren's whelp. She did not even think to check that the Book of Eight was within this reading device?"

"Well, lucky for me, right?" I say.

"Yes," the Shepherd says, "lucky. If this is how the next generation conducts its affairs . . . I shudder to think. You are both incompetents. Necromancers cannot make such errors."

"So what do I do?" I ask him. "Can you help me or not?"

The Shepherd sighs and takes off his glasses. I look into his wet black eyes. They don't scare me like they used to, if I'm honest. I meet his gaze without even shivering.

"Elza Moss is gone," the Shepherd says. "Whichever luckless warrior slays a demon is consumed by the creature's own fire. This has been the way since the first man drew breath. Her animus has been consumed. She is part of the nonpareil now."

"So how do we—"

"Ashana Ahlgren has this nonpareil, correct? Even now she travels through the lands of the dead with this precious object."

"Yes, so I need to—"

"You cannot." The Shepherd spits the words across the stone circle. "Elza is gone. You cannot bring her back. Live your life, boy. She is gone."

"No," I say. "I know there's a way."

"You asked my advice. I have given it to you. The girl is gone."

"So there's nothing you can do."

"I did not say exactly that—"

"Well, that's a shame," I say, raising my sigil once more to dismiss him.

"Wait," the Shepherd splutters, "wait!"

"So there is something you can do?"

"Perhaps," he says, muttering something. "Perhaps if we . . . When did the Ahlgren girl cross over into the world of the dead?"

"I don't know. Yesterday. She was gone by midafternoon."

The Shepherd mumbles to himself, counting on his fingers.

"It is difficult to make proper calculations," he tells me, "seeing as time between the two worlds does not run concurrently. But the journey she intends to make is long and arduous."

"What is Ash doing?" I ask him.

"Acquiring a nonpareil is difficult in itself," the Shepherd says. "I have only seen one before, and that was hundreds of years ago. But to properly make use of a nonpareil . . . it is no small task. Ashana Ahlgren must travel to a deep region of the spirit world. It lies far beyond this land of the living. She must travel through the Gray Meadows and the lands beyond. . . . She must reach the source of the underworld's eight rivers, the Shrouded Lake, and offer the nonpareil to the entity that resides below its waters."

"She's going to the Shrouded Lake?"

"An ancient place. There is strange power there. But it is far away. Without a copy of the Book on hand, the world of the dead is ten times more arduous to traverse. She will make slow progress."

"So someone could catch her," I say. "They could go into Deadside, catch up with her, and take the nonpareil for themselves."

"You do not know what you ask," the Shepherd says. "The spirit world is no place for a living person to go. Few dare to tread those lands. Your father never set foot there."

"But you've been, haven't you?" I ask him.

"I have," the ghost says. He replaces his glasses.

"I want you to take me there," I tell him.

The Shepherd chuckles.

"You are my sworn foe, Luke," he says. "You have gone mad. The loss of the witch child has dulled your reason."

"Take me to Deadside," I tell him again. "I want to catch Ash and take the nonpareil for myself. And then we'll offer it to the Shrouded Lake—"

"Madness," he says. "You will perish."

"I'll offer it there. And I'll have Elza back."

"Do you understand what you are asking?"

"Something difficult and dangerous," I say. "I don't care. Can you take me or not?"

The Shepherd licks his lips.

"What do I get from this, exactly?" he asks.

"The satisfaction that comes from helping your fellow man," I say.

He just smiles. Says nothing.

"I'll set you free," I tell him.

"In what sense?" he asks.

"Free," I say, waving my hand. "You can go where you like. You won't be in Hell."

"I want a new body," he says. "Another life."

"Can I give you that?"

The Shepherd looks at me hungrily.

"If I am present at a conception," he says, softly, "I can do the rest."

So this is what it comes down to. More debts and pacts. Remaking Dad's Host, bringing my old enemy back into my life. Promising him something I don't even want to think about. I don't have a choice. I need a guide. I can't just wander into the world of the dead on my own. Ash has the Widow, and she has a head start on me.

I have a good reason to do this. It's either this or let Elza go, let Ash win, and the moment I saw Elza lying in the dirt under that plastic sheet, I knew I couldn't let that happen. I don't have a choice.

"If that's your price." Think of Elza. Just think about Elza, and try not to think of what she'd say about this deal. "I'll do that for you. If we get back from Deadside with Elza. Not before then."

"Of course," the Shepherd says.

"Then . . . I'm going to bind you into my Host once more," I tell him.

"You say that as if I have a choice in the matter."

"I know that if you accept the role, the ritual is much shorter."

"You truly do love this girl, don't you? It's absurd. You're prepared to make your foe your brother in pursuit of the slightest chance that she may live again."

"Do we have a deal, or not?" I ask.

The wind rummages in the oak boughs overhead. The Shepherd examines the tattooed palm of one hand. "The task you wish to undertake is difficult in the extreme," he says quietly. "Even with my great expertise and skill, I make no guarantee of success. If we cannot resurrect the witch girl—"

"As long as I think you've wholeheartedly helped me," I say, "I'll keep my side of the bargain. I promise."

"Swear by your sigil," he says.

"I swear by my sigil that if you wholeheartedly help in this matter, I will keep my promise to you," I say.

"Excellent," the Shepherd says, clapping his hands. "Excellent. Onward to the Gray Meadows, then. Onward, on this ridiculous quest. Name me your Shepherd."

I raise my sigil above my head. The ring pulses with cold.

"*Honorable leader*," I say. "*Beloved left hand. Speaker for the dead. I name you Shepherd.*"

"*I accept this name in turn*," the Shepherd replies. "*I bind my soul to the Manchett Host, now and for eternity.*"

My sigil hums, and I feel a rush of coldness as the Shepherd's power joins with mine. For a moment the clearing is frozen in place, and we exist together outside time, an endless instant in which no wind blows and no grass grows and the secret language of the world seems written on the sky in the spread of the oak trees' branches.

The feeling subsides, and I'm left standing in my magic circle, bound to a spirit I thought I'd defeated and sent into Hell. And this is my best plan. This is absurd. I feel like I'm climbing a tall, dangerous cliff face, and I need to remember not to look down. Keep going forward. You need to save Elza. That's what this is all about.

What was it Dad said, that night when I saw him again?

You've got to live the life you have, rather than the life you wanted.

Experimentally, I step out of the magic circle. The Shepherd does the same, and we stand facing each other, just in front of the tallest standing stone. Then, as the wind rises, the ghost bends on one knee, and plants a cold kiss on my sigil ring.

We make our way down the path from the stone circle to Dunbarrow High in awkward silence. The Shepherd is one of my least favorite people, alive or dead. I just promised him something so horrible that I don't even want to think about it. I know what Elza would say about all of this. *Just let me go.*

No. How could I let you go? You didn't know what you were asking. If you could feel what I felt when I saw you lying dead in the dirt, with leaves in your hair . . . you'd know why I'm doing this. You'd realize, Elza, that I can't do anything else.

The Shepherd has a sour expression, like there's something offensive about the spring woods. He walks stiffly, with his shoulders held rigid. I'm shocked, as I sometimes am, by how real the ghost is, how vivid and present. I can see a loose thread hanging from one of the buttons on his waistcoat. There's a tiny yellow stain on the white collar of his shirt. The toes of his black boots are scuffed and worn.

"This isn't going to be like last time," I say.

"Whatever could you mean, Luke?" he asks.

"Any of it," I say. "I know what I'm doing this time. So behave."

"Yes," the Shepherd says, "you have every appearance of a man utterly in control of his destiny."

I don't dignify this with a response. We walk across the playing fields in silence. We walk through the high-school grounds, empty on a Saturday afternoon, and down the same hill I've walked down from school a thousand times before. As we pass through the school gates, I remember seeing Elza smoking just beside them, that first day we spoke properly, and it feels like being stabbed. I have to look away.

The silence lasts through Dunbarrow, which is heaving with weekend traffic. The Shepherd makes no comment on any of it. We walk across the bridge, up the hill to Wormwood Drive. There's a familiar silver car parked in our driveway, alongside Mum's yellow one. I should have been expecting this . . . too busy thinking about magic. I see Mum standing at the front window, looking right at me. She turns to speak to someone else in the room. If I run away now, it's going to look bad. There's nothing I can do. I'll just have to deny everything. I walk up the driveway like I haven't got a care in the world and open the front door, which is unlocked.

Ham comes rushing out of the kitchen to greet me, and then sees the Shepherd. His ears flatten back against the sides of his head, and he snarls at the ghost.

"It's fine, boy," I whisper. "He's with me."

Ham gives me a disbelieving look and backs off into the kitchen, still growling.

"Luke?" Mum calls to me from the front room.

"Yeah?" I say with feigned lightness.

"Could you come in here, please?"

Her voice is stern. I go to find her.

As expected, Mr. and Mrs. Moss are sitting on the sofa with Mum. Mrs. Moss is small, broad-faced, with curly rust-colored hair. Mr. Moss, Elza's dad, is tall and stringy, with thick glasses, a sparse beard, and receding brown hair. His smile is always apologetic. Elza gets her long, sharp face from her dad, but almost everything else from her mother. They've got cups of tea on the low table in front of them.

"Would you sit down, please?" Mum asks.

I sit in an armchair opposite the sofa, one that's rarely used because you can't see the TV from here.

"Hey," I say to Elza's parents. They give me thin smiles.

"Luke," Mum says, "Mr. and Mrs. Moss wanted to speak to us. It's about Elza."

"Has something happened?" I ask, trying my hardest to look puzzled.

Unseen by the adults, the Shepherd is standing in the corner of the living room. His hands are clasped at his waist. It's impossible to see where exactly he's looking, because of his eyeglasses. His expression is equally opaque.

"We haven't seen Elza since Wednesday morning," Elza's mum says. "It's now Saturday. She was supposed to help her father with the gardening. We were wondering if you knew where she was."

She's wrapped in plastic in the woods on the far side of Dunbarrow. I can take you all there now. It's my fault.

"I thought she was at home?" I say.

"She called me on Thursday evening," Mr. Moss says, "to say she was staying here again with you, like she did on Wednesday."

I haven't been thinking about this. I've been thinking about the Book, the Shepherd. I've almost lost track of our lies.

Mum rang Elza's mum on Wednesday, but on Thursday evening, we'd just captured the demon. We drove back to Pilgrim Grove with Ash. And we both called our parents and said—

"Luke," Mum says, "you told me you were staying with the Mosses that night. Elza didn't stay here. What were you doing?"

"We changed our minds, stayed at a friend's," I say. "The blond girl, Ashley. You met her on Wednesday. Remember?"

"We haven't heard from Elza since then," Mrs. Moss says to me. "We've tried calling her, and she doesn't pick up. Her phone isn't receiving calls."

"I don't know anything," I say, immediately realizing how guilty that makes me sound. "Last time I saw her, she said she was going home."

"Luke," Mum says softly, "this is serious. We're all really worried about Elza."

"It's not like her," Mr. Moss says, frowning. He's a strange person, quiet almost to the point of being comical, but the fear in his voice now hits me harder than Mrs. Moss's anger. I feel the chair moving under me, like I'm floating in space. I keep seeing Elza lying in the dirt. Keep folding the tarpaulin back over her face.

"She's a very conscientious girl," Mrs. Moss says to Mum.

"She'll be fine," I say, feeling my tongue move by itself.

There's a general silence.

"How do you know that?" Mrs. Moss asks me. "You just told us you didn't know anything."

"She's . . . busy," I say. "Elza is busy."

"Luke, if you know where she is . . ." Mum begins.

"Where is our daughter?" Mrs. Moss asks.

"I don't know," I say. My body feels hot and enormous, like I'm inflating. Guilt. I'm being pumped full of it.

"Where is she?" Mrs. Moss asks again.

"Luke," Mum says.

Mrs. Moss is breathing hard. "We'll have to get the police," she says.

I want to scream. How am I going to get out of this? Every moment I sit here is a moment I'm not busy saving her. Ash is getting closer to the Shrouded Lake with every second that passes. I give the Shepherd a despairing look.

"There's really no need," I say.

Mrs. Moss looks at her husband and Mum in disbelief. "Why is he lying to us like this? What are you hiding?"

"Luke," Mum starts to say, "if you and Elza are in trouble—"

She stops halfway through the sentence. She seems like she's having trouble moving her mouth. Her eyes roll up into the top of her head, and she collapses onto the sofa. Her eyes close. She's snoring. Elza's parents are also asleep, Mrs. Moss's head resting on Mr. Moss's shoulder.

"Our time is not endless," the Shepherd announces.

"Did you . . . ?"

"I have induced them to sleep. It is no great sorcery.

No harm will come to them, I assure you. But we cannot delay. If you mean to catch up with the Ahlgren girl, we cannot wait another moment."

"Sure." I look at the parents, asleep on our big sofa. I take a deep breath. Part of me is just glad he stopped Mr. and Mrs. Moss from looking at me like that. I walk over to the window and draw the blinds. "Will they really be OK?" I ask. The scene is quietly gruesome, three limp bodies with their heads lolling against the cushions. You can hear them breathing, but they look dead.

"They will sleep until you return to the house, or until three days have passed, whichever arrives first. They will awaken disoriented and remember little of the circumstances that brought them to this room."

"All right," I say. I can't think what else to do with our parents. "So what do we need to do?"

"Preparations . . ." The Shepherd strokes his beard. "You will leave your body behind at the threshold of the gateway. It would be wise to provide shelter for it, while you are occupied."

"So a tent," I say. "We've got one in the garage."

"As for what we will need in the spirit world, the Book of Eight and your sigil are paramount, for they are the tools with which your will may be imposed. You should feast before you attempt the crossing: your body needs sustenance while the spirit wanders. I might also suggest you bring your familiar."

"What? Ham?"

"He may accompany you. It is his right. I have no love of the beast, but he is an extension of your spiritual power. If he agrees to the journey, it would be to our advantage when it comes to battle."

I find Ham cowering in his crate in the laundry room. He whines bitterly when me and the Shepherd come to find him. Ham's such an incredible coward, and the idea of him following us into Deadside is bizarre. But if the Shepherd thinks it would help, then I suppose I should try and convince him to come along.

"Look, boy," I say. "I'm going on a journey. I want to get Elza back. He thinks we can do it. If you don't want to come, then I understand. But I'd really appreciate your company."

Ham looks from me to the Shepherd and back again. He whines and flattens his ears against his head. Then he gets up out of his crate, with a long-suffering look, and pads over to lick my hand.

I've only ever backed Mum's car out of the driveway before, but driving on the roads doesn't seem too difficult.

I have this unfortunate incident with a delivery van just at the bottom of Wormwood Drive, but we don't actually hit it, and we head on up to Pilgrim Grove without further excitement, with Ham lying on a sleeping bag in the backseat. At first I was convinced we'd meet a police car at a corner, get pulled over, and be put in jail, but with a bitter thrill I realized that it doesn't matter. The Shepherd can take care of that. I can do whatever I need to do. We make our way through the half-finished houses and the fog.

"Rather extraordinary," the Shepherd remarks, looking out through the passenger-side window at the mist.

"I know. I'm actually a natural at driving! Who knew?"

"I was referring to the gate to the spirit world," he says without a trace of mirth.

"You're really easy to tease," I say, and then realize it was what Elza used to say to me. *Will* say to me, I decide. She will say that again, and she'll give me one of her infuriating grins as well.

We drive through the development and across the field until we find the place, then get out of the car. Elza is still where I left her, hidden under plastic. The Shepherd kneels beside her. His face doesn't show any emotion. She's just a minor detail to him, her corpse only a small variable in our plan. He wets two fingers in his mouth and strokes them over her forehead. Somehow they leave a black smudge, like ink, trailing from Elza's hairline down to the top of her nose. The Shepherd leans back on his heels, examining the corpse from another angle.

"The decay is not too far advanced," he announces, "and I have halted it, for a time. Worms will not make a meal of her today."

I hadn't thought about that. A few hours, and she was already starting to rot. I don't want to think about it.

I lift her into the trunk of the car while the Shepherd goes to examine the gateway Ash made into Deadside. I've lifted her up before, carried her on my back and stuff, but she seems heavier now, and she's cold, too. Her arm hangs down and swings as I walk. I feel like a murderer, wrestling Elza's body into the trunk of a car.

"I'm sorry," I say as I close the trunk. "I'm going to fix this."

Ham gazes anxiously over the headrests. I leave the car and walk through the thickening fog to find the Shepherd. He's standing right where the front gate to Ash's place used to be. He seems to be feeling for something in the air, some kind of flaw or opening. I wait silently.

"No," the Shepherd says, almost to himself, "no."

He turns and sees me standing beside him.

"How did she do this?" I ask.

"The Ahlgren girl chose her plot well," he says. "There are hidden pathways in the earth. Lines of force. Where they converge—"

"Yeah, ley lines. Mum's always talking about those."

"Where they converge," he continues, "you will find a passing place. The stone circle you called the Devil's Footsteps is one such location. This house appears to have been built at another."

"She chose this place deliberately?"

"It would appear so. The house itself is built upon a passing place of sorts. A minor spot, apparently not even worthy of the attentions of the ancient people who first settled in Dunbarrow. There most likely was a single oak tree growing here, before the development began. Perhaps a ring of mushrooms . . . no matter. Even a minor crack between the worlds can become a great gateway, if opened with enough force. The Ahlgren girl appears to have transported her entire house into the spirit world."

"You can do that?"

"King Solomon supposedly had an entire wing of his palace that existed only within the realm of the dead. It's uncommon, but quite possible. The spirit Kasmut, the Ahlgren Host's Widow, has considerable power at her disposal. I knew her in life, and I have no reason to believe time has lessened her abilities, nor increased her supply of mercy. The opening of this new gateway would not be possible without an enormous reserve of magical strength. We must be cautious when meeting that woman in battle."

I remember the way the Widow fought the demon: the delirious fluidity of her movements, the terrible force behind her spear thrusts. Scary as the Shepherd can be, I've never seen him actually fight anything. I'm not sure how I'd rate his chances against Ash's bodyguard.

"Do not fear," he says, clearly reading my unease. "You have a powerful spirit at your disposal as well." He flashes his rank of gray teeth. I grimace back. "Powerful and cunning. In life, there were kings who came to me on bended knee. We will vanquish this upstart coven of women. You have my word."

"Glad you've got my back," I say.

Probably he's got my back just long enough to slide a knife into it. Plus who says stuff like "upstart coven"? Why am I trusting this ghost? This is insane.

I need to get Elza back.

This is going to work.

Trust yourself. Not him.

Trust yourself.

"So what do we do?" I ask.

"I had hoped we could force an entry here, perhaps even find Ashana's body unguarded. But the gateway is warded. I cannot break through."

"So?"

"You will open the gateway at the Devil's Footsteps, and we will proceed from there."

The drive out of Dunbarrow and around to the Footsteps, mimicking the drive we made with Ash on Thursday evening, isn't as tense as making our way up to Pilgrim Grove was. Seeing Elza's body, touching it, has reminded me that the worst has already happened. The idea of being stopped with a corpse in the trunk doesn't scare me like it ought to. She's already gone. Every mile we drive is another mile closer to bringing her back. In the end, we barely even see another car on the country lanes. I don't think the Footsteps is a particular draw for weekend sightseers. We make our way down the rutted path, stop more or less in the same place where we came just days ago with Ash, the same spot where I found Mum's car that morning last October. I remember Ham running to it, Elza getting out, the smile on her face when she saw I was alive—

I cut the engine. The Shepherd waits without speaking a word while I cry. When I'm done sniffling, he says in a voice like ice, "The world is cruel."

"What?" I say, realizing there's snot on my upper lip. I dab it with my sleeve, not caring. The Shepherd gives me a look of disgust.

"The world is cruel," he says again. "It does not care about your suffering. Magic is the art of changing the world to suit you. In order to bend the world to your will, you must be cruel as well. Mastery and empathy do not complement one another."

"Why are you telling me this?"

"Because," the ghost says, "you are forcing me into a dangerous journey with you. I want you to understand what may be necessary in order to achieve your goal. The spirit world, Deadside, is not Dunbarrow."

"I've seen it," I say. "I know."

The Shepherd snorts. "You were under the influence of the Black Goat. That spirit moves at will through both worlds like a great shark in a reef. This time it will be different. We must travel on foot, with only our will and our wisdom as guides. We will be vulnerable to the spirits that dwell there. Do you understand?"

"I think so," I say.

"You *think* so?" The Shepherd reaches out and sinks his spectral fingers right into my arm. I feel a cold bite, like someone laid ice on my skin. I shudder. "You must *know* so," he hisses. "You must know that you want what we seek, that you truly want it. You do not have *this* in the spirit world. You will leave your flesh behind. What is the spirit?"

"I don't know. Ectoplasm? It's made of dark matter?"

"Your spirit"—his mirrored glasses are inches from my eyes—"is what dwells within the flesh. It is *will*, Luke.

Will, and wisdom. Do you understand me now? It is not your muscles that will make you strong in the spirit world. It is your will, the will to power, the will that drives you to dominate and destroy. This is how you can survive."

"I understand."

"Do you really? You want what you say you want? You want it so badly you are willing to risk all?"

"I do," I say. "We've come this far. I'll do whatever it takes."

"I hope that you do," the Shepherd says. He lets go of my arm. "I do not know what we will face in the spirit world, but we will not reach the Shrouded Lake without incident. All that men fear in life is death, but within death itself, there are fates far graver. If your will is weak, turn back now, not once the threshold is crossed. I do not wish to find myself tethered to a master who lacks the courage to see our journey to the end. It would go badly for us both."

"No," I say. "We're going on."

Before he can say another word, I open the car door and get out. It's late afternoon now, with crisp air and long shadows. Birds squabble in the oak trees overhead. I decide to head down to the Footsteps with the tent first, set it up, and then get Ham and Elza. I shoulder it, make my way down the muddy path, over the stony bank, through the bracken. As I reach the stone circle, I hear someone break a branch behind me. I turn.

It's a boy wearing a rain jacket, tracksuit pants, dirty hiking boots. He's got his hood raised, and although his face is wild and gaunt, I recognize him. It's Mark Ellsmith, my old mate. He seems to be pointing a gun at me.

"Mark?" I say slowly. "Ash said you were in a hotel—"

"Luke," he says. He's got a look in his eyes that I don't like, as though he's been staring at the sun too long. He moves his mouth several times without speaking, like he's trying to choose the right words. The gun—a shotgun, with a smooth, oily barrel and an expensive walnut stock—remains trained on me, visibly trembling, along with his arms.

"That's your dad's, isn't it?" I ask, being sure not to make a sudden move. Mark's dad is one of these types you'd think was born in a Barbour jacket and flatcap, even though he actually grew up in West London. He likes nothing better than blasting pheasants out of the sky, wringing fluffy rabbit necks with his bare hands.

"Yeah," Mark says.

"How about you put that down?" I say.

"She said she'd make it stop," Mark says. "Said to wait in the woods and see if he comes."

"She" has to be Ash, surely? She trapped me in the mirror and warded off the passing place she made, but just in case . . . she left someone to guard this one as well. Covering all possibilities.

The Shepherd is approaching through the trees. She didn't anticipate that I'd summon him again. I try to catch his gaze, signal with my face that Mark has a weapon.

"Ash," Mark's saying. "She's got a way to make me forget. Forget what you told me. And she said I could have it. Just wait out here, she said. What's so special about this place anyway, Luke?"

"What did Ash promise you?"

"What you said to me, that day in the park. She said there was a way I could forget. If I just—" He swallows. "She called me. Said to wait at the stones, and if you come, I should stop you."

"Stop me how?"

"Not shoot. I don't have to shoot. I just need you to . . . sit down. She said not to let you near the stones. That's what I have to do. . . ."

"Mark," I say, "please put the gun down. Ash isn't a good person. She's using you."

The Shepherd is standing right beside him, unseen, examining the angle of the shotgun. What's he going to do? Why doesn't he help me? Maybe he'll let Mark shoot me. He'd be free. It depends how much he wants what I promised him. I'm imagining the gun firing, the bullets embedding themselves in my chest. . . .

"Why would you say that to me?" Mark screams suddenly. "*Why?*"

"I don't know what I said to you," I say. "It wasn't . . . Mark, it wasn't me."

"I haven't been able to forget," he says. "I can't forget. Ash said there was a way. . . ."

"What did the de—What did I tell you, Mark?"

He swallows. The gun remains aimed at my chest.

"You said—"

The Shepherd grabs the barrel of the shotgun and yanks it upward. Mark whoops with fear and pulls the trigger, both barrels discharging their shot into the canopy of trees. I feel the reverberations of the gunshot in my bones. My ears are ringing like a fire alarm.

"Mark!"

Mark is still staring at the shotgun in disbelief. The Shepherd has wrestled it from his grasp and now swings the butt directly into Mark's face, cracking his nose open. Mark goes down, howling with pain. I'm not sure what's affecting him worse: the nose, which looks broken, or the fact that, from his perspective, his shotgun just decided to float into the air and beat the shit out of him. The Shepherd throws the gun into the undergrowth. The ghost raises his hands, and to my astonishment, green flames boil out of his fingers, flowing over Mark's body like a rippling cocoon of fire.

Mark convulses, clutching at his burst nose, blood streaming over his chin. The Shepherd smiles, and green fire erupts again from his hands, oozing through the air and landing on Mark's fallen body. Mark's feet drum against the earth. His fingers clutch at nothing. There's white foam coming from his mouth, mixing with the blood.

The Shepherd raises his hands a third time—

I come back to myself.

"*Stop!*" I scream. "You're going to kill him!"

The ghost pauses, flames dripping from his white fingers.

"That was my intent, yes," the Shepherd says.

Mark is trying to crawl away, but he's so disoriented that he's crawling toward the Devil's Footsteps, toward me.

"*Please, Luke,*" he says, "*please . . .*"

"He was my friend. We're not going to *kill* him."

"He is an agent of Ashana," the Shepherd says.

"He barely knows what's going on! The demon told him something that's been eating his mind! Ash said she could help him! I hardly blame him!"

"I have sympathy for my enemies only once they are defeated," the Shepherd says, and unleashes a third barrage of flames onto Mark. This time they hit his back and thighs, boiling their way into his clothes and skin. Mark clutches at the dirt as if he's trying to dig into it and get away from us.

I raise my sigil, and it blazes with cold. A wave of power strikes the Shepherd, knocking him backward into the dirt. White lightning crackles around his chest and head. He yells in anger. I stand over him, pointing the sigil down at his chest.

"You know what I can do with this," I say. "You're my Shepherd. *My* Shepherd. If I say not to kill someone, I mean it."

"You are weak!" he spits. "Does my counsel mean nothing to you? The realm of the spirits has no place for mercy. Without the will—"

"I have plenty of will," I tell him, voice steady. "I'm using it now. Mark is already defeated. I'm not letting you torture him to death."

The Shepherd seems about to say something more, but then his face hardens into its usual mask-like stillness.

"I have overstepped," he agrees, and calmly gets to his feet. The flames around his hands evaporate. "I hope," he says as Mark groans in the mud, "that you will not hesitate to do what needs to be done when we face the Ahlgren party, however."

"Don't worry," I say. "We'll handle them."

"I am worried," the Shepherd says, giving me a hard look. "But I suppose the time for objections is gone. What shall we do with the boy?"

I look down at Mark.

"Send him to sleep," I say. "*Actual* sleep. That's not a euphemism."

Here's how our journey begins: I set up the tent near the Footsteps, behind a thick wall of bushes. Even if you approach from the path and stand right by the stones, our campsite isn't visible. It's a six-man tent, plenty big, and I haul Mark into one sleeping compartment, blood drying on his face. I wish there was time to take him to the hospital or something, but there's just no way. The Shepherd put him under, so at least he's not in pain.

I carry Elza's corpse to the tent and put her in the other compartment. When she's lying there, I stop and kneel next to her, quaking as I cry silently. I don't want the Shepherd to hear me. He doesn't understand. He never even liked Elza, and she hated him. She'd have hated this, me crossing over, all of it. For a moment I feel like I ought to stop, call the whole thing off, send the Shepherd back to Hell, but as I look at her lying there, I realize I can't. While there's even a chance of seeing her again, I can't stop.

I zip up the compartment. She's safe in there. There's no other option for me. I have to do this. I take a breath and go back outside. The tent should spare us the attentions of any wandering animals, at least for the few days

I'll be away. I hope it'll be only a few days, anyway. I seem to be trusting the Shepherd on a lot of the details. He waits silently by the Devil's Footsteps while I prepare, gathering stones and arranging them around the tent in the pattern he showed me. This is the other part of our defense: a ward against wandering spirits who might want a ride inside one of our bodies while we're gone. Yes, our bodies: me and Ham will be lying here, too. Apparently spirits like that are rare, but I don't want to take chances.

The next step is gluttony. I eat the biggest meal I can, cereal bars and dried fruit and as much milk as I can manage without puking. It's not quite feasting for eight days and eight nights, like the shamans used to do, but it's close enough. When I'm full, and my stomach feels like a bloated bag of rocks, I lie down in the tent, in the "lobby" area that separates the two sleeping compartments. Ham pads in to join me, and I zip the door shut behind us. We lie down, me with one hand resting on the back of his neck. It's uncomfortable and humid, and I'm already feeling sweaty. To my left Mark sleeps, and on my right Elza lies dead. I wear my sigil on my finger, and the Book of Eight is tucked inside my raincoat.

I lie still next to Ham and stare unblinking at the ceiling. I focus on the play of light that the low sun shining through tree branches makes on the tent's roof.

I step outside of myself. I pass through the wall of the tent, cross my ward of stone, and I'm standing in the clearing next to the Shepherd. He looks me up and down.

"You have the necessaries?" he asks.

I show him my sigil and unzip my jacket to find the Book of Eight nestled inside.

"How can I take this with me?" I ask him. "I'm a spirit, but I still have the Book."

"The Book is a creation of both worlds: therefore, it can travel between them."

"That's all the explanation you'll give?"

"I told you, magic is not about asking why. That is science, which I gladly leave to the scientists. Magic is beyond why. Magic is about changing what is."

"Good answer," I say. "Where's Ham?"

"Call him," the Shepherd says.

I turn back to the tent and raise my sigil.

"Ham!" I shout, a strange echo of every time I've waited by the kitchen door for him to come in from the garden. The sigil flares with cold. I'm not exactly sure how this is going to work, but the Shepherd assured me it would.

After a moment, Ham leaps straight through the wall of the tent and bounds up to us.

"How's that for you, boy?" I ask.

Ham barks and cavorts. He looks different in spirit

form, more smoky than flesh and blood, lit in a strange way, as though there were some distant spotlight that highlighted only him. He looks unearthly, in a way me and the Shepherd don't.

"Why does he look like that?"

"As I said, the spirit world is a place of will. Your beast does not have as strong a sense of how he should appear as you and I, so he appears vaguer and less defined."

Ham the luminous spirit dog licks my hand.

"So what do we do?" I ask the Shepherd.

"The gateway is before us," he says. "It remains only for you, the Necromancer, master of two worlds, to open the gate and pass through it."

At first, as I make my way across the clearing, I can't see what he's talking about. The stone circle looks no different than it did when I had a body. Then I catch a strange glimpse, a seam in the air, and I know in that moment the gate is open.

(asphodel)

I'm standing in long gray grass, in the middle of the standing stones. The Devil's Footsteps don't look any different in the world of the dead. They're the same size, the same shape, with the same cup- and hoof-shaped patterns etched into them. They even have the same patches of lichen dappling them. The stones are the only thing that hasn't changed.

When I crossed over, moments ago, it was evening. The trees around us were painted in sunset colors, dull orange trunks casting long violet shadows. There's no color in this place. The mist around me is gray. The stones are gray; the sky overhead is gray. My skin is gray; my hands have gray fingernails. My raincoat, which is supposed to be red and blue, is now two shades of gray. The Shepherd's black suit and hat are deep charcoal-gray. Ham, who's gray anyway, is even grayer than me and the Shepherd put together. He still looks strange and wispy, like he's a cloud of smoke someone formed into the shape of a dog.

There's something curiously lifeless about the grass beneath our feet. I brush one foot through it, and it rustles like grass should. But there's something off about it, all the same. We've been drained of color, bleached of something vital. I feel like if we got any grayer, we'd become part of the mist itself.

"Welcome," the Shepherd says. "The Gray Meadows."

"I remember this place," I say. "This is where I met Mr. Berkley."

"Best not to speak of that one," the Shepherd says. "Not here. There is power in the names of great spirits. Even in the names they have chosen to hide behind. To speak of that being here could be to behold it."

I nod. Ham is investigating the base of one of the stones.

"So which way do we go?" I ask.

"I believe we will find the Ahlgren girl's house in this direction," the Shepherd says, pointing. "We may pick up their trail from there. But first we must explain our business to the Gatekeeper."

"To who?"

"As I said, your powerful friend may roam where it pleases, and such a being as a lowly Gatekeeper would not dare to question its movements. You and I are not so exalted, and abide by different rules."

The Shepherd sets off downhill, and I follow him. The mist makes it difficult to see much, but I can tell already that the landscape of Deadside is different from that of Liveside. In Dunbarrow, the Devil's Footsteps are set in a hollow, a clearing in dense woodland. In Deadside, they're set at the top of a steep hill without an oak tree in sight. I follow the Shepherd down a narrow path, the only plant life the still, gray grass and some thornbushes. Ham trots behind me, seemingly unfazed by the strange new world he's followed me into.

At the bottom of the hill, we come to a large expanse of gray sand, in which a white tree seems to have fallen. The Shepherd comes to a halt, and I stop beside him. I start to speak, and he silences me.

The fallen tree moves, flexing in the mist, and I realize with horror that what I thought was a tree trunk is actually an animal, the biggest snake I've ever seen. It must be longer than a truck, thicker than an ogre's arm, and it rears up out of the dirt, turning to face us. The snake's skin is crusty and white, reminding me of the dry, dead skin you get on the soles of your feet. Its eyes are a piercing sapphire-blue, without pupils, the brightest color I've seen since arriving in Deadside. The snake opens its mouth, and I see that it has unmistakably human teeth lining its jaws, and a pink human tongue.

Yes? The snake addresses us, its voice surprisingly gentle.

The Shepherd looks at me with an expression I can't interpret. Is this the Gatekeeper? I suppose it must be. What am I supposed to do?

"Um, hello?" I say.

And you are? the snake, the Gatekeeper, asks me.

"I'm Luke Manchett," I tell it.

The Gatekeeper doesn't respond.

"My name is Luke Manchett," I say a little louder, guessing this is a test of some kind, "and I'm a necromancer. This is my Shepherd, and my familiar, Ham."

Luke Manchett and retinue, the Gatekeeper says. *What is your purpose in crossing the threshold, Luke Manchett? What do you seek?*

"Er . . . just passing through," I say.

The Gatekeeper grimaces, exposing its large teeth.

Where did you find him, Octavius? it asks the Shepherd.

"I apologize on my master's behalf," the Shepherd says, taking his hat off and dipping his head in a bow. "He is not of the old school. The accepted ways are a mystery to him."

You can say that again, the snake grumbles.

"If you will allow me to announce you?" the Shepherd says to me, replacing his hat. His tone suggests that I've messed up yet again and he's about to bail us both out.

"My, uh, powerful servant," I say, "will announce my business."

The snake nods.

"Mighty Gatekeeper!" the Shepherd says, raising both arms, projecting his voice like an opera singer. "Terrible serpent of the underworld! Before you stands Luke Manchett, a powerful necromancer! Son of Horatio! Only sixteen summers he has, yet here he stands before you! Raiser of the dead! Master of the Book of Eight! His mind consumed by shadow! His heart heavy with regret! He has parleyed with the Black Goat and lived to tell the tale! Look also upon his fearsome hound, Ham! A pitiless beast, consumer of spirits, scourge of deer and cats! I am his Shepherd, once known to you as Octavius, the King of the Dead! By my presence as his servant, you may gain some measure of Luke's power and wisdom."

Good, good, the Gatekeeper says, looking at me with what I take to be new respect. *And what is your master's purpose in the realms I guard?*

"Luke seeks the traitorous sorceress Ashana Ahlgren, daughter of the great sorcerer Magnus Ahlgren. Under the guise of friendship, she sought to steal my master's copy of the Book, and she has killed his beloved, the witch child

Elza Moss! Ashana's treachery knows no bounds! She has sworn to aid my master and has reneged on her promises! Shame! Treachery! Shame!"

Disgusting, the snake says, shaking its horrible head.

"The she-dog, this oath-breaking cur, she heads for the cradle of the eight sacred rivers, the Shrouded Lake! Accompanied by her crippled sister and her faithful retainer, Ashana seeks to offer a nonpareil to what sleeps beneath the water, and return her sister to true life! My master intends to stop her and take revenge! Blood! Treachery! She has no shame!"

A nonpareil, the Gatekeeper says eagerly, *a rare and precious treasure indeed.*

"Total nightmare to get hold of them," I say conversationally.

The gigantic snake and the Shepherd both give me the kind of look you'd give someone who farts in church.

A sorcerers' feud, then, the Gatekeeper says to the Shepherd, ignoring me. *Treachery. Blood. A battle between two dynasties. A young man questing to avenge his fallen beloved.*

"Truly," the Shepherd says, "this is a tale which will be sung throughout the ages. We beseech you, powerful Gatekeeper, let us pass. Let us avenge the witch child Elza Moss. Let us avenge ourselves upon Ashana."

Very well, the Gatekeeper says, smiling at me with its

human teeth. *Far be it from me to stand in the way of such a tale. Allow me to check your sigil, Master Manchett, and I will grant your passage into the underworld.*

I raise my hand with the black ring on it, and the Gatekeeper runs its pink tongue over my sigil, tasting it like you'd taste an expensive wine. I try not to shudder.

Yes. There is great power here. I will let you pass, brave sorcerer. May fate speed your journey. May you avenge yourself on this betrayer and eat her heart.

"Thank you, mighty Gatekeeper," I say, and for the first time, I sense I've done the right thing. The snake grins hellishly and coils itself back down into the sand. Its blue eyes close. I think it's gone to sleep.

The Shepherd leads us past the sleeping snake. Ham trots by my side. We move on, through gray grass and gray copses of fir trees, cross a narrow gray stream that somehow flows without making a sound. The mist is all around us, the dull light unchanging, the only noise the sound of my footsteps on the ground. After a while I ask, "So how did that go?"

"The thing to remember about creatures like that," the Shepherd remarks, "is they still think they live ten thousand years ago. They're older than the world itself. They spend a great deal of time doing very little, and they take their excitement when they can get it. They're cut from the

Heroic cloth. They know that era is long gone, of course. But if you humor them, they love you for it."

"Right," I say.

"I would judge you were perhaps a hair's breadth from it eating you," he continues. "So next time, I would try to pretend you are in an epic poem. A loud voice, strong posture; be sure you spend plenty of time on the declaring of deeds. That will usually suffice."

"I liked it when you described Ham as a 'scourge of deer and cats,' " I say.

"I was doing my best"—the Shepherd sniffs—"with what little I had on hand."

The mist eddies and flows around us, although I never feel any wind that could be pushing it. The mist is the only thing in this gray world that seems to move; everything else gives the impression that it's been in one place forever. I think that's what unsettles me about the grass: the sense that you could stand here for a thousand years and it would never grow one centimeter. The only time it ever moves is when we step on it. I don't hear any birds, don't see any squirrels or rabbits. There aren't even mosquitoes, and I never thought I would miss those. There's no sun, no clouds, no sense of day or night. The only way to track time passing at all is by your own movement through the landscape. We walk across endless expanses of heather, past lonely pine trees and hulking bare rocks. You can't fly in Deadside, I've found; I'm trapped on the ground the way I would be in my body back home.

"Where are we?" I ask after what could have been hours.

"We are approaching Ashana's house," the Shepherd responds without looking back.

"What is this place?"

"The ancients called this land Asphodel," he replies. "These lands lie closest to the world of the living. In a way, this country is England's memory of itself. Before human life existed."

"I see," I say, although I don't.

We move on, Ham trotting along at the rear. He isn't sniffing and dawdling like he does on walks around Dunbarrow. He seems to grasp that we have purpose.

After what feels like a long time, we come to a forest of some sort, slender gray trees with black apples growing from the branches. The Shepherd tells me not to eat them, as if there were any danger of me wanting to, and we pass into the forest. After a while we come to a clearing, and I see Ash's house.

It doesn't look much different from the way it looked when I first saw it. The house has two stories, a garage, a front garden with a fence and a metal gate. It has double-glazed windows and a chimney stack and a bracket for a satellite dish. It looks extraordinarily normal and just plain extraordinary all at once. The house has become as gray and lifeless as the rest of this forest.

"I don't for a moment expect she left it unwarded," the Shepherd says, "but it would be remiss of us not to make sure."

We approach the house. Sure enough, there's a line of silver flame that erupts from the ground, blocking our path. It makes a high chiming noise when you're close to it, and emits no heat. The Shepherd makes some half-hearted explorations around the ward but finds no weakness.

"As I expected," he announces.

Ham seems to be sniffing something on the far side of the garden. I make my way over to him. It's the remains of Ash's reading machine, broken apart, spokes and levers sticking out like the legs of a smashed insect. Inside I find part of a book, completely torn to pieces. It seems to be my French-to-English dictionary. For the first time in a while, I laugh.

"Here's where she found she didn't have the Book," I say to the Shepherd. "Elza even swapped something else in, to make up the weight."

He smiles a thin smile.

"Your witch child is not without her virtues," he remarks.

"So where do we go now?" I ask.

"The geography of the spirit world is complex," he says in his lecturing voice. "Where the living world is consistent and yet ever-changing, the spirit world is inconsistent and timeless."

"I don't understand even one little bit of what you just said."

"It means, dull boy, that Asphodel and similar realms are unmappable by conventional means. The landscape eddies. It flows. The configurations are infinite. A mountain may become a crevasse when the traveler turns his back. We could return to the Devil's Footsteps and find that one of the eight rivers runs between us and those stones. One never knows."

"So how do we find our way to the Shrouded Lake? How will Ash? How can we find her?"

"As I said, navigating this other world is partly a matter of will. As Ashana greatly desires to reach the Shrouded Lake, she will eventually do so. But it may take her some time. We have an advantage, as we have a map."

"We do?"

The Shepherd reaches over to me and pulls the Book of Eight from my jacket. I think it's the first time he's touched me in Deadside, and I'm alarmed to find that he's physically present. I can feel his wrinkled old hand against my chest. I really don't want him to touch me.

The Shepherd is holding the Book, oblivious to my distress. He strokes the green spine, and the Book of Eight falls open. He turns the pages, muttering, until he finds what he wants.

"Look," the ghost says. He holds the Book so I can see. It looks like it usually does, a bizarre jumble of shifting shapes and symbols, holding no meaning for my conscious mind whatsoever. It doesn't seem as hypnotic here in Deadside, though. I don't feel I'm in any danger of losing myself in its pages.

"We wish to arrive here," he says, tapping a strange mark with one long thumb. It lies in the center of the page, with eight lines spidering their way out from it in all directions. "The Book's map will alter itself, along with the landscape. An infinitely long volume has room to map every single configuration of the spirit world that could exist."

"So you can get us to the Shrouded Lake?"

"I can." The Shepherd gives me a graying grin. "Not only that, I believe we may find that we arrive before Ashana and her companions."

"Well, let's get going, then," I say.

The Shepherd keeps ahold of the Book, examining it now and then and talking to himself. We move off into the forest, Ham trotting along between me and the ghost. We walk through more of the apple trees, then up a barren slope dotted with thin, unwholesome-looking clumps of reeds, and from here, with the disjointed logic that a dream has, we're walking in a deep forest. The trees are taller than anything I've ever seen before, dark and elephantine, with bark like the scaly hides of dinosaurs. They loom over us, taller than those giant redwoods that grow in California. Some of their roots are the diameter of train carriages, maybe thicker. I can't see their summits, can barely even see any branches. The trees are monoliths of gray bark that vanish in the fog overhead. It's darker here, too, the fog thicker and closer to black. I almost bump into the Shepherd, who's peering down at the Book.

"Keep close to me," he says, and then strides off into the fog again. I follow as best I can. He and Ham scramble down earthen banks, ford through the stagnant pools of dark water that collect around the bases of the trees. At one point we pass a single fallen leaf, dead and gray, which I swear is larger than a racing yacht's sail. I feel as though we've been shrunk down to mouse-size, and that at any moment a silent white owl, grim and immense, could come soaring down from the treetops and carry us back to its nest. From what I've seen of Deadside this far, it isn't even that unlikely.

As I'm scrambling under a gnarled loop of tree root, I see a flash of white off to the left of us. It's a human figure, I'm sure of it, and from the pale clothing, it could be Ash. I freeze, trying to determine if she saw me. The fog is thick and dark, almost like smoke. I can't see anything anymore. I can see the ground beneath my feet, and that's about it. I realize I've lost the Shepherd and Ham.

"Hey!" I hiss. "Guys! I saw something!"

No response.

Maybe the Ahlgrens were waiting for us? This is an ideal ambush spot.

I silently press on, following the trail I know they were walking on. As I'm coming down a steep bank of earth, still afraid to shout too loudly in case Ash and the Widow are nearby, the fog lifts a little, like a breeze ruffled a curtain, and I see more clearly where I am. This is a hollow of sorts, a depression between two of the gargantuan trees, and to one side there's a cave that's formed where earth has collapsed away between two of the trees' roots. A figure is standing outside the cave, with its back to me.

It's Elza.

What's happening?

It's unmistakably Elza, just as I last saw her. How can it be her? Is this where she ended up? Her hair is long and wet and black, falling down her back, just like it was when she died. She's dressed in her leather jacket, black jeans.

She's pulling at a strand of her hair, just like Elza used to when she was stressed.

"Elza?" I call.

She stands still.

"Is that you?"

"Luke?" she calls back. It's her voice. She sounds afraid.

"Elza! I'm coming to get you! It's OK."

She doesn't turn around. I make my way across the hollow toward her.

What is she doing out here? I have a sudden rush of love, an urge to hold her and comfort her. She must be scared, terrified. . . .

"Where are you?" she asks.

She still hasn't turned around.

"I'm here, Elza! I'm here! It's OK!"

I'm nearly touching her. I can see the strands of her hair; her fingernails, painted black; the silver beads she wore around her left wrist.

"Do you love me?" she asks.

"I'll always love you," I'm saying, reaching my hand out to her, "always, forever. . . ."

Elza turns around. Where her face ought to be, there's just a mouth. It's a wide, ravenous mouth, toothless and tongueless, occupying her face from chin to hairline.

"Do you love me?" the monster asks, still using her voice.

There's no time to scream. The Elza thing jumps at me, clawing at me, knocking me to the earth. The being, whatever it is, is strong, and it tries to pin me to the ground so it can lower its mouth to my face. I'm looking into blackness, hungry blackness, and—

There's a blast of green light, and the mouth is screaming. The thing leaps off me and rears up to face this new threat. I hear Ham barking and the Shepherd yelling something unintelligible. The Elza monster roars, no longer sounding remotely human, and I see beneath the clinging layer of green fire that there's something else standing there, not Elza at all, something like a thin and faceless woman with impossibly long arms. She seems to be covered with fur.

The monster shrieks and leaps like a monkey up into the tangled roots overhead, scrambling away into the mist. The Shepherd and Ham are standing over me. I never imagined I'd be glad to see the black-eyed ghost. One of his hands still crackles with the green fire; the other cradles the Book. Ham licks my face.

"What . . . ?" I ask.

"A hungry spirit," the Shepherd snarls. "A ghoul. Shifting forms like the mist itself. Such is the fate of those who dwell in these deep woods too long. It nearly had you, Luke."

"I thought it was Ash," I say, ashamed. "And then it looked like Elza."

"Next time, raise your sigil. That ring commands some authority over the unbound dead here. You are lucky we came back to find you."

"I will." I start to get up.

"I want you to remember," the Shepherd says quietly, "your oath to me. What you promised. I said I would help you wholeheartedly, and I have. I could easily have left you."

"I know," I say.

"Keep close to us!" the Shepherd says.

I don't need telling again.

The monstrous forest stretches much farther, and I take utmost care to stay within touching distance of the Shepherd and Ham. We follow an arduous path over and around roots, through a system of caves, around the edge of a large chasm that seems to drop into nothingness. There's no more contact with the beings that live in this forest, although sometimes when the fog shifts, I catch sight of furtive human shapes ducking behind roots or vanishing into tunnels. The forest is clearly inhabited.

Whether they're scared of the Shepherd, or me, or perhaps just the sigil I carry, I don't know.

As suddenly as it began, the forest vanishes. We're walking through heather. The fog is thinner, more like mist. I don't have to stay within arm's reach of the Shepherd. We tramp along in single file. For hours we don't speak a word, don't see a soul. I wonder what it's like for Ash, moving through this gray silent world with the Widow. Did they bring Ilana? The idea of chaperoning that cheerful, strange girl through Deadside sends shudders through me.

We pass a hilltop where a black tower stands, its doorway empty and open, with no windows in its stone walls. None of us have even the slightest urge to look inside. We walk across a wide gray desert where boulders lie at disorderly angles, with trails in the dust behind them indicating that, at some point, they've been moved around. We walk through meadows and forests that could be England. We climb a mountain, which would be beautiful if the slopes weren't gray and the view obscured by fog.

While crossing a plain of dull, volcanic-looking rock, we come to our first proper river. I have to call it a river, because that's how the Shepherd refers to it, but you wouldn't immediately think *river* if you saw it. The river is a wound in the rock, a chasm, and at the bottom of this chasm is a slow-flowing stream of red fire. The flames are red in the way fresh blood is red, a clamoring crimson, with none of the yellow or orange tones you see in normal fire. There's heat coming off the river, and the redness is an astonishing contrast to the monochrome landscape we've been traveling through. Ham stays well away from the edge.

"The Phlegethon," the Shepherd says.

"The flegga-what?"

"Phlegethon, the ancients named it. There are eight rivers, boy, that flow through the underworld. Eight rivers of shadow and flame. The greatest of them is the Styx, River of Oaths, backbone of the underworld. The lesser rivers number seven: Lethe, Acheron, Phlegethon, Cocytus, Apelpsion, Algos, and golden Elys. We stand before the Phlegethon, the River of Rage. It flows into the heart of the darkness, Tartarus."

"It doesn't sound like we want to follow this river," I say.

"No," the Shepherd agrees. "This river does not lead anywhere we want to go, and we cannot travel upon it."

I don't have anything to say to that. We walk in silence alongside the chasm, the bloodred river below us, and eventually, as the Shepherd knew we would, we come to a bridge. It's roughly carved from the same volcanic stone, and fortunately seems to be unguarded. We cross, and when we reach the other bank I look back and the Phlegethon has vanished. We're in a barren gray field instead.

Things get bad again maybe hours or days later; without nights or the sun or even meals to judge time by, your perception swiftly stops having any meaning at all. My legs don't get tired, because, like the Shepherd said, you don't have muscles here. It's about will and wisdom. I'm feeling pretty short of the latter.

We're descending a barren slope, heading toward who-knows-what, when the fog lifts again the way it does sometimes in this place, and I find I can see farther down the slope into a stony valley dotted with fir trees. There are figures, only specks, moving toward the tree line. Two of them are bright white, the third wearing gray.

"Is that . . . ?" I ask.

"Having never laid eyes upon them, I could not say," the Shepherd replies.

The specks have vanished into the trees. They must've been miles away. The fog thickens again, almost as though the landscape itself were taunting us. It was Ash and Ilana and the Widow, I'm sure of it.

"That was them," I say. "I know it was. We're gaining on them."

"We are still far from the Shrouded Lake," the Shepherd says, examining the Book of Eight. "However, I see no reason why catching the Ahlgrens before they reach its shores would be to our disadvantage. Do you believe they saw us?"

"Who knows?"

"We shall assume that they did, and hope that they did not. Let us make haste."

We break into a jog, Ham scampering downhill, sending small flurries of gray pebbles skittering around his paws. I've never seen the Shepherd run before, I realize, and it looks strange. In his three-piece suit and glasses, he's dressed more for a long night at the library than running a marathon. When I went up against him, he never had to run anywhere—he always gave me the impression that he was three moves ahead, that I was turning up late to the places he already wanted me to go. As we pelt down the mountainside together, I'm wondering how great this plan of ours really is. Any scheme that involves an elderly master tactician hurtling downhill at a breakneck pace seems like it's got a loose thread somewhere.

The three of us reach flatter ground, run on into the woods. This forest is normal-size, the trees lifeless grayer versions of the trees you'd see around Dunbarrow. We push our way through low bushes, strange black clumps of flowers. I'm peering into the mist, convinced that at any moment I'll see Ash's pale hair, the Widow's white gown, perhaps hear a snatch of Ilana's muddled twin-speak. I nearly walk right into the Shepherd, who's crouched down like a hunter.

"What is it?" I whisper.

He shushes me, pointing at the forest floor. He's looking at a small silver coin, not a sort that I recognize. It looks ancient, rough, and chipped. There's a bird stamped into the metal.

Ham sniffs at it, then recoils as though it tried to bite him.

"It is a problem," the Shepherd says quietly.

"Are we in danger?"

"Yes. But not from the Ahlgrens," he says. He examines the Book of Eight, ripples and eddies of ink swimming across the double-page spread. He frowns, not liking what he sees. "No choice," he says to himself. "Having found its mark, we cannot retreat. We have to go past it."

"Go past what?" I ask.

"The less you know of such matters, the better," he says, closing the Book. "It will really do you no good to understand. Do not speak to them. Whatever you do."

"Speak to who?" I ask.

He leads off without another word, leaving me and Ham to skulk along in his wake. What on earth is happening? I notice more and more coins, all the same sort, silver with a bird stamped into them. I think it might be a raven or a crow, some kind of carrion bird. At first it looks like someone dropped a purse; and then, as the coins grow more numerous, like we might be walking through a grove of money trees that are dropping ripe fruit; and finally, when you can't even see the ground anymore, I imagine a blizzard of silver pieces, blanketing the earth in money. Our feet slide in the coins, sending them jittering and jangling over one another. It's impossible to walk quietly, and again I'm seized with the fear that Ash might be lying in wait for us.

Then I hear the voices, and a different kind of fear grabs at me.

They're low, urgent voices, chanting like monks at prayer. They seem to be coming from all around us, echoing through the fog and the trees. I clink my way across the coin-strewn ground, the voices growing louder with every step, knowing that whatever we're about to see, I desperately don't want to see it. We move out of the forest, onto a great plain that shimmers with drifts of silver pieces, and I see the source of the noise.

The plain is covered with stakes—long, sharpened poles of wood, a little taller than I am. On each stake is a severed head, all facing the same direction, positioned at regular intervals across the plain, and they're all chanting, or perhaps babbling; it's hard to tell. The sight is so gruesome and strange that I barely know what to do. The Shepherd forges ahead, boots scattering the coins underfoot, and me and Ham follow him, afraid of this place but more afraid of being left behind. Ham's tail is between his legs, and he refuses to look up from the silver-coated ground.

The heads are all human, and they're mostly men. Some are bearded; some aren't. There are men from every country and nation you can think of. As I pass, the heads see me, tilt downward to catch my eyes. Their lips move.

"I say, boy," one says.

"*Agua,*" another says, wheezing. "*Agua . . .*"

Some of them wear helmets: bronze helmets, steel helmets, helmets made from dried bamboo padding. Some of them wear the full-faced helmets of medieval knights; others wear a wreath of leaves. I see one head wearing a gas mask, a housefly spliced with a morose elephant.

"You there, who are you?" a head asks me, in the tone of someone used to being obeyed. I walk on, ignore him. The Shepherd is just ahead of me, his hunched shape half-visible in the mist, silently winding his way through the stakes.

"If you could just loosen my bonds," one sweating, sallow head pleads as we pass him.

"I'll tell you where it's buried," a man with no teeth and a huge black beard promises.

"Please help us."

"Boy!"

"Pardon me, sir . . ."

The heads harangue and plead, wheedle and beg; they mock and abuse us as we pass. I don't speak to any of them. I put one foot in front of the other.

The Shepherd walks onward, occasionally checking to make sure me and Ham are still behind him, sometimes looking down at the Book of Eight. The stakes grow thicker and more numerous, the heads closer together, chanting and babbling, all facing the same direction. When the stakes are so thick that we're knocking into them as we walk, the mist thins, and I see what stands at the center of the plain.

It's a tree, I think, or something like a tree: a black spiky shape breaking through the earth, coins heaped in shimmering drifts around its trunk, and enormous swords, eight of them, stuck into the earth in a circle around its base. Every part of the tree seems to have a bird perched on it, more black birds than I've ever seen in one place before; the tree itself isn't visible, I realize, only the birds sitting on it, ravens or crows or something, cawing and squabbling and flapping their wings as they jockey for position, sometimes taking flight and landing on another spot of the tree. It's like on a nature documentary when you see ants swarming over a hapless bug — the birds are that dense, the kind of creepy repetition you don't often see outside of a computer screen. The tree, if that's what it is, is mesmerizing. The heads cry louder as the tree comes into view, although I still can't understand most of what they're saying.

I fix my eyes on the coins, the ground, and hurry onward. The stakes become less dense again, the chanting of the heads less fervent. And then I hear a voice I recognize:

"Boss."

I look up at the stake right in front of me. It's him.

"Seriously, boss, I'm glad to see you!"

Shaved head, scar down his left cheek, a cross tattooed on his forehead. A flattened nose, gray eyes, snaggle teeth. Three gold rings punched through his right ear. And I'd know that voice anywhere.

"Please, boss," the Judge says, "you gotta get me out of here."

I swallow.

"You promised, boss," he says, "remember? Said you wouldn't send us to Hell. Well, look at me now. Help me out. Get me down off here."

"Sorry," I say under my breath.

The Judge's head looks at me with openmouthed glee and begins to scream. It isn't his voice anymore: it sounds like a bird, the cry of a vicious hawk with a baby rabbit in its claws. The other heads take up the bitter scream, their voices becoming an inhuman noise, beyond words.

The Shepherd is looking back at me, horror on his waxy white face.

"RUN!" he screams. "RUN, YOU STUPID BOY!"

I don't need telling twice. The heads are screaming, and I hear the beating of wings. Me and Ham take off like rockets, dodging between the stakes, my feet slipping on the coins, convinced at every step that I'll fall and whatever's after us will have me—

The Shepherd's moving faster than I thought possible, sprinting like a champion athlete across the terrible plain. Ham's running flat out, whimpering, coins spraying around his paws like sea foam. I chance a look behind us as we run.

The black tree is exploding in slow motion, unraveling, birds flying from its branches and trunk into a whirling cloud that seems to cover the gray sky. As I take a second glance, I see them diving down at us.

I scramble up a bank, coins jangling and rolling, grabbing desperately at roots and stones beneath them.

We're in the woods again. The heads are behind us. Ham yowls madly in the trees. I can't see him. I can't see the Shepherd, and I—

Something black flies down through the mist, cawing.

It's a bird, a raven, with a stone beak and silver coins for eyes. It dives at my face and I thrash it away, still running, my hand throbbing with cold where I hit the creature.

There are more of them, black flashes above me as I run. I'm hurtling through gray woods, no idea where I'm going. I skid down a bank, sending coins flying, the birds crying harshly in the gray mist. I'm completely out of control, and when I trip over a root and fall flat on my face, it's almost a relief.

The birds land in a circle around me. They're made of shadow, the way the Fury was, although whether they're demons or some other kind of spirit isn't clear to me. There's a pause while we look at one another, me on my hands and knees, them glaring back with glinting coin eyes. The nearest shadow bird screams, a high, horrible sound like a chain saw ripping into metal, and they leap at me.

I do the only thing I can do: I cover my eyes with one hand, frightened by the birds' cruel flint beaks, and lunge at them with my sigil. The ring blazes with cold, sending shock waves of icy power through my body, and I convulse like I'm having a fit. The birds scream louder, and I feel their wings beat at me, their stone beaks tearing at my back and legs, but I swing my sigil toward them. The coldness grows, white light streaming from my sigil ring, and when it fades, the birds are gone. I'm on my own in Deadside, crouched in the gray forest, surrounded by a freshly fallen pile of silver coins.

I trek through the forest alone and across a barren gray moor, concentrating on walking forward, keeping one foot in front of the other, not sure what my plan is now. I try to hold my companions in my mind as I walk, remembering what the Shepherd said: that to will yourself to find something in Deadside is how you will come upon it. Ham and the Shepherd. The Shepherd and Ham. Did the birds take them? What happened?

I shouldn't have spoken. What even was that place? The Shepherd should've . . . but he told me not to speak. He told me what I needed to know.

Ham and the Shepherd. Ham and the Shepherd. I'll find them, and we'll make our way to the Lake. Save Elza. We can still do this. I'll do it alone if I have to. Without the Book . . . no, keep walking. I can't give up.

Ham and the Shepherd.

Ham and the Shepherd. I try to hold them in my mind as clearly as I can. Ham's stupid marmalade eyes and the Shepherd's cruel black ones, Ham's long fluffy tail, the Shepherd's hooked nose and full waxy lips.

This is where I'll find them, I insist as I climb a low hill.

This is it. They'll be right here.

To my amazement the mist clears and I come upon them, waiting at the base of a huge dead tree. The Shepherd is leaning against its gray trunk, examining the Book, and Ham is lying on his side in the grass at its base.

"Hey!" I shout.

It worked! I can't believe it actually worked. I never thought I'd be glad to see the Shepherd, but here he is, and despite his sour ways, aren't we starting to get along—

The Shepherd walks up to me and, without a word, he strikes me across the face. It doesn't hurt the way it would in the living world, but he's strong enough to knock me flying, sending me thudding to the ground. He draws his boot back and kicks me in the stomach, and then in the throat for good measure.

"Damn idiot!" he yells. "You bungler! Do you understand what nearly became of us?"

Ham snarls and leaps between us, baring his teeth at the Shepherd. The ghost looks from me to my dog and backs off, still glaring with cold fury.

"Sorry," I say, holding my hands up, both in supplication and to remind him who's wearing the sigil. "I'm sorry! I just—"

"You just did the *exact thing* I told you *not* to do! You spoke to them!"

"It was the Judge—"

"Those *things* are no longer men! They are worshippers now!"

"What . . . what was that place?"

The Shepherd adjusts his hat, which had come askew when he hit me. He seems calmer now. Ham drops his hackles but still stands between me and the ghost.

"We had the misfortune to come across the Ravendark Tree," the Shepherd says. "An old power. Older even than the Black Goat, though that one would never admit it."

"It's a . . . a god?"

"A shrine, of sorts. A living temple. As to what power is honored there, I think it is best not to know. An ancient and nameless spirit."

"I'm . . . I'm sorry."

"This world is not a game," the Shepherd says. "If we had been slower, less lucky, it would be our heads on those poles, too, alongside the rest, singing that tree's endless song."

"We got away," I say, getting to my feet. Ham presses himself against me, whining, and I stroke his head to soothe him.

"We did," the Shepherd agrees. "Unfortunately your mistake has put us far off course. I had intended to leave the tree's sacred grounds via an entirely different route."

"We can't catch them?"

"I do not believe so. Not now. Not on foot."

"So what do you suggest?"

"There is a river nearby," he says, pointing to a long ribbon of black ink that's scrawled across his current page of the Book. "I believe we may be able to arrange transportation."

We walk through gray heather, past gray copses of trees. Beyond a long stretch of dim marshes, we come to a stony riverbank and a fast-flowing black river.

"The Cocytus," announces the Shepherd. "The River of Lamentations."

The river water is strange, I realize: there are no reflections within it. The Cocytus is a swift flow of darkness, moving without sound or ripple. When I peer down into it, I can't see the mirrored image of my own face. Nothing but blackness.

"Immerse the sigil in the river," the Shepherd tells me, "and we will see what its Riverkeeper has to say to us."

"What is a Riverkeeper?" I ask.

"A powerful spirit. Do nothing to incur its anger."

"You're sure about calling this thing?"

"With the time we have lost, I do not believe we have another option," he says, not entirely reassuringly. "The Cocytus flows from the Shrouded Lake. If the Riverkeeper agrees to transport us upstream, I believe this to be our best chance of making it there before the Ahlgrens do."

I don't argue. I dip my right hand into the black water,

immersing the sigil. It's cold, unsurprisingly, although it doesn't feel like putting your hand underwater. The sigil pulses with power. I withdraw my hand, and we wait.

For a while we get to rest. The Shepherd sits down, pores through the Book, occasionally removing his eyeglasses and peering intently at the pages.

Ham sits next to me, looking at the river with curious eyes. The trip's been longer and more dangerous than I could've imagined, and we're not done yet. I'm glad I didn't leave him at home, though. I run my hands through his strange spirit fur. He grumbles. We sit like this for a while, and then without warning, the Riverkeeper emerges from the mist.

The spirit travels the Cocytus in a boat that reminds me of a gondola. The Riverkeeper's boat seems to be made of bronze or brass, some dull-hued metal, elaborately engraved with spiraling designs. The gondola looks like it has been through a lot: it's streaked with grime, some parts are dented and battered as though someone went at them with a hammer, and furry patches of white moss are clinging to the bits of the boat that ride higher above the water.

The Riverkeeper is a monster; there's no other way to put it. The thing has to be eight feet tall at the least, more ogre than man, silently punting the gondola through the river of shadows. It wears a gray robe, something like a toga, spun from wool.

The monster's boat glides closer to the shore and comes to a halt right in front of us, its brassy prow riding up onto the gray banks of the Cocytus. The enormous boatman steps lightly off the vessel and looks me up and down. *Boatman* might not be quite the right word, I realize now, because the left-hand side of the Riverkeeper's face is unmistakably a woman's. She has a sharp cheekbone, flowing blond hair, an eye as blank and silver as a ball of mercury. The right-hand side of the Riverkeeper's face is male, head shaven, with half a blond beard and mustache, and an eye that seems to be a glowing red ember. Whether these differences in anatomy extend below the neck, I'm mercifully unclear, as the creature's robe is all-concealing. The feet that walk across the gray stones toward our party are bare and look more animal than human, with clawed hairy toes. I notice that the Shepherd is kneeling, and I decide it would be best if I did likewise.

Ham cringes beside me. I keep one hand resting on his paw. I press my forehead to the riverbank.

The Riverkeeper speaks, two voices as one, a low masculine rumble and a lighter, colder female tone. I don't understand a single word the creature says.

"I will parley with them," the Shepherd hisses to me.

"What language is that?"

"A spirit tongue. It was spoken when our world was young. Fortunately I am fluent."

"So parley, then," I hiss back.

The Shepherd, still kneeling but now looking up at the creature, answers in the same language. When he speaks, it still sounds like nothing on earth. The Riverkeeper responds, perhaps impatiently. The Shepherd says something else. He gesticulates. He bows his head to the ground at one point, and I do the same. The Riverkeeper laughs, a horrible sound, and gestures at us in a way that seems indulgent somehow. I'm looking up at its long, split face, half male and half female, yet strangely coherent as a whole. The silver eye blinks, I notice, but the red-ember eye never does.

After a while the Shepherd stands upright, and I do, too. The Riverkeeper is making an extended point. It holds up two fingers, and then says something else and holds up one. The Shepherd nods and turns to me.

"The Riverkeeper is moved by our tale," he says, "and is prepared to offer us passage so that you may avenge your beloved and return her to life."

"Well, that's very kind of it."

"They do not offer us passage for free," the Shepherd continues, smoothly. "A toll must be paid to sail the River of Lamentations."

"Right." I look at the monster's strange face. "So what does it want from me?"

"The standard rate," the Shepherd says.

"Which is what, exactly?"

"A tooth for each supplicant," he says, as if we were discussing the weather, "and a finger for the master."

"Wait—"

"These are reasonable terms," the Shepherd tells me. "If you refuse, we will not make it to the Shrouded Lake in time."

"Whose teeth are we talking about? Whose finger?"

"Yours, of course," the Shepherd says, as though talking to a child.

The Riverkeeper addresses me in its doubled voice.

"They say you are free to choose which teeth, and which finger. The Riverkeeper is not ungenerous in these matters."

"Shit," I say under my breath. "Is this going to hurt?"

"I have never paid a river toll myself," the Shepherd says. "But from what I have heard, it is one of the less painful ways to lose a finger."

I look at the monster, at the bronze boat, at the dark, silent river flowing past us. Time's running out. Ash already had a lead on us, and after that horrible incident with the Ravendark Tree . . . I don't know what to do. I like my fingers, and my teeth as well. We've all had a good run together. But I want Elza back. I didn't come this far to turn back now. You have to choose what you'll give up to get what you want. With magic, I'm learning, nothing comes without a price. And I mean, fingers, what are they good for, really? Pressing buttons? Pointing? If you didn't have a little finger, if you were just born without one, would you even really consider yourself at a disadvantage? It's not like losing a hand. Worst that'll happen is I can't look posh and drink tea with my pinkie in the air.

"All right," I say. "Fine. Let's get this over with."

"I would advise that you offer up the back teeth," the Shepherd says. "Less visible."

"Just what I was thinking," I say, sounding braver than I feel.

The Riverkeeper motions with one long-fingered hand, a *Shall we move along?* sort of gesture.

"Tell it one back tooth from the left, one from the right," I say to the Shepherd. "And the little finger . . . on my left hand. That's my offer. And I want to be taken right to the Shrouded Lake."

The Shepherd speaks again in the spirit language. The Riverkeeper nods.

"They accept," he tells me.

I swallow. This is for Elza. If I don't do this, I'll never see her again. What's a pair of teeth and a finger compared with that? A finger for her whole body and mind? A couple of teeth so I can see her smile again? It's a bargain.

"Get on with it, then," I say.

The Riverkeeper motions for me to open my mouth, and I do; the creature reaches inside, stooping in order to do so, and its long, spiky fingers jostle against my tongue and teeth. The giant's hand tastes of metal and earth, a dull, sour flavor. The fingers find the teeth it wants, the molars at the very back, top left and bottom right, and they twist and tug at them as if trying to undo a knot. With a rush of heat, I feel the teeth give way—it doesn't hurt, not the way it would in Liveside, because they're just the spirit of my teeth—and the creature withdraws its hand, two of my white teeth stuck through with its bronze fingernails. The Riverkeeper holds them up to the gray light of Deadside, examining them with its silver eye and burning eye for flaws or weaknesses, and then, satisfied, it takes a small leather bag from inside its robe and stashes my teeth inside.

"And now the little finger," pronounces the Shepherd.

I hold out my left hand, quivering only slightly. The Riverkeeper smiles for the first time, revealing bronze teeth that are shaped like trowels: blunt scraping instruments. It bends down toward me, gently fitting my little finger inside its mouth. I close my eyes and try to think about Elza's face.

o o o

Our passage along the Cocytus, the River of Lamentations, is swift and mostly silent. We travel against the current, the logic of Liveside's rivers having no hold over this flow of shadows. The Riverkeeper stands at the back of the bronze boat, punting us along with a wooden pole. The monster is silent as we travel; it sings no songs, neglects to point out notable features of the spirit world as we pass them. I sit in the middle of the gondola, legs crossed, with Ham's furry head resting on my lap. I stroke his ears and rub his snout. The Shepherd sits at the boat's prow, silent, unmoving, like a figurehead.

The sky overhead is hidden by gray fog, the banks of the Cocytus equally gray and barren of feature. We pass gray sandbanks, gray rocks, the occasional gray willow tree that droops down into the black water. The river runs through gray canyons of dizzying sheerness and steepness; runs through gray fields of astonishing flatness and drabness.

There's no blood on my hand, no pain at all. It looks like I was born without a finger. There's just a nub, a strange absence. The Riverkeeper sheared it off with a single bite and then let my finger drop from its mouth into its clay-colored hands. It examined the digit with the pride of an angler who's reeled in a big fish, with the avarice of a diamond merchant presented with a flawless stone. Then the Riverkeeper took a golden box from its robes, the sort of thing you might keep a wedding ring in, and carefully tucked my finger away.

The river runs on. Nothing seems to swim in it, fortunately. We pass through a landscape of standing stones, each monolith higher than a house, arranged in a monotonous pattern that stretches as far as I can see. We pass under an elegant bridge, lit by hanging lanterns, and for a brief flash, I think I can see a child looking down at us. We sail through areas where the river is so wide and slow you'd be forgiven for thinking it was a lake, a swamp, and I see islands crammed with gray mangrove trees. We sail through narrow chasms where the Cocytus runs fast as a fairground ride, the Riverkeeper expertly punting us upstream through ferocious rapids without the boat ever seeming in danger of capsizing. We sail past a bank where a herd of black horses with human heads are drinking from the water. They look up at us as we pass by, their eyes white and blank as marbles, but none of them says a word.

"Is this what happens when you die?" I ask as the monstrous horses fade into the fog.

"Pardon?" the Shepherd asks. He doesn't turn around.

"This," I say. "Is this it? Because I used to think, how sad to hang around on earth when you're dead. But now . . ."

"You have started to see it as the better of two bad choices," the Shepherd says. "You feel that the underworld is a place apparently designed to blaspheme against all that men feel to be good and decent. You see that Asphodel is a labyrinth built by a madman, a twilit chaos, where water flows uphill and night never falls and man and beast have become intertwined."

"Something like that."

"I cannot say I disagree," the Shepherd says after a pause. "There are places worse than Asphodel, hard as that may be to believe. Tartarus, for example. The darkness."

"I mean, this is where I'm going when I die? Where everyone goes? Gray mist and horrible things trying to eat you?"

"Perhaps," the Shepherd says. "I have come to believe that, if there is a realm of perpetual mist, and a realm of perpetual darkness, there must be a realm of sunlight to match."

"You think that?"

"I will never see it," he says. "And I have never spoken to any who have been there and returned from its borders."

The river flows. Our gondolier pushes against the riverbed, lifts the pole, pushes again. All I can see is fog, black water.

"Then again," the Shepherd says at last, almost to himself, "who would be willing to leave Paradise?"

Hours, maybe days, pass, and then we come to a waterfall.

The falls are silent as the river, a colossal torrent of shadows, plummeting down a high ridge of gray granite. My questions about how we'll navigate this obstacle are answered when we sail up to the fall of darkness and then, without any apparent effort, are punting up it. The waterfall is below us, with the river rising behind our boat like a wall. There's no sense of gravity changing, no vertigo. We were traveling horizontally, and now we're sailing vertically instead. There's no more and no less to it than that.

The fog thickens as we ascend the black waterfall, the grayness gathering so close around our boat that I can't see the Shepherd, can't see Ham, can't even see myself. And just as I think things can't get any grayer, as I start to believe time itself has stopped, that I'm only a mind floating disembodied in a void, we break through the fog into a vast open space, and I see that we've come to the end of our journey.

(the shrouded lake)

We're under a clear night sky, a sky full of stars, more than I've ever seen before, stars glittering like tiny gems laid out against black velvet. The constellations are vivid and numerous, moving like a film set to fast-forward, stars rising from one horizon and making their way across the entire sky in a matter of minutes.

There's fog here, thick and white, but it only sits around an inch or so above the surface of the Shrouded Lake. The fog is flat and sluggish, dry ice spread over a dance floor, and it parts smoothly around our prow as the gondola moves through it. The lake itself is hidden from view by this fog, but the rest of the landscape is remarkably clear, lit with the same kind of crisp, cold light that shines from a full moon, although no moon is in view overhead. The Shrouded Lake is enormous, spreading in all directions around us, but I can pick out distant shore-lines, and even what seem like islands, sitting low in the fog.

Ham is staring around at this strange new place. The Shepherd and the Riverkeeper seem unmoved.

"Is this it?" I ask, although I already know the answer.

"Indeed. We are sailing upon the Shrouded Lake," the Shepherd says, "source of the underworld's eight rivers."

The Riverkeeper continues to punt, as though pushing against a riverbed. I wonder how shallow the Lake must be, or, alternatively, how long the Riverkeeper's pole is. Our passage is totally silent, with no indication that we're sailing on water at all.

"What do we do now?" I ask.

"There is a shrine," the Shepherd says, "where offer-ings to the sleepers beneath the Lake are made. We will await Ashana and her sister there."

We sail on. The Shrouded Lake is eerie but beauti-ful, a surprising contrast to the life-leached terrain of Asphodel. The landscape here seems fixed; the trees and hills at the shore stay in place as we approach. It's the sky that changes, a gleaming river of stars flowing ceaselessly overhead.

"What's happening to the sky?" I ask after a while.

The Shepherd chuckles, a hoarse sound.

"You don't recognize it?" he asks.

"Why should I?"

"Because it is part of you, and you are part of it," the Shepherd says. I don't answer. Eventually he sighs and says, "I would have expected you to know the Book of Eight when you saw it."

"*That's* the Book of Eight?" I ask, but even as I say the words, I know he's right. The constellations are sigils, magic marks, flowing across the blackness in an infinite procession.

The Shepherd holds up the green-bound Book itself. "It is. And this is the Book of Eight as well. They are one and the same."

Ham whines. I stroke his neck and ears until he calms.

"I don't understand," I say.

"Neither do I," the Shepherd replies, looking up at the swirling stars, and for once he doesn't sound smug or annoyed. He sounds almost wistful.

We make ground on the lakeshore with a dull grinding of stones against the boat's bronze hull. I step carefully from the boat's prow onto the shore. The blanket of mist makes it difficult to tell where the lake ends and the shore begins, and the fog laps at the pale shoreline like a silent tide. The lakeshore is steel-colored sand mottled with small stones. Pine trees stand in solemn groups, everything highlighted in silver, bathed in a strange moonlight glow.

The Riverkeeper is standing on the shore beside the boat, looking at us with an air of satisfaction. The monster bellows jovially.

"It wishes to extend its hope that we vanquish our adversaries," the Shepherd explains, "and inform you that if you ever wish for passage along the Cocytus again, it will be glad to answer your sigil. The price will remain the same, of course."

"Please thank the Riverkeeper sincerely," I say. The Shepherd delivers a short speech in the giant's strange language, and the monster nods, giving me a bronze smile, apparently satisfied with whatever he said. Without another word, the Riverkeeper steps back into its boat and begins to punt away from us, out across the milky surface of the Shrouded Lake. I watch it leave, thinking about my teeth in the leather bag, my little finger locked away in a golden box. Wondering what exactly the creature wanted them for.

The Shepherd is already examining a page of the Book.

"Follow on," he says, striding off. "The shrine is not far. We are nearly at our journey's end, Luke."

I don't know what's going to happen when we see Ash and the Widow. I haven't really thought this far ahead. Whatever happens here, on this silent shore, is going to affect the rest of my life. I can't get this wrong.

"Come on, boy," I say to Ham, who barks and trots

ahead, following the Shepherd. I set out behind them. The Riverkeeper and its boat have already vanished, leaving by whatever route we took to arrive here. Stars race overhead. The shoreline is like a black-and-white photograph you're somehow walking through.

We come to the shrine without me even noticing it. I was expecting some kind of white marble temple, a ring of standing stones, perhaps an altar surrounded by flickering torches. If it weren't for the Shepherd, I'd have walked right past it.

It's a flat jetty of black stone, barely higher than the mist that covers the lake's surface. It extends maybe ten feet out from the shoreline. I walk the length of it, stop, look out over the lake. Nothing but a flat, unchanging blanket of fog, and the dim suggestion of silvery hills far away on the opposite shore. The way the stars move gives you the impression that you're falling forward, toward the lake's surface. There's a single mark, a sigil or rune of some kind, cut into the jetty, right at the end of it. It means nothing to me.

I turn away from the lake, and see that Ham and the Shepherd are sitting on the shallow steps that lead from the lakeshore to the shrine itself.

I sit beside them. There's no wind here, no animals foraging in the undergrowth. None of us is even breathing. Again I feel as though I've fallen out of time. Even the silver light falling on the shore and the trees and hills beyond them is changeless, the shadows unmoving.

"How long do we have to wait?" I ask.

"Who knows?" the Shepherd says. "There is no time here. Days and years are for the living."

The stars flow from the horizon like white embers rising from a hidden fire.

"I do not believe we will wait for them long," he says after a while. "We seek them, and they will be drawn to us, just as they draw the lake toward themselves. They will come."

"What will we do when they get here?" I ask. I hadn't even thought about how we'd stop them. The Widow . . . I don't know if we can fight her.

"You told me the Ahlgren girl bears a sigil minor," the Shepherd says. "In which hand?"

"Left."

"As soon as she is within range, I will strike directly at her sigil. I will be able to destroy it, and thus break the Ahlgren Host. She will have no dominion over her servant."

"That'll work?"

"A single sigil minor, the last remnants of a broken Host? We can overwhelm it. Her sigil will shatter before our combined power like glass beneath a hammer blow. And once her sigil is useless . . ."

"The Widow will turn on her," I say.

"I believe Kasmut will. At the very least, she cannot be compelled to attack us. And I do not see any gain in such a conflict for her."

"And without their Host, Ash and Ilana—"

"Are easy prey." He gives me a cold grin. "We will take the nonpareil from the girls without effort, I assure you."

"If you're sure," I say. I don't like the thought of letting him loose on Ash and Ilana, especially not Ilana, who's never intentionally hurt anyone. We're going to have to fight, though. Ash didn't give me any choice in this.

"Do you really love this girl?" the Shepherd asks. It's such an unexpected question that I almost think I've misheard him.

"What?"

"The witch girl. Elza Moss. Do you love her?"

"I mean . . ." I begin, feeling like I'm talking to a distant, awkward relative. The Shepherd is one of the last people, living or dead, I ever imagined having this conversation with. "Yeah. I do. We haven't been together that long . . . but I think so."

"You are not sure?" He sounds amused. "We have come a long way for a woman you are not sure about."

"OK, yeah. I love her. I know that I do. Going through life without her . . . it would be like losing my eyes. I couldn't do it."

"Or a finger," he says.

I raise my maimed hand up for him to see it.

"This is nothing," I say. "I'd have given the Riverkeeper a hand, if it got Elza back."

"Why do you love her?" the Shepherd asks.

"Because . . . she's a good person. She's honest. She cares about other people. She's funny. She's beautiful."

"Surely you have met others who have those qualities as well." The Shepherd doesn't seem like he's taunting me. He sounds genuinely interested.

"You know what? It's partly because of you that we fell in love. You and the rest of the Host. Going through what you made us go through . . . that was what brought us together. So in a way, I should thank you. I'd never have loved her without you."

"It was unintentional, I assure you," he says.

"She just . . . she really cared about me. She put herself in loads of danger for me, and there was nothing making her do that. That's why I love her. That's why I'm going to get her back."

Ham scratches at his spirit ear with a spirit paw. He's quite relaxed, seemingly content to sit and wait on the shores of this strange place. The constellations flow and morph above us, and I wonder whether they're pages of the Book that I've already seen, or pages that nobody alive has read. If you can even call what's above us a "page" at all.

"What does it feel like?" the Shepherd asks me.

"Love?" I ask. I take a hard look at his waxy white face, the drooping nose, the gray beard, his mirrored round glasses. I try to detect any hint of mockery there.

"I have never felt it," he says. "I am aware that the emotion exists, but I have never felt affection for another soul. I do not understand it."

"It's like . . ." I stop. How do I begin to explain? How do you explain love to a being like this, someone who has never felt anything other than contempt or hate for another person? How can I explain what goes through my mind when I see Mum or Elza or Ham? How can you explain the mysteries of the heart to a creature that doesn't seem to have one?

"It's, like, someone you can't be without. You want to be near them. You want them to be happy. Because you need that for them. You're tied together, and you can't be happy if you know they're not."

"So it is selfishness," the Shepherd says.

"No—"

"You have shown me this emotion only through the prism of your own self. If you act according to your own desires or happiness, how can you say you do not act from self-interest? Love, as you speak of it, is a mask for self-interest. Elza gives something to you that you cannot find within yourself, therefore you jealously covet and protect the source of this feeling, and now that she is elsewhere, you have gone to insane lengths in order to bring her back to you. It is greed and self-obsession. A weakness that weak men call strength."

"It's not just about me," I say. "If you love someone, you do things for them, even if it's against your own interests. I got my finger bitten off."

"You weighed up what achieving your own goals was worth, and paid that price. It was not for Elza's sake you paid the Riverkeeper. It was for your own."

"You don't understand, and you can't ever understand. You're a monster. It's like trying to describe red to someone who's color-blind."

The Shepherd smiles. "I have often been called a monster. It is strange, the way we speak of those who dare to be honest about their own desires."

"So everyone's selfish? Love is just an excuse so we can tell ourselves we're not?"

"All men are driven by the desire to remake the world into one which better suits them. I believe there are varying degrees of self-deception which the weak practice, excuses they give themselves for not doing so. Strong men, sorcerers, act. I do not trouble myself to find excuses for doing as I please. *Love* is only a man's way of hiding his selfishness from himself."

I'm trying to think of something to say to this, because

I know he's wrong, but then the Shepherd rises to his feet. I look where he points, squinting to see into the silvered distance.

Three figures have crested the farthest hill.

The Ahlgrens stop when they see us, clearly surprised to see figures already standing before the shrine. They turn around and vanish below the summit of the hill. I'm tense, hopping from foot to foot, wanting to run after them, but the Shepherd stays put, and me and Ham stay beside him. They have to bring the nonpareil here. We can let Ash come to us.

Eventually she reaches the same conclusion, and two white figures appear once again over the lip of the hill. Ilana isn't with them. Ash and the Widow make their way down the slope, and then thread their way between the trees toward us. They make no attempt to hide—the lake's shoreline is so wide and open that there's no possible way of approaching the shrine unseen. Ash and her body-guard pass the last of the pine trees and advance on us, feet crunching in the gray sand and stones. Ash is wearing white jeans, Converse sneakers, her white denim jacket. She has a backpack slung over one shoulder. The Widow looks the same as ever: wrapped in a white robe, broken spear stuck through her chest. She walks in front of Ash, approaching with a weary determination.

They halt a short distance from us. Ash looks drained and ill, her mouth set into a hard line.

"Luke," she says, "don't make us—"

The Shepherd raises his hands and speaks a ringing, terrible word, and my sigil burns with cold. He's drawing power from it somehow, and before I can move, a bolt of white lightning jumps from my ring into his hands. The power crackles around his long fingers, and the Shepherd casts the lightning in a blinding stream at Ash. The energy is drawn into her left hand, the power from my sigil coursing into hers. She screams, and the white light flashes so bright that everything—the lakeshore, the Shepherd, Ham—is obscured.

I take my hands away from my face. Nobody has moved. Ash's left hand is gone, blown out of shape, like smoke in a strong wind. Her left arm now ends in formless mist, with white fire dripping from the stump. She stares at the remains of her sigil in disbelief.

"Priestess! Kasmut!" the Shepherd says. "The Ahlgren Host is broken. You are free."

The Widow looks at Ash, still gaping at her shattered hand, and turns back to us. She draws the spear from her chest with one smooth gesture, weighs it in her hand.

Dark blood seeps into her white robe. A droplet falls from the tip of the spear and stains the gray sand.

I'm waiting for her to strike, to attack Ash, maybe to run, but she doesn't move. The Widow shifts her weight, curls one bare foot in the sand. The Shepherd faces her, hands still raised in his spell-casting gesture. Ham seems to have vanished, in a typical display of cowardice.

"I did not serve from fear," the Widow says, and before anyone can reply, she charges across the lakeshore toward us.

The Shepherd bellows in response, green fire erupting from his hands in a great wave. The flames warp and flow like molten glass, spreading over the lakeshore, but the Widow leaps higher than I thought possible, far above the flames, and she falls onto the Shepherd and buries her spear in his chest.

He gasps. The Widow lifts him bodily from the ground, holding the Shepherd aloft like a hunting trophy. His hat has fallen from his head, and his glasses, too, baring his straggly gray hair and his tar-black eyes. Their gazes meet in a look of hatred so pure, I'm surprised it doesn't scar the air between them, and then the Shepherd's hands spout with more flame. This time it meets its target, enveloping the Widow, distorting her body like she's trapped at the bottom of a green bottle. She doesn't cry out, but moves with a terrible swiftness, taking two quick steps toward the lake itself, fire still coursing over her, and then tosses the Shepherd into the air like a terrier throws a dead rat. He flies from her spear, fire still trailing from his hands. He falls and disappears without a sound into the mist-shrouded waters of the lake. There's no splash, and he doesn't cry out. His black body parts the mist and vanishes in an instant.

I feel his power leave me in the same moment, my sigil dulling on my finger, becoming just a useless ring. The lake's covering is unbroken, calm and white, with no sign of the Shepherd ever having existed. He's gone.

He was carrying the Book as well.

How am I going to get back home?

No. One thing at a time.

It's me and the Widow.

Her spear is balanced in one hand, pointed right at me. I retreat up the shallow staircase, out onto the long platform that makes up the shrine. The Widow's spear tracks me as I move from side to side, aimed at my heart.

I don't have a plan.

Her eyes are like dark holes in her face.

I have absolutely nothing.

She steps up onto the shrine, her bare feet making soft sounds on the stone.

Does it hurt if you die in the spirit world?

I open my mouth to say something to her—I have no

idea what—and in that moment, the Widow lunges at me. I fall backward, hitting the stone shrine hard, flailing with my hands as she plunges the spear toward my head. I hit the shaft of the spear with my forearm and it goes wide, striking the dark stone next to my head.

The Widow presses a cold foot on my chest, pinning me to the ground.

I strike at her leg, but it's like punching a statue. She could be cast of iron.

I see that she's smiling, the first expression of joy I've ever seen on her face.

She raises the spear high for another blow.

I know she won't miss again.

Why did I come here?

What did I think I would achieve?

I hear Ash screaming something.

The Widow turns her head, and at that moment, a gray furry body hits her in the chest, knocking her back. Ham's a hunting dog, bred to bring down a stag, and he puts the full force of his weight into the blow, raking her with both huge paws. Ham's jaws latch onto the shoulder of her spear arm, and I hear him snarling, angrier than I've ever heard him.

The Widow takes another step backward, shrieking and beating at Ham with her free hand, but he forces her back another step, and she falls off the side of the shrine. She topples back with a wail, Ham still snarling and struggling against her. They vanish into the Shrouded Lake in the blink of an eye, and all that's left of them is a swirl of mist.

I get to my feet. I keep hoping Ham and the Widow will reappear from the lake, rear up out of the waters, still fighting, but I know that won't happen. Once you fall through that curtain of fog, there's no coming back. They've gone to another place, become part of whatever lies beneath the Shrouded Lake. Ham's gone. I've known him since he was eight weeks old, since he was only the size of a rabbit, and I won't see him again. He died to save me, and I don't even have time to think about it, not while Ash is still between me and the nonpareil.

She's waiting for me on the lakeshore, backpack left on the sand behind her. Her left arm ends in a strange swirl of fog, with flickers of white lightning playing through it. They look a little like finger bones. Ash holds the witch blade in her remaining hand, point angled down to the gray shore.

"Listen—" she begins.

"I don't care," I say. "Give me the nonpareil."

Ash smiles, a bitter, hopeless smile. "You know I can't, Luke."

"I don't want to kill you," I say. To my surprise, I find that it's true.

"Me neither," she replies. "So get out of my way."

"You know I can't," I say.

Ash gestures with the witch blade. The pale knife gleams in the strange silver light. Sigils shine in the darkness above us. "You're defenseless, Luke," she says. "It's over. Let me through."

"While I'm still standing," I say, "it's not over."

This is stupid. She's right. She'll cut me to bits.

"I don't want to kill you," she says. "I really don't."

"Did you want to kill Elza?"

"I had no choice about that. Someone had to die to get the nonpareil."

"Nobody had to die, Ash."

"Somebody did. It was Ilana or Elza. Your girlfriend or my sister. I chose us over you."

"You had no right to do that."

"I love her," Ash says with a bitter smile. "You love Elza. One person's love had to destroy the other's. There wasn't a way for both of us to get what we wanted."

She's edging toward me as she talks, knife held tight in her hand. I know absolutely nothing about knife fights, except that it's probably bad if your opponent has one and you don't. I think I'm in a bad spot.

"I do like you," Ash continues. "I am sorry. I kept you alive, and I didn't have to. I think we've got a lot in common."

"We're nothing like each other. I'd never do what you did," I say. "You can't just use people. Me, Elza, Mark . . . we're people, not tools for getting what you want."

"And what was Octavius to you? What was your dog? You used them to get here, didn't you? How did that work out for them?"

"They chose to help me," I say.

"You're no better than me," Ash says. "Don't kid yourself that you're the hero here."

"Everything I've done, I did to get Elza back. You forced me into this."

"Luke," she says again, gray eyes glittering, "this is stupid. I've got the witch blade. I'll cut you to pieces. Just let me pass."

"No," I say.

"Half my inheritance," Ash says. "I'll give you half. I don't want anyone else to die because of me and Ilana. Just let me pass. You'd be one of the richest people on the planet."

"No. I don't want money. I want Elza back."

Ash lunges forward at me, slashing with the knife. I duck backward, almost falling over, and the blade slices the air right in front of my face.

"Last chance," Ash says. "Next time it's for real. Get out of my way."

"No."

Ash lashes out with the witch blade again, leaping at me. I stagger, lurching drunkenly to one side. The Shrouded Lake is just behind me. If I keep retreating, she'll drive me right into it.

Ash advances, and this time I move toward her, catching her knife arm just as the blade is about to slide into my eye. She pushes against me, and we fall to the ground. Ash is above me, pressing down with all her strength, and even though she's five foot nothing, a girl with arms like lengths of string, the blade is still moving toward my face. I can't hold her off.

How can Ash be this strong?

I'm using both arms to stop her, and it's still not enough.

"You're making . . . me . . . do this. . . ." she hisses through gritted teeth.

She strikes me with her ruined left hand, white lightning flickering through the warped remains of her fingers.

It isn't her real left hand.

What did the Shepherd say? Will and wisdom. I'm not fighting Ash's body. I never have been. That's what he was telling me all along. We left our bodies back in Liveside. I'm fighting her will. It's not her muscles that give her strength on this shore; what gives her strength is Ilana. Her love.

I push back against Ash's body, push against the slow advance of her knife. I push against her, and I think of Elza. I remember Elza the day Kirk kicked a ball at her and she whirled around to face us. I remember the first day we talked about the ghosts, in the graveyard at Saint Jude's, gray clouds overhead and pigeons slapping their wings against wet branches. I think of how she helped me when she didn't have to, put herself in danger for someone she barely knew. I remember Elza sprinting across a lonely field, my body pursuing her; the way she outwitted the demon. I remember seeing her holding the Book of Eight by lamplight, the first moment I realized I felt something for her. I remember coming up the path from the Devil's Footsteps and seeing her get out of Mum's car, still alive, and feeling joy like I haven't felt before or since. I remember how it felt to kiss her. I remember Elza out on the moors with me and Ham in January, the day she photographed us in the snow. I think of Elza laughing, Elza frowning as she tried to finish a poem, Elza falling asleep during the epic final fight of *Starkiller 3*. The way she'd dismiss bands she didn't like as "utterly inconsequential." The meticulous way she'd spread Marmite on her toast.

I realize what the nonpareil is, the thing that's truly without equal.

It's her.

All of this is what Ash took from the world. Tried to take from me.

I twist Ash's wrist, twist until I think it's about to break, until she screams and drops the knife, the witch blade falling to the ground beside us.

I can be as strong as she is. Stronger.

Will and wisdom.

But mostly will.

I throw Ash off me, and she feels insubstantial, flat, like a doll made of paper. I'm above her, one hand wrapped around her throat. She's screaming, trying to kick me off her, grabbing at a gray stone with her good hand and beating at my face, but I can barely feel it. My right hand is groping for the hilt of the witch blade.

We're beyond words now.

She hits me so hard that the rock splits. In Liveside the blow would've killed me.

I find the knife's rough hilt.

Ash's fingers scrabble at my eyes.

Without another thought, I plunge the witch blade into her chest.

There's no blood, just a strange burst of light.

Her hands go limp.

I stand up. Ash doesn't move. The knife is still buried in her spirit body. She looks different somehow, duller and less solid, like her body's turning to fog.

She's dead.

I kneel down and slide the knife out of her chest. There's no resistance; it's like I stabbed smoke. The blade doesn't even leave a wound. Her eyes are open.

"I didn't have a choice," I say to what's left of Ash. "I'm really sorry."

I find the nonpareil inside her backpack, wrapped in cloth. It feels warm, almost weightless, like fresh-baked bread. I make my way down to the shrine, past Ash's dissolving body, up the shallow steps and along the promontory of dark stone, until I'm standing at the very edge of the shrine, looking out over the mist-shrouded waters.

The mark carved into the stone looks the same as it did before, but now that I'm holding the nonpareil, I find I can understand it. It's not a complicated mark. I feel like I've known what it meant my whole life.

The mark means: SPEAK.

"I am the necromancer Luke Manchett, son of Horatio Manchett," I say to the Shrouded Lake. "I need your help. I have a nonpareil."

No voice answers me.

I look again at the mark cut into the stone, and I realize that it means something different now, or rather something new. I see that the mark is a word that can mean whatever the person speaking wants it to mean.

The mark now means: WHAT DO YOU DESIRE?

"I want Elza Moss, whose spirit is held within this nonpareil, to return to life," I tell the lake, or whatever power lives beneath it. "I want her to return to life, just as she was."

The mark means this: IT CAN BE DONE. MAKE YOUR OFFERING.

I remove the cloth and look at the nonpareil for the second time. It's as beautiful as I remember it being. The nonpareil is like a soap bubble, a glass bowl, a heart, a pearl. Its surface is silvered like fish scales, with the texture of sun-warmed stone. Well-being like I've never known flows through me as I look at the object in my hands. I can smell summer grass, taste fresh chocolate. The patterns of light and color within the nonpareil are forming pictures: faces, bodies, smiling people. I see a man with slicked-back hair, a pencil-thin mustache, and I know it's the Vassal. He waves to me and fades. I see a man with thinning blond hair, wispy and long like a dandelion that's spreading its seeds, a man dressed in white, wearing rimless glasses, and I know without being told that it's Magnus Ahlgren. I see people without number, men and women and children, and I know they're the spirits that the Fury ate and burned away within itself. Each of them could be saved, but they're not the one I'm looking for.

And then I see her.

Elza smiles out through the glassy wall of the nonpareil, and I smile back at her.

I raise the nonpareil above my head, and in response, the mist that covers the Shrouded Lake melts away, and I see the true surface of the water.

The Shrouded Lake is black and flat as glass, mirroring the stars in the sky, a perfect reflection of the strange constellations that warp and flow overhead. And then, as I look at the lake, I realize that's not quite right either. It's not the lake's waters that reflect the sky. The sky in Deadside is a reflection of the Shrouded Lake. The lake is made of night sky, stars and galaxies beyond counting, symbols and magic marks flaring in the darkness, a depth of infinite light and volume. No wonder there was no sound when Ham and the ghosts fell. They went into the void itself. It's dizzying, incredible. I'm standing on a short spur of rock that juts out over unbelievable emptiness.

I kneel at the end of the shrine and lower the nonpareil gently into the blackness. I let it go, and it falls into the infinite depth of the Shrouded Lake, flaring brighter and whiter as it falls like a meteor, and in just a brief moment, the nonpareil's glow is lost among the uncountable mass of stars, and I know it has become one of them.

The mark carved at my feet means this: WE HAVE RECEIVED YOUR OFFERING.

The white mist flows back across the surface of the Shrouded Lake, hiding the bottomless sky from view.

The mark means: TURN AND GO, LUKE MANCHETT. RETURN TO LIFE. YOU WILL NOT BE HARMED.

"What about Elza?" I ask the mist.

THE BELOVED WILL FOLLOW. BUT YOU MUST TRUST IN HER.

"Trust how?" I ask.

DO NOT LOOK BACK.

I stand on the edge of the shrine, looking out over the mist, hoping against hope that I'll see something rise up out of it, Elza or Ham or someone, but nothing happens. The stars flow silently overhead.

I turn around.

Ash is gone. Her backpack is still there, but her remains have vanished. Maybe they melted away, became part of the gray mist? Maybe something carried them away? What about Ilana? The idea of the one-armed girl, set loose on her own in Asphodel, doesn't delight me. But I don't see what else I can do. I can't talk to her; she won't trust me, and I don't know how I could help her.

I stay on the shore for a short time, hand on the hilt of the knife, waiting to see if anything will come at me out of the pine trees or over the hills, whether Ash had one last trick up her sleeve. Nothing happens. The urge to turn and look over my shoulder, back toward the lake, is an almost physical pressure, like there's a fishing line stuck into my forehead, but I resist. I press forward, through the tree line and over the hill that the Ahlgrens crested minutes or hours ago.

I walk downhill, and before long the fog of Deadside is rolling around me, dulling the bright landscape, obscuring the stars that flow overhead. I have a sudden intuition, as the stars dim, that this is what the sky looks like above all of Deadside, but it's only when you stand at the edge of the Shrouded Lake that you can see it.

I return through Asphodel without anyone; no Shepherd, no Ham, no Elza, not even the Riverkeeper or Ash. Everyone's gone. It's just me, walking through the grayness with my head down, moving toward the land of the living with nothing but a knife and a promise. Whatever spoke from beneath the lake told me Elza would be following me, and that I would be protected. On the second count at least, its promise seems to hold. I don't see any spirits, human or otherwise. The closest I come is when I'm walking a narrow mountain path, gray fog swirling around me, and somewhere below me I hear soft voices singing.

I walk alone, in silence, leaving Ham behind me, hoping that Elza follows. I walk alone, through gray fields and gray forests, alongside silent black streams and across a crumbling bridge over a mist-filled chasm. I walk alone, without the Book of Eight to guide me, holding the image of the passing place in my mind, willing it to emerge from the fog. I walk alone, with only my thoughts for company, and I don't look back.

I have no idea how long the journey takes, but I arrive at my destination with a suddenness that jars me. I climb a low ridge, clinging to gray tree branches for leverage, my eyes fixed on where I'm going, and I find that I've scrambled up into a wide patch of gray sand and an enormous white snake is rearing up before me. I raise my arms like the Shepherd did and begin to declare.

"Mighty Gatekeeper," I begin, "I am the necromancer Luke Manchett, returned—"

There's no time for that, the Gatekeeper replies, interrupting me.

I fall silent. The snake runs its fat pink tongue over

its teeth. Have I done something wrong? If I got this far, beat Ash, reached the lake, only to get eaten by the Gatekeeper . . .

He awaits you at the threshold, the snake continues.

If I had a heart, it would be racing.

"Who?" I ask, but I think I already know.

He of Many Faces. Speaker of Secrets. The Black Goat. He awaits.

It's all I can do not to turn and run. I think of Elza. If I turn back now, it was for nothing. I have to be brave. I've met him before.

"Thank you," I say.

I bow to the Gatekeeper, and the snake bows its white head in turn. I walk past it, feet crunching in the gray sand, heading uphill, toward the passing place. The hill seems shallower than when we descended it, without plant life, just barren earth and stones. I reach the lip of the rise, the Devil's Footsteps, and I stop walking because there's something in the middle of the stones and it's worse than anything I've ever seen, a choking clot of darkness with something moving inside it, something stillborn but still living, moving inside a womb of oil, and its head turns and I close my eyes—I don't want to see I don't want—

"My boy?"

I want to scream, but I don't.

I open my eyes.

He's there in the middle of the stones, exactly as he was the last time I met him. An aging, handsome face, the skin honey-tanned, white hair slicked back from his forehead, laughter lines by his mouth and eyes. A neat white beard and big white teeth. Always smiling. A wolf-gray suit and a shirt that's deep midnight-blue. Hungry eyes and arms held out like he's expecting me to hug him. Mr. Berkley.

"Is something the matter, Luke?" he asks. His voice is deep and cheerful, commanding without seeming bossy or mean, a voice you ache to trust. "You look like you saw something terrible."

"I did," I say.

"Manners," he says, but still smiling, without anger. "This can't be a surprise, surely? You've had rather a busy week. Taken up your father's mantle again, summoned one of my children, slaughtered it at dawn, freed Octavius from the darkness, promised him a new body, made him your Shepherd once more, parleyed with a Riverkeeper, journeyed to the Shrouded Lake, made an offering to those that sleep there . . . Am I missing anything?"

I can't think of anything to say.

"You can't have thought I wouldn't notice any of this happening, Luke. Did you really think I'd pay no attention?"

"I hoped," I say.

Berkley laughs. "I do find your naïveté rather endearing, it has to be said."

"What do you want from me?" I ask. He's standing between me and the gateway, preventing any hope of escape, although I'm not sure it would work anyway. He can find me in the living world as easily as he can here.

"I want us to sit together," Berkley says, and as the words leave his mouth I find that we are sitting down, facing each other across a small round table made of gold, in golden chairs with places set before us, golden bowls piled with dark meat and fruit, golden goblets and a jug that looks like it ought to hold wine. We're still at the passing place, the three stones standing around our table like guards. Berkley takes a long drink from his cup. What's going to happen to Elza? Isn't she supposed to be following me?

"Don't worry about your friend," he says. "She'll find her own way."

I swallow.

"If you're angry about us killing the demon—" I begin.

"Luke. If I am ever angry, you will be aware of it, I assure you. Happily I have been visited with more children than it is possible to name or number, so the loss is of no particular consequence."

He takes another draft of whatever it is he's drinking.

I have my hands folded in my lap. The witch blade is still tucked into my belt, although I doubt it would be much use against him. The table's piled high with food, but there's something wrong with it, some kind of corruption or taint to the meat and soft fruits that makes me feel ill just looking at them.

"What do you want from me?" I ask. "Because I really wanted to go home."

"And so you shall. I merely desired to sit and speak with you. I do like to reach out to my supplicants now and again, to keep our bond fresh in their minds."

I look at my hands. I remember touching him, my fingers held in his lineless palm. I invited this creature into my life. I signed his contract, and then, on Halloween, I called him back with my own blood and bargained with him. I've tried my best to forget about him, but I know I never will.

"You don't like me very much, do you?" Berkley remarks.

It's such an unexpected turn to this conversation that I start in my seat. He's looking at me intently, his eyes bright, seeming to reflect firelight without a source.

"Now, why is that, I wonder?" he continues, taking a black peach from the nearest bowl.

"You're the Devil," I say.

"So you dislike me *a priori*? You dislike the Devil

because he is the Devil? The Devil exists to be hated, reviled, feared?"

"You're evil," I say. "You torment people. You trick them. You tricked me."

Mr. Berkley takes a bite of the black fruit. Chews thoughtfully, swallows.

"In my long experience," he says, "evil tends to be a matter of opinion. I exist to offer knowledge. To the weak-minded, that is seen as evil. I exist to bestow power to those who dare ask it of me. To the weak of heart, the timid souls that shuffle through their lives and deaths as though both were a dream, I am known as evil. I hoped you had started to grow beyond that, my boy."

"That's what evil people always say," I reply. "They say they're not evil and nobody understands them and they had to do what they did."

"Does the Devil know he is the Devil?" Berkley says, looking at me. "When he gazes at his own reflection, is it the face of the Devil that he sees?"

"What are you trying to say?"

"I offer knowledge and I offer power. I did not trick your father, and I did not trick you. You knew my terms, and you accepted them. Attempting to distance yourself from me after the fact is unbecoming."

"I had no choice! It was that or death at the hands of my Host!"

"So there *was* a choice," he says, amused. "And you came to me."

"I—"

"It is a sorry definition of freedom to apply the term only to choices between palatable options. Ashana saw she could either let her sister die or allow your witch girl to die instead, and she made her choice. To say she did not have one is nonsense. You chose to pursue her, chose to plunge your knife into Ashana's chest to save your beloved. You chose to raise the dead, bind them to your will, plunge headlong into their world. You chose to lead your hound, who would have followed you anywhere, into danger and death. You chose to call upon me, and now complain I am a disagreeable presence in your life. Do not speak to me of having no choice."

"I want to go home," I say. "Just send me home."

Berkley laughs.

"Demanding to be returned home," he says. "A formidable philosophical defense. I shall have to employ it for myself at some point."

I don't say anything.

"Do try the peaches," he continues. "They're exquisite."

"What do you want?" I ask.

"Only that we sit and speak."

"No. We made a deal. What do you want? Is this the lead-up to you asking me?"

Berkley places the peach stone, shiny with juice, on his empty gold plate. "I told you," he says, "I want something equal in value to your father."

"A nonpareil?"

"No. I have no use for such objects."

"When will I have to pay you?"

"Perhaps I will never collect my debt. Perhaps I will allow you to live out your life, day by day, the sun rising and falling, the moon blossoming with light and devoured by darkness, never knowing when you will round a corner and see my face. Perhaps you will hear my voice in your dreams. Perhaps you will try to forget your debt, bury it like a seed beneath frost-hardened ground, but you will never forget me. Perhaps you will live your entire life never knowing when I will collect, with the debt forever in your thoughts like a scratch on the surface of your eye, and when you lie on your deathbed you will realize that every moment you lived was poisoned by the waiting, the fear, and then you will know that the debt has been paid."

His smile is wide and white, his eyes alight with a monstrous radiance.

"Or perhaps," the Devil says, almost in a whisper, "I want something else."

The gray mist of Deadside swirls and thickens around us, and all I can see are eyes shining like poisoned blue stars, and when the mist clears again, he's gone.

The table is empty of food and drink, and there's only one thing, lying in the center: a small book bound in green leather, with an eight-pointed star engraved on the cover. I should have known it wasn't gone for good. There's no choice. I know Berkley won't let me leave it behind.

So I pick up the Book of Eight, tucking it into my jacket, and then, without a backward glance, I pass through the gateway.

It's late afternoon, with gnats looping in the air overhead and a low sun falling softly through the trees. A perfect Dunbarrow afternoon, as nice as you could hope for in early April. After the gray of Deadside, the warm colors of the bracken and grass and moss are intoxicating. I feel drunk on the blue of the sky, the green of new leaves. Even after everything that has happened, I can't help but be happy to see the sun again. I feel like I was underwater for a thousand years, stuck at the bottom of a murky ocean, and I just broke the surface.

I turn, taking in the rest of the Devil's Footsteps, and stop short when I see a figure in white, standing at the tree line back toward the road. Is that Ash? How can it be her? I killed her . . . I'm sure of it. Her spirit vanished. How did she . . . ?

I dart out of the stone circle, hurtling through the air toward the tent, toward my body, to Elza and Mark. How did she get back here? What if she already moved my body? She could've done anything—I was so sure she was dead.

Luckily, nothing in the tent seems different. I dive back into my body. I open my eyes to see sunlight dappling the roof overhead, and Ham's furry body, gone cold, beside me. I quickly check the other sleeping compartments, moving quickly, aware that Ash could be on us any moment. Elza is lying in the compartment next to me, still apparently lifeless. Mark is asleep. I've got the witch blade in my hand, and I'm fumbling with the zip of the tent when I hear a voice from outside.

"Luke?"

I don't move a muscle. The only sound is my breathing.

"Luke," the voice—American, female—says again, "come out."

"What do you want?" I ask. I was so sure this was over.

"I'm not going to hurt you," Ash says.

"Oh, yeah?"

"You should really come outside," she says. "I've been here for hours. I could've hurt your body and I didn't."

She has a point, I suppose. This doesn't quite make sense as an ambush. Who knows how she survived or what she wants?

I unzip the tent and climb out. There's a girl standing a few feet away, dressed in white Converse, white jeans, a baggy white sweater. She has Ash's face, Ash's build, but her hair is long and unruly, and her eyes are the blue of sun-bleached denim. She raises a hand in greeting.

"Ilana?" I ask.

"Sort of," Ilana Ahlgren says. "It's complicated."

I'm still holding the witch blade. I take a slow step toward her.

"What are you . . . I mean, how are you here?"

"I came down to see if you were all right," she says.

"Why? I mean, I . . . I killed Ash, Ilana. She's dead. I killed her."

"Not exactly," Ilana says.

My throat tightens. "Ash? Is that you?"

"Like I said," Ilana continues, "it's a little complicated."

"You're in Ilana's body?"

"We both are," she replies. "Ilana hid while you fought Ash and the Widow. We, she, saw everything. We

(344)

saw the servants fall. We felt the blow you dealt to Ash and watched it from the safety of the tree line as well. As Ash was dying, Ilana knew what she had to do. It was so simple. We'd been sharing our spirits for so long . . . and maybe we were always supposed to be one person. We began as one person, after all; it was only later that we divided. It was so clear. Ilana took the rest of Ash into herself, and we became one whole spirit."

Ilana seems strangely calm as she relates all of this.

"So you're both in there?" I ask.

"Yes. Ashana and Ilana. All of our memories, all of our thoughts. But we're one person now. We will be one person from now on."

"I don't really know what to say to you," I reply.

"Say you're happy for us."

"Happy? Ilana . . . I killed your sister. I murdered her."

"I'm still alive, Luke," Ilana says.

"Aren't you angry with me?"

"Ash wasn't happy," Ilana replies. "It's strange how clearly we see everything now. She wasn't well. Neither of us was. The way Ash—the way I—treated you and Elza was wrong."

This is so bizarre.

"Are they . . . are you happy now?"

Ilana looks up into the trees. She frowns.

"We think so," she says. "But then, Ilana always was

happy. That's something Ash never saw. Her sister was happy, even though she was dying. It was Ash who suffered."

I remember the first time I met Ilana's ghost, the way she reached out to the night sky. The joy in her face.

"Maybe there's something in that," I say.

"We feel better than we have in a long time," she says, brushing hair back from her face. "Maybe things turned out for the best."

I think of Ham, lying cold just behind us.

"It doesn't feel like that," I say.

"We're sorry for what we did to you," Ilana says.

"Ash said I could drink from the chalice of Lethe water," I say. "She told me I'd forget what I read in the Book of Eight. If you want to make things right, you can start there."

"We can help your friend Mark," Ilana says. "That was true. But Ash was lying to you. The waters of the River Lethe cannot erase pages from the Book of Eight, for the Lethe flows from the Shrouded Lake, and that place—"

"It *is* the Book, somehow, right?"

"In some way, yes. We can't erase the Book's pages. It's like using fire to extinguish fire."

"Will I really go crazy?"

"It might happen. It might not."

"That's comforting."

"It wasn't meant to be," Ilana replies. "It was the truth."

"I need to check on Elza," I tell her.

"She may not return immediately," Ilana says. "She has to find her way back from the lake, follow the path you made for her."

I turn and crawl back into the tent. Ham is still lying where I left him. He looks like he might be asleep. Ilana bends down beside me and gives him a gentle rub on the head.

"He was a brave dog," she says. "Very loyal."

"Yeah," I say. "He was."

Ilana opens the compartment where Mark sleeps, and she somehow produces the chalice of river water from her pocket, using a hand motion I can't follow. She tilts his sleeping head forward and pours dark water into his mouth. She whispers into his ears, and he mumbles softly in his sleep as she speaks. Ilana lays Mark's head back down. "He will forget," she says. "The Fury's words are gone."

"What did the demon say to him?" I ask.

"Who knows? Demons have their own language, and we are not supposed to hear it. Their forbidden words can implant ideas, terrible false dreams. . . . No one knows what it said to him. To know would be to suffer the same torment he suffered."

"What about his nose?"

"He was drunk, out in the forest. He must have fallen. He can't remember what happened."

"Could you have made me forget Elza?" I ask. "After she died? Would that have worked?"

"No," Ilana says. "Your mind is linked with that lake. The Book of Eight resides within you. The river water won't erode your memories."

Elza hasn't moved, but there's something about the body. It feels expectant, on the edge of something. She has to return. I didn't look back. I did everything right. She's still lying on her back, hair pooled around her neck.

"Maybe we could bring her out to the passing place," Ilana says.

"Would that work?" I ask.

"It might help."

As I reach down to Elza again, I notice that my little finger is missing. The digit the Riverkeeper took is gone, like I was born without it. I don't mention it to Ilana.

We carry Elza out of the tent and across the sunlit clearing, and lay her gently down on the moss in the middle of the standing stones. The light plays on her hair, on her freckled face. She looks peaceful somehow, beautiful, like she's posing for an oil painting.

"So now what?" I ask.

"Have faith," Ilana says. "Hope."

We sit down on the flattest stone.

Ilana brought a bag of food: sandwiches, apples, chocolate bars. They taste like the most delicious food I've ever eaten. She tells me that it's Sunday afternoon, Easter Sunday, April fifth. I was in Deadside for less than a day. It feels like I spent months there. Ilana nods when I tell her this.

"We left the lake just ahead of you, but we arrived back in Liveside twelve hours earlier than you."

I doubt they ran into Mr. Berkley on the way back to Dunbarrow, but I don't mention that part. Best to have some secrets.

"So we don't know how long Elza will be?" I ask.

"She'll come back."

"I hope."

"The Shrouded Lake isn't a joke, Luke. If the sleepers beneath the waters said she'd come back . . . she will."

"What are you going to do now?" I ask her.

"Us? We're going back to California."

"What are you going to do when you get there, though?"

Ilana frowns.

"All Ash really thought about was Ilana. How to keep her alive. How to get her back. Now that we're together . . . I don't know what we'll do. Live, I suppose."

We sit together in silence, looking down at Elza.

"You know, I'm going to have a lot to explain when she comes back," I say. "It might be better if it's just me here at first. Easier."

"Of course," Ilana says. "I'll wait on the path."

Ilana embraces me, then walks away through the clearing, back toward the road. I assume she's got a car parked out there somewhere. I'm glad Ash seems to have found what she was looking for.

I sit alone and wait. Birds trace intricate patterns in the sky, snatching insects from the warm air. I run my thumb over my sigil, over the gap where my little finger used to be. I run my mind over the gap where Ham used to be. I'm going to miss him.

As the sun sinks behind the low hills, as the last hint of light is fading from her face, Elza breathes in and opens her eyes.

We bury Ham on Monday evening. It's almost dusk, a clear sky, the sun setting on the horizon. We've dug a grave for him right at the end of the garden, by the stone wall. The apple trees are starting to blossom, their branches decked out in delicate white blooms. Elza said that in some cultures, white is the color of death.

Mum stands next to me, wearing her poncho, with a wreath of flowers in her hand. She remembers Ham having a stroke, dying in his sleep. She remembers that I never had a little finger, was born without it. Elza stands beside Mum, holding one of Ham's old chew toys. He never showed that much interest in them, to be honest, but this is the one he seemed to like the best: a ball with a knotted rope stuck through it. I'm holding the spade.

Ham lies in his grave, wrapped in his favorite blanket. As a puppy he'd crawl underneath it and stay there all day, with just his little black nose peeking out. I remember that, back when we first got him, and he was as tiny and sleek as an otter. I think growing up to be so big was always a surprise to him. The blanket, which used to cover him completely when he was young, is now wrapped around his chest and back like a shawl. He looks peaceful.

"I suppose this is it, love," Mum says.

"I can't believe it," I say.

"Maybe we should say something," Elza suggests.

They both look at me.

"All right," I say.

My mouth feels dry. I still expect him to wake up at any moment.

"Ham was our friend," I say. "We all loved him. Whenever you'd had a bad day, Ham was there. He was one of the cheeriest, kindest dogs I ever knew. I think we gave him a happy life. I hope we did. I know I owe him a lot and I'm going to miss him."

"He had a wonderful soul," Mum says softly. "You could see it in his eyes. They were such lovely eyes. I know wherever he's gone to now, it's a good place. I feel sure of it."

I remember the Shrouded Lake, those depths, the darkness and beautiful stars. I don't know what's under the lake, what that place even was. But I hope it was something good.

"I think you're right," I say to her.

Mum places the wreath of flowers in his grave.

"Ham," Elza says, "I didn't know you nearly as long as Luke or Persephone did. But I think we hit it off immediately, and I know Dunbarrow will feel a lot emptier without you. I loved you because you were a big, kind beast who wasn't afraid to break the rules, and you came through for me and Luke when it counted. We're all going to miss you, Ham."

She drops the chew ball into his grave.

"Good-bye, boy," I say, and shovel the first clump of earth onto his body. It falls with a soft sound on his blanket, the flowers, the toy.

Am Ham, I think as I scoop up another shovel load of earth.

Am Ham.

Mum drinks several toasts to Ham's memory and goes up to bed by ten thirty, leaving me and Elza the sole attendees of his remembrance party. We're sitting out in garden chairs, wrapped up in my duvet, with stars overhead and a bonfire burning. It's clear and cold, and I can see an airplane moving high above us, red lights flashing on its wings.

Elza is a miracle. To feel her sitting next to me, her

warmth, to look down and see her face, her freckles, her perfectly arched eyebrows: a miracle. Her eyes, the fire reflected in them: masterpieces.

"So what did they find?" she asks me.

"Who?"

"The doctors. You had your MRI, right?"

"They said my brain activity was unusual. But not, like, diseased. I don't think they knew what to make of it."

"That's about what I expected," she says.

"How do you feel?" I ask her.

"About what?"

"Being alive again. Everything."

"I shouldn't be here," she says.

"I thought I'd never see you again," I say. "Like, not even that we could meet again in Deadside. You were gone. Vanished into the nonpareil. I couldn't deal with that."

Elza runs her hand over the place where my little finger used to be.

"I told you not to come after me," she says softly. "I said if something does happen to me, don't try and bring me back. Let me go."

"I couldn't—"

"I did mean it, you know."

"I didn't have a choice, Elza," I say, remembering Ash saying the same thing.

"I knew you'd try and do something. I saw it in your eyes when I was dying," she replies. "And don't think I'm not grateful. I like being alive."

"I like you being alive, too."

"But I don't know if you understand why I said that to you. I don't want you reading the Book of Eight again. I don't want you using your dad's sigil, raising a Host, getting deeper into this mess. You brought the Shepherd back into our world, Luke. You gave your finger to this Riverkeeper creature. You lost Ham. I'm not worth that."

"You are," I say.

"I'm serious," she says. "I'm really serious. Black magic, necromancy . . . this stuff will eat you up if you let it. The price is just going to keep getting higher. What happens next time you lose someone?"

"It was my fault," I say.

"It wasn't. I made my own choice to help Ash. We both should've known better."

The bonfire spits, sparks rising up into the night air.

"You know this isn't over, right?" I say.

"Berkley," she says.

"He says I still owe him. He wants me to have the Book. Whatever's happening to me . . . it hasn't stopped yet."

"So," Elza says, "we fight back."

"How?"

"He's the Devil," she says. "People have been writing about him since the dawn of time, with one name or another. Someone's been in this position before."

"You really think that?"

"Well," she says quietly, "it's that or give up and wait for him to come back. Give him what he wants."

"So don't you think we'll need the Book of Eight for this?"

"For all we know," Elza says, "he wrote it."

She rests her head against my shoulder, and we sit, watching the fire.

"What do you think Ilana will do?" I ask after a while.

Later on Sunday, we'd had a very awkward group discussion at the stone circle, and then drove to my house to alter our parents' memories. Ilana didn't stay long after that. She said she had a plane to catch.

"I really don't care that much," Elza says sleepily.

"It's just her now. Her and Ash. They say they're happy, but . . . I mean, the Widow's gone."

"Honestly?" Elza says. "She's a young, rich, beautiful girl with an American passport and more money than she could spend in ten lifetimes. I'm not feeling that worried about her."

"Still not an Ahlgren fan, then?"

She laughs.

"She did kill me."

"Ash wasn't evil," I say. "She had reasons for doing what she did."

"Everyone is the hero in their own story."

"Is that a quote from somewhere?"

"I don't know," she says. "Maybe."

"So what do we do now?" I ask Elza.

"Well," she says. "I'm alive. You're alive. Ham's gone. We live, I suppose. We try and get on without him. We've got exams in a few months. I'm thinking about that."

"Right. Exams."

"We should draw up a schedule or something," she says.

"That's really what you're thinking about?"

"What else is there?" Elza says. "It's important. I can't skip our exams just because I died. Life isn't just about the big adventures. It's all the boring parts as well."

I lean down and kiss her.

The Shepherd said he didn't believe love existed, that he couldn't feel it, and I suppose in a way it's the same thing. To people like him, me and Elza might look deluded, crippled, like two people who've chosen to struggle through our lives lashed together, a weird stumbling animal, drunks in a three-legged race. And in my darker moments, I do think he might have had a point. But here and now? Out here under the stars, with the fire warming my face and Elza breathing against my neck, her fingers playing along my wrist? If our love is selfish, all some big delusion, I think I'm OK with that.

We sit in silence, watching the fire. A log collapses in on itself, sending sparks spiraling up into the darkness. We sit hand in hand, the night drawn around us like a black blanket, until the bonfire is nothing but embers.

ACKNOWLEDGMENTS AND NOTES

First I'd like to thank my agent, Jenny Savill, for her guidance and wisdom, as well as the steak lunches, which are creative stimulants of great potency. I'd like to thank my editors, Kate Fletcher and Jessica Tarrant, for their hard work and sensible suggestions, as well as everyone else at my literary agency and publishing houses who had a hand in bringing this book to you.

I'd like to thank my family for their love and support, and I'd like to thank the many people who read early drafts of this novel.

The ancient Greeks only spoke of five rivers that flowed through the Underworld: the Styx, the Lethe, the Acheron, the Phlegethon, and the Cocytus. Since the magic of Luke's story hinges around the number eight, I've fabricated the rivers Apelpsion, Algos, and Elys.